The ties that bind may be the ties that kill as these extraordinary women race against time to beat the genetic time bomb that is their birthright....

Lynn White:
With enhanced senses, and superspeed and strength, this retrieval specialist can breach any security—but has she been working for the wrong side?
DECEIVED by Carla Cassidy—January 2005

Faith Corbett:
This powerful psychic's secret talent could make her the target of a serial killer— and a prime suspect for murder.
CONTACT by Evelyn Vaughn—February 2005

Dawn O'Shaughnessy:
Her superhealing abilities make her nearly invincible, but can she heal the internal wounds from years of deception?
PAYBACK by Harper Allen—March 2005

* * *

ATHENA FORCE: The adventure continues with three secret sisters, three unusual talents and one unthinkable legacy....

Dear Reader,

Silhouette Bombshell is dedicated to bringing you the best in savvy heroines, fast action, high stakes and chilling suspense. We're raising the bar on action adventure to create an exhilarating reading experience that you'll remember long after the final pages!

Take some personal time with *Personal Enemy* by Sylvie Kurtz. An executive bodyguard plans the perfect revenge against the man who helped to destroy her family—but when they're both attacked, she's forced to work *for* him before she can work against him!

Don't miss *Contact* by Evelyn Vaughn, the latest adventure in the ATHENA FORCE continuity series. Faith Corbett uses her extrasenory skills to help the police solve crimes, but she's always contacted them anonymously. Until a serial killer begins hunting psychics, and Faith must reveal herself to one disbelieving detective....

Meet the remarkable women of author Cindy Dees's *The Medusa Project*. These Special Forces officers-in-training are set up to fail, but for team leader Vanessa Blake, quitting is not an option—especially when both international security and their tough-as-nails trainer's life is at stake!

And provocative twists abound in *The Spy Wore Red* by Wendy Rosnau. Agent Nadja Stefn is hand-picked for a mission to terminate an assassin—but getting her man means working with a partner from whom she must hide a dangerous personal agenda....

Please send your comments to me c/o Silhouette Books, 233 Broadway, Suite 1001, New York, NY 10279.

Best wishes,

Natashya Wilson

Natashya Wilson
Associate Senior Editor, Silhouette Bombshell

Please address questions and book requests to:
Silhouette Reader Service
U.S.: 3010 Walden Ave., P.O. Box 1325, Buffalo, NY 14269
Canadian: P.O. Box 609, Fort Erie, Ont. L2A 5X3

CONTACT

EVELYN VAUGHN

Silhouette®
BOMBSHELL™

Published by Silhouette Books

America's Publisher of Contemporary Romance

Special thanks and acknowledgment are given to
Evelyn Vaughn for her contribution to the
ATHENA FORCE series.

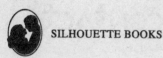 SILHOUETTE BOOKS

ISBN 0-373-51344-5

CONTACT

EVELYN VAUGHN

has written stories since she learned to make letters. But during the two years that lived on a Navajo reservation in Arizona—while in second and third grade—she dreamed of becoming not a writer, but a barrel racer in the rodeo. Before she actually got her own horse, however, her family moved to Louisiana. There, to avoid the humidity, she channeled more of her adventures into stories instead.

Since then, Evelyn has canoed in the East Texas swamps, rafted a white-water river in the Austrian Alps, rappelled barefoot down a three-story building, talked her way onto a ship to Greece without her passport, sailed in the Mediterranean and spent several weeks in Europe with little more than a backpack and a train pass. While she enjoys channeling the more powerful "travel Vaughn" on a regular basis, she also loves the fact that she can write about adventures with far less physical discomfort. Since she now lives in Texas, where she teaches English at Tarrant County College SE, air-conditioning remains an important factor. Feel free to contact her through her Web site, www.evelynvaughn.com, or by writing to: P.O. Box 6, Euless TX, 76039.

For my sisters at Silhouette Bombshell.

Chapter 1

It was sensory overload. Especially for her.

"You been here before?" shouted the bartender over the noise. He was a gruff old Vietnam-vet type with a long cowboy moustache and tattoos, but Faith didn't sense any threat off him. Of course, in this chaos, he'd have to come at her with a switchblade before she sensed a threat.

Maybe noise created its own kind of pseudo-silence—a benefit to partying with her new roommates that she hadn't expected.

"Here, New Orleans?" she shouted back from the sanctuary he'd allowed her on his side of the bar, out of the worst of the crowd. "Or here, DeLoup's?"

With a bottle of tequila he pointed at her green crop top which read, *Tulane University*. Ah, proof of her previous life. He could see she'd been in New Orleans awhile now. He grinned. "DeLoup's."

Faith shook her head and grinned back while, ever in motion, the bartender set some tourists up with shot glasses, lemon and salt. She usually avoided places like DeLoup's. She wouldn't be here now except that she hated to back down from a challenge.

Like she'd told her mom in that last, ugly argument before she'd moved out, she was through hiding in the shadows. Faith wanted people in her life, even if only people on the margins of society could really accept her. And people—social people—went dancing. And drinking. And...

And other things she'd avoided.

On that determination, she said, "It's fun!"

And despite her enhanced senses, inexplicably keen for as long as she could remember, it *was*. Fun. In a throw-you-in-a-blender-and-hit-puree kind of way.

Jazz music bounced off walls hung with crooked neon beer signs and dented license plates. It mixed with laughter and shouted conversation—and heartbeats, the vibration of dozens of thudding heartbeats. Bare, multicolored bulbs dangled from ceiling fixtures, not quite reaching some of the bar's intense shadows, but Faith could see in the dark almost as clearly as she could in the light. Frigid air-conditioning fought a losing battle against the hot, humid Louisiana night that poured into the bar every time the doors opened, not to mention the heat rolling off of its gyrating patrons. The aromas of beer and rum, sweet fruit drinks and fried appetizers mingled with colognes, breath mints and sweating, pressing humanity.

Faith could also smell the emotions, almost like perfume, could hear them on intermingled heartbeats. Currents of attraction. Patches of jealousy. Pockets of lust. From more than one area she smelled the decay of unhappiness and uncertainty.

And a whiff of...fear?

Faith frowned. Surely she'd imagined that amidst all the confusion. But real fear had its own scent, cold and acrid like metal. She did a quick head count of the roommates who'd brought her here.

Absinthe, a kohl-eyed Goth, dirty-dancing with a frat boy.

Evan, the unassuming, sandy-haired boy-next-door type, dancing with the kind of wiry, sharp-eyed guy who never pledged a fraternity.

Innocent Moonsong, hair dyed far lighter than her brown skin, rings and necklaces and piercings glistening as she belly danced in solo circles, with at least three admirers looking on.

And Krystal…

Where was Krystal?

The bartender's hand settling onto Faith's bare shoulder might as well have been an exposed power line. But instead of electricity she got a hard shock of concern, curiosity, wary attraction. Now she sensed that he smoked more than cigarettes… took pain pills for old pains…*had pins in his knees from that wreck, shrapnel from when he saw some buddy blown up—*

She stumbled back, away from the uninvited information dump, away from her own freakishness. She caught herself with an elbow on the bar's sticky wooden surface. Jazz music swirled back in around her.

When the bartender reached for her again—"You okay, kid?"—Faith ducked quickly back, avoiding contact.

"I'm—" But what could she say? She was a freak, strange enough that even her mom couldn't explain it, strange enough that the most accepting friends she'd found so far were French Quarter psychic readers, not exactly mainstreamers themselves. That wasn't new. But tonight, she was a freak with a missing roommate. "I have to go find my friend. I haven't seen her come back from the restroom."

Which lay across a sea of dancing, mixing, pressing people.

Not that Faith had a choice. Something was wrong.

Like a swimmer taking one last breath before diving into freezing water, she braced herself, then stepped into the dancing crowd.

Every person who brushed or bumped her brought a static jolt, a blare of fragmented sound, a blast of intense scent. Like being in a pinball machine. She was the metal ball, drawn by a force as sure as gravity in one direction while too many uncaring obstacles knocked her everywhere else. *Zap. Ring.* In the confusion, she got only flashes of real or imagined information.

This one told her husband she was at a girlfriend's house. That one lost out on a raise. Another just tried E for the first time.

Faith gritted her teeth as she waded through them all, finally pushing into the moderately quieter back hallway with the pay phone and the bathrooms. The door marked *Filles* was closed, so she knocked. "Krystal?"

Nothing. Certainly nothing good. If she concentrated, Faith could hear a heartbeat, but there was something strange about it. Something...*off.*

She tried the doorknob. If she wound up invading someone's privacy, she could always claim to be drunk. The door opened barely half an inch before catching, latched with an old-fashioned hook-and-eye to go with the Old N'awlins flavor.

It was enough for Faith's gaze to track three things.

The back of Krystal's pale-blond head, where it lay still on the linoleum.

The faucet, pouring water into the pedestal sink.

And a booted foot seeming to levitate upward off of that sink to vanish, ghostlike, into the ceiling.

Faith jammed her hand into the crack and sliced upward, hard. The hook snapped free. Then she was in the room, skidding to her bare knees onto the gritty linoleum beside...

Beside a human shape that used to be her friend, one of her new roommates. *No.*

Faith didn't have to feel for a pulse. She could hear Krystal's lifelessness in her silence—no heartbeat, no breath. She could see the purpling stripe, like a gory scarf, around her friend's throat, could smell death amidst the usual toilet smells, a stagnant scent, along with the remnants of that cold, metallic fear and…

And something that turned her stomach even more harshly than this violent death. That scent was also an emotion, but one she'd never caught before. And it came from—

She looked up at where the booted foot had vanished—presumably with a killer attached—and at a white ceiling panel that hadn't been replaced quite straight in its channel.

No time to think. If she stalled on the enormity of what must have just happened in here, like a normal human would, any chance she had of identifying Krystal's killer would vanish.

Good thing Faith wasn't normal.

Springing to her feet, she kicked the door shut and jammed the hook back into place—protect the evidence, right? Then she scrambled onto the sink's edge and rose, stretching upward for the metal runner that supported the drop ceiling. She had to go on tiptoe, precariously balanced on porcelain, to wedge her fingers around the metal bar. The I-shaped runner gouged cruelly into the flesh of her hands. Wishing she'd done more chin-ups at the gym, Faith had to make do with swinging herself once, twice.

On her third try, she kicked a second panel loose and caught that runner behind her knees. Now she hung like a scantily dressed *U*, shoulders straining, but it was enough. Stepping her feet closer to her hands with awkward lurches, glad she'd worn running shoes instead of heels, she edged her knees close enough to give her leverage.

She wedged her head and arms up past the wood-fiber panel into the narrow crawlspace of the drop ceiling.

She heard a slither of movement, rapidly retreating.

Crawl was the right word for this suspended space, Faith thought, wriggling quickly in after the fleeing suspect. The drop ceiling, a precarious collection of acoustical tiles balanced on an exposed framework of metal channels, lay barely a foot below the wooden joists of the upper roof. Her view up here was obstructed not just by the darkness, which she could handle, but by lengths of taut hanger wire and aluminum air-conditioning ducts swathed in paper-wrapped, pink fiberglass insulation. But she could hear him—statistics told her it would be a *him,* as surely as did instinct and smell. She twisted in the direction of the telltale scuffling and caught a glimpse of retreating boot soles, barely ten feet ahead of her.

Faith launched herself after them, not on hands and knees but on thighs and forearms, her bare tummy and legs rasping across years of accumulated dirt. Her neck ached with the strain of keeping an eye on her quarry as she wriggled after him. The ceiling panels felt horribly unstable beneath her. They probably were—those yard-by-yard squares—barely an inch thick, suspended from the joists by mere wire. From beneath her she caught wafts of jazz music, shouted conversation, blurred heartbeats and breaths and mingling emotions. But ahead of her…

She heard the distinct rhythm of her quarry's pounding heart and breathed in his smell as it faded from that strange, stomach-turning scent to surprise and distress at her pursuit.

Not surprisingly, he was bigger than her. The crawlspace was even tighter for him. It was slowing him down.

Faith was maybe eight feet behind him now. She dragged herself closer, digging with her elbows, scrabbling with her arched feet.

One of his shoulders glanced off a metal duct.

Now she was barely six feet behind him, putting her hips into it.

He had to flatten onto his stomach to avoid a low-hanging swag of electric wiring that had pulled free of its staples.

Now she was barely four feet behind him. She caught her hand on an exposed nail and barely noticed the slice of pain. She kept crawling.

He stopped. Why? Three feet, two...

Faith reached out her hand, ready to grab the killer by the ankle if that's what it took. She doubted she could capture him alone, but she'd come to know evidence. She could damn well tear some vital clue off him.

But with the appearance of a sudden square of light, he vanished.

At least, that's what it looked like. Even as she gaped, Faith realized that the man had punched out another ceiling tile and dived, headfirst, into whatever lay below.

Wriggling closer, she peered over the edge of the runner and saw metal racks, industrial-size bottles, cardboard boxes. *Storeroom.* She pivoted onto her hip, her shoulder brushing a joist above her as she rolled on her side and dropped her feet down first. Then she levered herself the rest of the way through the ceiling and let go.

With a light thud, she landed in a crouch on the floor below.

The storeroom was empty—of everything but storage, anyway. Faith shouldered quickly out the door....

And found herself behind the bar again. The man she'd been after could be anybody amidst the milling, churning crowd now. And the bartender wasn't there to say who'd just appeared from the storeroom.

Like everyone else, he'd apparently been drawn away by the shrill screaming coming from the bathrooms.

With a deep breath, Faith dived back into the crowd, an overly aware pinball trying to go in one inexorable direction.

"You touch anything?" demanded the first officer on the scene, a tall brown patrolman named Lee. He'd responded not to the bartender's 9-1-1 call but to one of DeLoup's customers rushing out onto Bourbon Street to fetch help.

"Of course I did," admitted Faith. "But I've contained the scene since."

The shrieking CPA who'd found Krystal had not pushed the door hard enough to force the hook-and-eye latch a second time. Apparently, when she'd looked in, she hadn't wanted to.

Faith had gotten there just as the bartender shouldered his way through—in time to keep him from compromising evidence.

The patrolman, after an unsteady look at poor Krystal's blue-tinged face and a grateful check of Faith's ID badge, agreed to leave the bathroom to her while he worked crowd control.

"Not like you can go anywhere," he said, as if the ceiling panels weren't gaping like missing teeth above the still-running sink.

One down. But Faith wasn't worried about patrolmen.

"Did you throw up?" asked a kindly EMT not ten minutes later, about the running water. A good-looking guy named Steadman, he was careful to step only where Faith had indicated he should. The likelihood that the crime-scene investigators could pick up a single distinct boot print off the chaos of a bathroom floor were low, especially with something gritty, like sand, crunching underfoot. Faith should know. But it didn't hurt to be careful.

"No. I found the water that way."

"Did you check for the victim's pulse?"

"She was already dead when I felt her wrist." And she hadn't needed to check for a pulse to know that. But Faith had wanted to leave a fingerprint, just in case. Her mother had stressed the need for paranoia about Faith's freakishly acute senses since childhood. Leaving proof of an unnecessary assessment had seemed a better idea than trying to explain that she could hear the absence of her roommate's heartbeat.

Steadman crouched easily beside Krystal's body and eyed the straight-line bruising around the neck and the welts where, if Faith had to guess, Krystal had gouged her own throat trying to dig away the killer's garrote. Steadman, too, seemed to check for the absent pulse more out of procedure than practicality. "She looks familiar. Didn't she read tarot in Jackson Square?"

Faith stiffened, concerned he would recognize more than Krystal. Not that Faith had been on the Square for a while. She'd only been…experimenting. It had been a failed experiment.

"Yes," she said. "She did."

He swore under his breath and stood. "Well, ma'am, this is one for the cops, the coroner and the crime scene unit."

Two down. But Faith wasn't worried about EMTs, either.

Again she found herself alone with the body. She looked into Krystal's staring eyes, not quite able to reconcile the corpse with the tall, vivacious young woman who'd offered to style Faith's hair before they'd headed out that night. *Krystal.*

It had always been one of Faith's favorite daydreams, to live with a bunch of other women. Roommates, sisters, dormmates at some kind of boarding school—no matter the details, she'd always imagined it would be like an endless slumber party. Like…belonging. This new apartment—rather, her newly rented half room in a very *old* apartment—was her first real effort toward that.

But slumber parties usually didn't include murder.

Now she wished she'd accepted Krystal's offer, despite her dislike of being touched and Krystal's overreliance on hairspray. Krystal had been teaching her breathing and relaxation techniques to control her oversensitivity. They'd been friends, though maybe not as close as normal people got. Faith wasn't sure she knew how to get close to other people. Now she'd lost any chance to get closer to this one.

She hadn't expected losing someone to hurt like this.

Still, the worst part about standing here in the bathroom, alone with Krystal, wasn't that guilt. It wasn't the eerie stillness, a now blatant absence of jazz music, laughter and shouted conversations that made the simple gurgle of water running down the drain become deafening. It wasn't even being this close to a dead person.

The worst part was the lingering...*smell* was what Faith could best call it, but that wasn't wholly correct. A perverted sexuality hung in the air, part musk, part heat. It had been left by the killer and this horrible, irrevocable thing he'd done. It smelled like power. Dominance.

Evil.

More than the corpse's presence, that atmosphere of evil twisted deep in her stomach.

"So," drawled someone loudly. Though the man in the unbuttoned coat didn't throw the door open hard enough to bounce it off the wall, he might as well have, the way Faith jumped at his arrival. "What do we know?"

Damn. Not only had the detectives arrived, they included Roy Chopin.

Faith had been around Chopin only a handful of times. He was a rangy man with a rolling walk, blunt and expressive. He wore his brown hair styled back from his long face, to keep it out of his tired eyes. His mouth alternated between threat-

ening and mocking, and his jaw looked like a dare. His sheer
physicality made her uncomfortable, even without touching.
He didn't *have* to touch. A cop in every sense of that word,
Chopin seemed to expect the whole world to get out of his
way. To judge by his cocky attitude, the world usually did.

Tonight, though, his presence felt welcome as it washed
over the crime scene like a rainstorm clearing out the gutters
of Bourbon Street. Imagining all this ugliness through his de-
tached gray eyes demoted Krystal's death from a scene of horror to a mere shame and, more to the point, a puzzle to be
solved.

Faith grasped gratefully at that air of detachment. She
would return to the horror soon enough, after all. And she
would need all her wits. Where Chopin went...

Well, when his partner arrived, she'd be three down. The
detectives were the ones who had worried her all along.

For good reason.

In the meantime, Chopin was already looking impatient.

"This is Krystal Tanner," she reported. "I found her like this
at about ten-fifteen. Someone was climbing out through the
ceiling. I went after him, but he had a pretty good head start,
and— What?"

Chopin had shaken his head, his tired eyes widening.

"You *went after him?*" he demanded.

"Yes."

He looked her up and down. She sensed the way he saw
her as surely as she could read his perusal of the scene. She
was a blond-haired, ponytailed coed with full lips, unusual
green-gold eyes and tanned arms and legs, bared by the miniskirt and crop top. The outfit had seemed a better choice before her crawl through the filthy roof space.

"*Alone?*"

Her chin came up under the challenge of his gaze. "Yeah."

Chopin leaned closer, faux conspiratorial. "And why would you do an idiotic thing like that?"

Well, duh. "Because the alternative would have been *not* to go after him?"

He grinned as he straightened, fishing a notebook out of his shirt pocket. "Krystal Tanner," he muttered, making a note. "Ten-fifteen. You're not on the force, so how is it I know you?"

She was surprised he'd remember her, even vaguely. Then again, powers of observation went back to his cop-ness. "I'm an assistant evidence technician for the city. Faith Corbett."

She fisted her right hand, hoping he wouldn't want to shake. The man was intense enough without risking direct contact.

"Yeah, that's it." He nodded and, to her relief, kept his own hand busy taking notes. "You're one of Boulanger's day shift, working the desk, right? Sometimes you make pickups and drop-offs at the station. So Corbett, how is it you know the deceased?"

Poor Krystal. One minute she'd been dancing, drinking, celebrating life. Then she'd headed for the ladies' room and... God. *The deceased.*

"She's my roommate."

Chopin stopped writing and angled his wide gaze back to her, brows furrowed. "Oh. I'm... uh..."

Why was it some men had trouble expressing even the most conventional courtesy, lest it betray some emotion? Faith saved him the effort. "Thanks."

"So, Bernie, you went charging after this killer and...?"

Had he just called her Bernie? Unwilling to be distracted, Faith repeated the story as quickly as she could without looking too suspicious, increasingly aware of him studying her as he listened and took notes. She felt as if he could see every hair on her arms, every piece of grit embedded in her tummy, every scrape on her knees. It wasn't sexual—there was a corpse at their feet, after all. Well…not any more sexual than any man staring at a woman's bare tummy, anyway. But such intense scrutiny made her uncomfortable.

Like he could maybe *see* just how weird she was.

"You didn't get a good look at him?" Chopin demanded, when she finished. At least he hadn't interrupted her.

"Just the bottom of his feet."

"And you didn't ask anybody if they saw him leave the storeroom?" His mouth had gone back to threatening. His questions were starting to feel like little shoves of energy.

"No, everyone was distracted by finding Krystal."

"And how was your relationship with the vic?"

Faith's mouth fell open. "Why are you questioning me as if… oh." But she knew the answer to that, too. "The first person on the scene's always the first suspect, right?"

"Yeah." Chopin didn't even bother to apologize for his suspicions. But he did include her in another mocking grin. "Nothing personal, hon. It's one of those hard truths, like 'everybody lies.' Statistics would put the odds on either you or her boyfriend-slash-husband."

"She didn't have a boyfriend or a husband."

"Could I see your hands, please?" *Shove.*

Faith spread her bare palms for him. Only when she felt his interest spike—a minute change of his temperature, a sharp inhale through his teeth—did she notice the pink lines where she'd pulled herself up through the ceiling, the bleeding cut from that exposed nail. "Oh…" she whispered.

For a moment she felt dizzy with the very real possibility that she might be charged with this crime. So much for keeping a low profile!

"Don't sweat it. If you'd done the deed, you'd have lines on the sides of your hands, too. Here—" to her relief, he indicated where he meant with his pen, not his finger "—and here. Besides, she's fashion-model tall—pushing six feet? I'm no M.E., but I'm betting the ligature marks on her neck would be a lot lower if you did her. Unless you somehow made her kneel first, which, how could you without imminent threat, and I don't see anyplace you could've hidden a gun. Or much of a knife. Nice shirt, there."

"You're smarter than you look," said Faith, fully aware it was her own way of shoving back.

"'Cause of my fashion sense, or 'cause I'm not hauling you down to the station yet?" Detective Chopin looked less exhausted as he eyed her. "Usually I'm the brawn of the outfit. Right, Butch?"

Strike three.

"Now, Roy," demanded Chopin's partner from the doorway. Here stood the sweet, trustworthy man whose arrival Faith had feared even beyond the slap-in-the-face energy of the younger Roy. "What are you doing harassing this here helpful citizen? Sugar over vinegar, son. Sugar over vinegar. How do you do, Miss? I am Detective Sergeant Butch Jefferson. I am most terribly sorry to have to meet you under such clearly distressing circumstances, and I apologize for my partner's appalling lack of manners."

"He's the Good Cop," muttered Chopin amiably, still taking notes. Which made him what?

Butch, who had more than twenty years on his thirty-ish partner, extended both a genuine smile, which made his dark eyes crinkle at the corners, and his worn brown hand. There was no way Faith could refuse to take the latter. Not without rousing suspicion and requiring more conversation, which—around Butch Jefferson, anyway—she wanted even less than touching.

With a determined smile, she allowed Butch to envelop her hand in his.

It wasn't anywhere near as unsettling as touching his partner would have been. Butch's personal energy was slow and easy, like the Mississippi in the summertime. The flashes of possible information that accompanied his touch—*widowed, volunteered with Big Brothers, loved beer and boiled crawfish*—he released it all so freely, it didn't carry the unsettling jolt of so many other people.

"Faith Corbett," she said—the first time she'd ever given this particular cop her real name. *Please don't recognize me.*

"From evidence," added Bad Cop, who proceeded to take over most of the talking.

The older detective didn't seem to realize he and Faith had spoken before, much less that it had had nothing to do with her job with the crime-scene unit.

Then again, she'd chosen Butch Jefferson last year specifically because he didn't have a terribly suspicious nature— not for a homicide detective, anyway. She'd always used a fake accent, the dozen-or-so times she'd telephoned him. And she'd given him a fake name, Madame Cassandra. But the information she'd passed on as Detective Jefferson's anonymous contact with the psychic community had always been real.

As long as the information stayed anonymous, Faith could remain useful. But if he recognized her voice, or learned the tips came from her…

Well, either he'd see her like Chopin had—young and blond and thus somehow unreliable—or he'd see her like the few other people who had learned her secret.

Freak.

Worse, they would want to know how she did it. And that, not even Faith could tell them.

She honestly didn't know what she was.

But whatever she was, keeping quiet about it was one of

the few things her nervous mother had gotten right. *Look what happened to Krystal.*

The thought caught Faith by surprise. How could Krystal's murder have anything to do with the tarot reader's special abilities?

She stiffened, increasingly aware of the gurgling drain beneath Roy Chopin's surprisingly accurate narrative of her night. It would keep running until the night shift for the crime-scene unit arrived.

Running water?

She might only do glorified clerical work for the crime-scene unit, so far. She might only be an assistant crime-scene technician. But she knew the water had to mean something.

What?

Amidst the Bourbon Street crowd that lingered into the night, attracted by flashing lights and yellow police tape, He closed His eyes to savor His…His amplification.

Strength. Meaning. Confidence. Yes!

That last time hadn't been a fluke, after all.

He stood for what may have been hours, too powerful to tire of it, relishing how helpless the so-called authorities looked. Patrolmen had come and gone, as had an ambulance. Now the photographers and the crime-scene investigators, the night shift, had arrived. But He waited.

He wanted to see the detectives leave as ignorant as when they'd arrived. Stupid, arrogant suits. He wanted to gloat.

When finally they emerged, a younger man with an old black partner, they didn't seem as helpless as He'd hoped. The younger one looked dusty enough to have been clambering around the crawlspace over the ceiling.

But they didn't look satisfied, either. Or done.

Both seemed distracted by the blond bitch who'd chased

Him from His kill before he was done. The one with the green tank top and the miniskirt. He didn't like that one at all.

"Let me or Roy get you a cab now, Miss Faith," He heard the black man say. "Gang activity's gotten worse, not far north of here. No need for you to take chances."

"No," said the girl, all but backing away. "Really. My roommates will walk with me. We'll be safe together."

The trio who shuffled nearer, red-eyed and lost, looked as if they needed more protection than they would provide. Even the man among them had the posture of a girl.

Those three looked familiar—from Jackson Square.

More psychics?

Even as He thought that, as His breath fell shallow and His heartbeat sped and his groin tightened, the one called Miss Faith suddenly turned her head. Her unnerving green gaze raked across the remaining onlookers as if she knew what she was looking for.

He leaned back just enough to hide behind the shoulders of some good ol' boy. When He dared look again, she'd gone. She seemed to deliberately ignore the detectives staring after her. She was too busy dividing her attention between her friends and the street around them, like a little blond bodyguard.

He dared breathe again after they turned a corner. More than one psychic there, for sure.

The kind of people with power to spare.

A few more like tonight, and even the Master could no longer control Him.

Chapter 2

Faith couldn't tell if she'd really sensed the killer among the onlookers, or if it had been her imagination. Sure, she was weird. But could she really recognize a particular heartbeat, a particular smell, in that kind of crowd?

Probably she'd just been distracted by Roy Chopin and Butch Jefferson watching her retreat.

"They asked a lot of questions," noted Moonsong, after a block. "Who Krys dated, if we knew anybody who would want to hurt her. That was nice and thorough of them."

"Bull! Did you see how they looked at me when I told them I'd met Krys at an astrology class?" Between grief, guilt and frustration, or maybe the simple boredom of waiting out the administrative elements of a crime scene, Absinthe had chewed most of her black lipstick off. "Like I was crazy. Like *Krystal* was crazy. It's disrespectful, is what it is."

"Krystal would have thought it was funny," Moonsong insisted. Her real name was Emily, but a surprising number of psychics changed their names. It wasn't so much to hide their true names—like Faith masquerading as Madame Cassandra when she made anonymous calls to the police. It was more about…identity.

About making a fresh start, even honoring their unusual abilities.

"Well, it's not funny," said Absinthe who, because Faith had helped her through the paperwork of a legal name change, really was Absinthe. Faith had majored in pre-law, before dropping out.

Until she knew what she was, it seemed premature to settle on what she should do.

Moonsong's expression set. "But she would have thought it was. Remember? Whenever people got all cynical about what she did, she'd say, 'That is *so* Queen of Swords.'"

Absinthe laughed. "Or she'd say, 'Don't get all Virgo on me.'"

Then she pressed a black-nailed hand to her mouth as her laugh shuddered into a sob. Moonsong circled her dark arms around her, and the two of them walked like a four-legged, two-headed creature.

So much for an endless slumber party. Faith wrapped her arms around herself and tried not to picture Krystal's dead blue eyes and the welts on her throat. Mostly she tried not to imagine the moments before Krystal had died.

She and her three roommates took the same close, shadowed, cobblestone streets that had seen five of them heading out mere hours before. Never had the quieter, late-night backstreets of the French Quarter seemed so empty.

"Would you…?" Evan hesitated beside her, then forged on. "You don't like to be touched, right?"

Faith longed for normal contact at that moment far more

desperately than she feared the intimacy. "It's not so bad if you don't touch bare skin. I mean…yes. I could use a hug."

So awkwardly, like a junior-high kid learning the waltz, Evan positioned one hand on Faith's shirted back, the other on her denim-covered hip, and drew her tentatively against his shirtfront.

She laid her cheek on his shoulder and sighed. The worst of the night's horrors eased, if only a little, under the comforting thrum of his concern and his heartbeat, gently muffled by the pressed cotton of his shirt.

What a sweet, sweet man. They were kind, all of them.

Krystal. Tears of gratitude and loss burned in Faith's eyes.

Faith's roommates knew her secrets—the few she'd figured out herself, anyway. Better yet, they accepted her abilities without demanding explanations. They respected her need for privacy. And they were, for the most part, able to deal with her despite her issues. The so-called fringe really had become friends.

A little over a year ago, Faith had gone to a psychic fair to figure out if being psychic was why she was such a freak. She'd hoped that maybe, like in the *Ugly Duckling* story, she would discover she'd been a swan all along. A psychic swan.

It didn't happen that way. *They* turned out to be swans, all right, but *she* was still something different and strange. A heron, maybe. Maybe something weirder, like a platypus.

God, she'd wanted to be one of them. To be one of *anything.* But she couldn't predict the future. She didn't get reincarnation. The only impressions she felt off runes or tarot cards were a sense of who'd last held them, partly because of how they smelled. The true psychics used paranormal, *extra*-sensory skills. Faith's abilities seemed to be pure *sensory.*

Just…sensory with the volume turned up.

These weren't her people, after all. But she'd liked them—

and more important, they'd brought out her protective instincts. As Absinthe pointed out, a lot of people distrusted psychics. And too many psychics depended on ethereal defenses when they could use a good lesson in kickboxing. After an incident at the psychic fair's "open circle," when Faith had faced down some large, loud disbelievers, she'd realized that this half-hidden community needed someone like her. Someone who could kickbox, sort of, and who wouldn't hesitate to do so. Even the ex-military pagans, when in a sacred circle, had hesitated.

Faith had not.

She hadn't started protecting them just to buy their friendship. Between her mother's paranoid habit of relocating every few years, and Faith's own issues about touching, Faith had resigned herself to being a loner. But the psychic community had welcomed her. When one of Krystal Tanner's roommates had moved out, and they'd started looking for someone to pay a fifth of the rent, they'd asked Faith, who'd jumped at the chance to fulfill that slumber-party dream of sisterhood.

Now Krys was dead. Murdered.

Faith pulled back from Evan's platonic embrace, smiled her sad thanks, and continued walking.

Some protector she'd turned out to be.

"I heard what happened. Are you all right?"

The man who asked that, two days later, was Faith's supervisor. Black-haired, brown-eyed, bearded Greg Boulanger ran the day shift of the crime-scene unit. He was something of a Cajun science geek with the extra strike against him of being management. At almost forty, he was clearly too old for Faith's interest. And yet she liked him. A lot.

And not just because she felt loyal to him for hiring her.

The best way she could describe how comfortable she felt

around Greg was that he had a quiet presence. Kind of like her roommate Evan did. Besides, like so many of the people who worked evidence, Greg often smelled of balloons. It was because of the latex gloves, Faith knew. But the scent had remarkably pleasant, innocent associations, all the same.

"I'm fine," she assured him. He stood beside the desk where she sat. Although his brown eyes seemed concerned behind his wire-rimmed glasses, Greg didn't come at her with the shield of sympathy that so many other people in the office had…probably because, despite being a nice guy, he remained distracted by the job.

"Even coroners aren't cavalier about the bodies of people they know," Greg insisted. "People you know are different. They're supposed to be."

"I'm okay."

"You should probably take some time off."

"No. Really. I kind of like being here."

Greg's eyebrows rose as he looked around them. Unlike those on television, the crime-scene unit consisted of four rooms and one small hallway, crowded into too little floor space on the third floor of a generic municipal building. Faith's desk, up front, was open to a room with three other desks and two crowded worktables. Books overflowed on shelves. The place smelled like a cross between a library and a science lab, with an undercurrent of death because of the morgue down the hall.

"I've been handling the practical stuff," Faith tried to explain. "Calling her family—Krystal was from East Texas. Packing her belongings for when they come. Contacting a local funeral director to make arrangements for after…"

Her need for a deep breath surprised her. So much for Krystal's lessons in stress management through breath control. Maybe Faith wasn't so okay after all.

"After her body's released?" Greg finished for her, gentle.

Faith nodded. "And contacting the coroner to see when that will be. The family wants to have two funerals, one here for her friends and one in Caddo, just for them, so I've been help-ing to arrange that."

Greg picked up the sheaf of evidence reports that still needed to be entered into the computer system and turned it over. "All the more reason you need a break. Things are crazy with that gang shooting."

Krystal's death hadn't been the only murder that weekend.

"But this *is* a break. Everyone at home…well, they were friends with Krystal longer than I was." Her roommates smelled of salty tears and wet misery. Their very breathing sounded like an uneven dirge. The usually strong Absinthe's moods seemed to carry an unpleasant edge of guilt, too. Not that Faith blamed any of them. She felt more than a little guilty that her own grief felt so distant and so, well…mundane.

Absinthe had distracted herself by increasing the spiritual "shields" around their apartment, with incense and crystals; she'd stayed up all night making protective amulets for each of them. Faith wore hers even now, under her top, more for sentimental reasons than because she believed in it.

She didn't *dis*believe.

Moonsong had taken to bed, hoping Krystal's spirit could contact her in a dream so that they could say a proper good-bye—though Faith thought it was as likely that grief or de-pression had simply exhausted her. Evan, bless him, had run interference with Krystal's other friends, spending hours on the phone, answering the same questions over and over. No, they didn't know why anyone would have killed Krystal. No, the police knew nothing. No, they couldn't believe she was dead.

Maybe that was the difference. Faith was the only one among them to have spent time with Krystal's corpse. She very much believed her friend was dead, so she seemed best able to handle all the customary indignities that shouldn't be heaped on people in mourning, either her roommates or the poor Tanner family.

Greg sighed. "Then don't go home. Go to the zoo or the aquarium. Take a riverboat ride. Go shopping."

Faith shook her head. She could justify forgetting Krystal for whole minutes at a time, to focus on her work. But to shop? "I'm good here."

"That's debatable."

She stared, confused, and he sighed. "Since you're personally involved, you'll want to keep some extra distance from this case. You understand that, don't you? It's not that I distrust you, but if anything compromises the evidence…"

"I understand." Between this job, and her pre-law work at Tulane, she *got* evidence.

Her boss's pale eyes focused on her as intently as they might focus on a strand of hair, or a fingerprint, or a particular bug he might be studying. Which, from Greg, was quite a compliment.

She was still startled when she caught a whiff of attraction. Even more when, almost as if an afterthought, he tucked a strand of her blond hair behind her ear.

Because he was wearing latex gloves—he almost always did, around here—the touch didn't send an unpleasant jolt through her. In fact, she wouldn't describe the sensation as unpleasant at all.

He was a human. She was a human. It was human contact.

But here, it still unnerved her. To judge from how his eyes widened, it unnerved him, too. Greg stepped quickly back, fisting his hand as if he'd done something wrong with it. And he hadn't. It wasn't like he'd traced her lips, or her collarbone. It wasn't like he'd told her she looked hot in black.

"I…" he said, then cleared his throat. "Sorry. We've still got that Storyville shooting to deal with. I'd better go check on some ballistics results the lab was faxing over…."

To maybe the relief of both of them, Faith's phone rang.

She smiled reassurance at Greg as she picked it up, but he was already hurrying away. "Evidence," she said.

"I told you the Quarter was a dangerous place."

Faith hadn't had time to brace herself against this second wave of guilt. "Mother?"

"I just saw the news," insisted Tamara Corbett. "Krystal Tanner—she's one of your roommates, isn't she? The one from Texas?"

"Well…she *was.*"

"Please, Faith. Don't try to make light of it!"

"Trust me, Mom. I'm not making light of anything. But there's no reason for you to worry. You know she wasn't killed at the apartment, don't you?"

"But she was in the Quarter. Were you there, too?"

Faith scowled at her computer screen, not sure how to answer that.

"Oh, baby…" moaned her mother, which was even worse than lecturing. Tamara had always been overly protective of Faith. All they'd ever had was each other. Leaving home to move in with Krystal and the others had been one of the hardest things in Faith's life. Especially since she'd been able to hear the reality of her mother's despair in her catching breath, in her pounding heartbeat, as she left. She'd been able to smell it on her, to taste it in the air.

But that wasn't the only thing Faith had been sensing when she moved out. The guilt in the air hadn't just been her own. And until her mom was able to explain what *that* was all about…

Well, wasn't Faith's life complicated enough?

"I'm okay, Mom," she said now, feeling like the grown-up in this equation. "I mean, of course I'm not okay, but considering everything, I'm as good as can be expected. Try not to worry."

That was like saying *try not to fly away* to a frightened bird.

Or like saying *try not to wonder where you're from* to a fatherless girl, which was essentially what her mother had said whenever Faith tried to pursue the mystery that shrouded her past. Had she inherited her freakishly keen senses from her dad's side of the family? Was it possible she might have cousins, even distant cousins, even *one,* who understood what she was going through?

Tamara had always refused to talk about Faith's dad. He'd left them, he hadn't wanted them, he'd died, and that was that. Her stubbornness on that front made it easier not to bleed sympathy for her seeming apprehension now.

"I'm terrified you're going to pull a Thomas King," said Tamara, referring of course to the Navy SEAL team leader who'd vanished and been thought dead for over a year, until his recent dramatic rescue. Because of the political ramifications of his mission, he was still making news. "If something happened to you, what would I do? Maybe you should move back home. For a while. Just until things die down."

"What things? The funeral? My friends' grief? They need me now more than ever, Mom."

"But you're so close to Rampart Street, to Storyville…."

"You're the one who moved us to the murder capital of the United States." As soon as she said that, Faith regretted it. Not only was it cruel, but it put the city in far too dark a light. "I'm sorry, Mom—"

"No. You're right. I'm just glad to know you're safe." And Tamara hung up.

"Damn!" Faith hung up, too, and pressed fingers to her

forehead. She loved New Orleans. She'd been just as glad to leave Kansas City, where she and her mom had lived for two years before coming south. New Orleans had a dark side, yes. But the flaws of this old, magical, slow-moving city were what made it feel like home. It made her own flaws—or her eccentricities, anyway—more acceptable somehow. More normal, even.

Faith had longed to be normal her whole life. Living amidst the quirks of the Big Easy was as close as she'd come to it, especially once she'd found the psychic community. The older she got, the more aware Faith became of how guilty her mother felt. About *something*. Tamara wouldn't say and Faith couldn't—wouldn't—sense it off of her. It was one thing to stumble across a jumble of half-clear impressions about someone. It would be another thing entirely to drag out someone's hard-kept secrets. That would be invasive. A violation. Damn it.

But whatever it was, Tamara shouldn't also feel guilty about moving them here.

The phone rang again and Faith took a deep breath before answering it. "I'm *fine*," she repeated.

"Glad to know it," said a much deeper voice than the one she'd expected. "That's exactly the word I would have used."

His energy actually seemed to pulsate out of the phone. Or was that just the man's inability to moderate his voice?

"Detective Chopin," greeted Faith, sitting up. Like he could see her. At least he'd called, and not his partner. Faith had been on the phone with Butch Jefferson as an anonymous contact too often to risk letting him recognize her disembodied voice. "Do you want to talk to one of the technicians, or maybe Mr. Boulanger?"

"If I'd wanted to talk to them, I would've called them," he said. "I figured…that is, I thought I'd ask…"

Faith waited, feeling as handicapped as if she'd been blind-folded. All she could hear over the line in this busy office was that Chopin sounded frustrated. If he were here, she could have read his body language and his scent and even his temperature as if he were holding up cue cards with personal insights. On the phone...

Maybe that's why she and cell phones had such a bad history. She resented their limitations.

"You are Faith Corbett, right?" asked the cop, managing a slightly quieter voice after all.

"Yes, Detective. What can I do for you?"

"I just wanted..." Chopin swore, and his voice went normal again. Which meant, pushy. "Evidence. On the Tanner case. We're past the 24/24, and I need a damned progress report."

The 24/24 stood for the day before and the day after a murder, the time from which the most valid clues came. Soon, people's recall would fade. Undiscovered physical evidence might vanish. That's why the majority of murders were solved within the first forty-eight hours.

Krystal had been dead thirty-seven hours and counting.

"I'm not supposed to involve myself with the Tanner evidence, Detective Chopin."

"Which wouldn't keep you from looking from a safe distance, right? So what's the status? And call me Roy."

He had her there—she *had* looked, on the computer network. She just hadn't modified any files. "We're still waiting on the M.E. for the autopsy results, and so far Officer Hinze hasn't found concrete matches on any of the fingerprints from the scene. Considering that there were over fifty prints and partials, that's still going to take some processing. The foot-prints will be even more tricky—for some reason, there was a lot of spilled salt on the floor. You know this one went to the night shift, don't you?"

"Yeah, I know. So, is the body still there? Did it—" Then he said, "Aw, f—" He bit off the swear word. "I'm sorry. Hell. I almost forgot it was your friend. I mean…uh… *she.*"

"You were right the first time," Faith assured him. The evidence in the morgue was no longer Krystal. "I hope you've got some leads on the bastard who murdered her."

He knew better than to commit himself. "Just to humor me—the body's still there?"

As in many cities, the crime-scene investigators were not part of the police department, so they didn't have offices at the police station. Neither was this unit part of the parish— Louisiana talk for a county. As soon as the city coroner finished with the corpse, it would be released to the funeral parlor or moved back to the parish morgue. But as long as it remained evidence to be examined…

"The body's still here." Faith's fingers darted across her keyboard to access the proper file and confirm that. Looking only. No interference. "Why do you need to know? Do you need to see it for…something?"

"Unless the M.E. has something pertinent to the case, I'm just as happy leaving that part to you folks. Hell. Maybe I do need to talk to Boulanger."

"Hold a moment, and I'll put you through." Never had she felt more like a glorified secretary. But at least her job kept her near law enforcement. She'd dropped out of college the previous year when she was questioning everything, including why she'd thought she would even want to be a lawyer. But in the meantime, she had to pay the rent. This job felt… right.

Greg's voice mail clicked on, and Chopin swore again.

"Would you like to leave a message?" Faith asked.

"No. I'd like you to find him. I need to see if anything got—" Did he start to form the *T* from *taken,* or was Faith imagining it? "Hunt Boulanger down and have him call me. Got it?"

"Yes sir, detective sir," said Faith.

"You're cute when you're a smart-ass," said Chopin, as if he could see her, and hung up.

Faith let the phone roll off her shoulder into her waiting palm. Her neck felt cricked already. But once she had the receiver in her hand, she held it for a long moment, as if she'd be able to sense anything of importance off of it.

Other than the fact that Officer Leone had used her line recently, she sensed nothing. Not off the telephone, anyway.

Roy Chopin had called her cute. Actually, at the start of the conversation, he'd called her fine, too. Then he'd gotten self-conscious.

He'd called to talk to her? Using her friend's corpse as an excuse? Surely not.

She'd thought *she* was socially inept.

Since she'd been sitting too long anyway, Faith decided to head down to the autopsy room where the medical examiner would be working his magic. If Greg wasn't with him, she could work her way back from there, but there was no reason to waste time checking the nooks and crannies if she'd only find him where he usually was—with the evidence.

The frigid autopsy chamber was large for a room, but small for a morgue. Only a dozen stainless steel drawers fronted one wall, with three slabs—two regular steel tables, one with a trough underneath it—positioned down the room's center. Two of the tables had a sheet-draped body on them. It seemed sad, them left out like this, but Faith supposed bodies were too heavy to put away every time someone ran out for coffee or a bathroom break.

Either way, nobody was here. Nobody living, anyway.

She glanced toward the sheet that she thought hid Krystal's corpse. This time, she couldn't smell her friend's presence because she was breathing shallow, through her mouth. Although everything here had been made for easy cleaning—the floor, the tiled walls like a bathroom's, lots of metal—even the reek of disinfectant couldn't mask the odor of death.

"Tell me," she whispered, keeping her distance as she'd promised Greg she would. Never had she more fervently wished that she really was psychic. "Tell me who did this to you."

Then her head—Faith's head, of course—came up. She heard something in the hallway, male footsteps. Someone was coming.

Someone who didn't belong here. In fact...

She didn't know those boots. So why did they concern her?

She concentrated, straining to catch this particular heartbeat. It pulsed more rapidly than the heart of someone who was simply taking care of tasks at work. It sounded more like someone doing something they shouldn't. And in this otherwise lifeless room, surrounded only by hearts that never would beat again, she recognized it.

The killer was coming.

Time to leave, thought Faith—but her feet didn't move. It wasn't from courage. Some instinct more powerful than her desire to see the killer's face was holding her transfixed, listening to those footsteps, listening to that heartbeat. What was different about it? A murmur? A rhythmic anomaly? Could she even be sure it was the killer, and not her imagination?

Her head couldn't. But her instincts weren't letting her go out there, all the same.

The problem was, he was coming in here. She didn't have to be psychic to guess that. This room was at the end of a hallway. He was coming in here, and either she stood here and waited for him, or she left by forcing herself to walk right by him—

Her feet weren't cooperating.

He was barely ten feet from the door, if that much. She could hear it. Nine feet. Eight....

Faith wanted to stand her ground. But she'd been raised on paranoia for too long. Almost in defeat, she spun, tugged open one of the steel drawers at her feet—

A man's ashen face stared back up at her. One of the dead gangbangers. Being a crime victim, he didn't look happy, even in death.

The footsteps were only six feet from the doorway. Five....

She kicked that drawer smoothly closed and yanked the handle of another. It glided open, empty. She swung in, feet-first.

Three feet from the doorway...

Planting either hand on the disinfected, death-scented linoleum beneath the drawer, Faith pushed backward, sliding herself into the dark, steel confines of a drawer that normally held dead bodies.

Chapter 3

It was cold. Cold and dark, and so very, very close.

Not that the former residents of this drawer had needed to see or stay warm.

On her stomach, Faith tucked her arms beneath herself, both for warmth and to lever her face farther from the steel slab that had held countless corpses. She shivered. Even her extra-keen eyes could see nothing. She could hear nothing. Was this thing actually soundproof? If so, was it so the dead could sleep peacefully…or so that the living wouldn't hear them?

Stupid, thought Faith of her own fancies. *Stupid, stupid.* Now that she'd committed to this foolish course of action, she felt frustrated with her own cowardice. That, and its impetus.

A person couldn't really have such distinct hearing that she could recognize a specific heartbeat, from down the hallway. Could she? Not even a freak like her. It had to be her imagination. Or maybe she was mentally deficient. Her mother had never wanted to consult a doctor about Faith's "condition."

Even if she wasn't crazy, and the visitor to the morgue *was* the killer, why hide? She'd had a chance to see the man's face, to finally know who had done this horrible thing to her friend…

But even now, when she considered pushing out of this body locker, she couldn't quite summon the courage. She'd been in shock when she'd gone after the killer at the bar. Now, in daylight, facing him down seemed even more foolish than hiding from him.

Even in here.

She could feel her muscles stiffen, her breath strain in this cold, solid tomb of sensory deprivation. If she raised her head, she bumped it on steel.

Something felt sticky under one elbow—*don't think about it!*—and she shivered harder.

Minutes passed.

Desperate, she harnessed her thoughts back to logic. Okay, suppose the intruder really was the killer from the bar. What the hell would he be doing here? How could he have gotten past security? Why would anyone take such a risk?

The last question echoed through her skull as surely as her own heartbeat and chattering teeth echoed blindly, deafening, back at her in this closed metal drawer. *Why?*

Roy Chopin had almost asked if anything had been taken from Krystal's body. Faith felt sure of that. But shouldn't he be asking about Krystal's personal possessions rather than her corpse? What could be—

Taken from a corpse?

Oh, God. A trophy.

When the bodies on the slabs had merely been things, the empty remains of crime victims, hiding made sense. But when

Faith thought of them being further victimized—here, where they should at least be safe—she couldn't stand it.

She might already be too late. Safety be damned. Planting her hands on the sides of the drawer, wincing to imagine whatever else might have touched the same spot, she pushed forward—

And bumped her head on steel.

No.

She was locked in?

No! Barely swallowing back an embarrassing whimper, she fumbled at the front of the drawer. Oh, God, no. She couldn't have made such a horrible mistake. What if she suffocated in here? What if nobody found her for days? She would never have a chance to make up with her mother. She would die a virgin. It would be like being buried alive!

When her hands encountered a latch, her relief was dizzying. Her reaction to the snick of that latch, to the rush of air that now smelled fresh in comparison to where she'd been, was heaven itself. But she didn't have time to savor it as she threw open the door to the body drawer. She pushed the tray that held her forward, rolled stiffly off it, braced herself for an attack from—

From nobody.

Faith crouched there beside the open drawer, her heart pounding, her hands fisted, and faced an empty examination room. She spun one direction. Turned the other. Nothing.

Had she imagined it?

But no. She wasn't imagining the scent that lingered beneath this smell of antiseptics and death. It didn't matter if most normal people wouldn't be able to smell it; many smokers couldn't discern scents like baking bread or cheap perfume either, but that didn't mean the smells weren't there. This smell was here, too. Part musk, part heat. Power. Dominance. *Evil.*

If Faith needed further proof of intrusion, Krystal's corpse now stared blankly at the ceiling.

Someone had moved the sheet from her blue-lipped face.

Still catching her shuddering breath, skin crawling from her momentary entombment, Faith took a hesitant step closer to her friend's remains. The bruised horror that had once been Krystal's slim, smooth neck seemed all the more blasphemous. Her eyes were open, blank. Her pale blond hair…

Was something different about her hair?

Faith bent closer, peering at it. There was definitely a blunt wedge where a chunk of hair by Krystal's temple had been inexpertly sliced away. Someone had taken—

A knock at the open doorway startled her so badly, Faith sprang back from the corpse with a cry. Then she stared at her boss, confused. How had Greg gotten so close without her hearing him?

Just how upset was she?

Still, now that she did notice him, his heartbeat sounded comfortingly, familiarly like Greg. He wore Nikes, not boots. He, at least, wasn't the killer.

"This is your version of keeping distance from the case?" he asked, pale eyes frowning behind his glasses.

Faith flushed. "I came looking for you and I…I found her like this." It was technically the truth. She was just leaving out the middle part, where a more honest woman would say, *and I heard someone coming and hid in the drawer and then climbed back out once he was gone and* then *I found her like this.*

"Like what?" He came closer. He had a clipboard in one hand, a pen behind his ear, fresh gloves flapping out of his pocket. That was so Greg. Now that she'd noticed him, he wasn't the least bit silent. Just…quiet-natured.

Easy to be with.

"Uncovered. And…some of her hair's been cut off. Did the medical examiner take it to run tests?"

Greg took her by the shoulders—luckily his hands made contact with her sleeves, not her bare skin, but subtle sensations flowed across her all the same.

Nothing bad.

"That's it, Faith. You're done for the day. I don't care where you go, but you're too close to this case to be here until we've finished processing the evidence. Consider it bereavement leave."

This time, Faith was aware of someone else coming. He didn't sound like a threat. He sounded like the medical examiner. "But Greg, look. She's missing hair."

At least he looked—which meant he also let go of her. And he frowned. "That's odd."

"Then the M.E. didn't…?"

"Didn't what?" asked Dr. Mandelet, entering. He was a round man with café-au-lait skin, curly black hair and a neatly trimmed beard, his accent faintly touched by the Caribbean. His shoes, Faith noticed, had crepe soles.

"If you took hair to test, wouldn't you take it by the root?" asked Greg, using his pen to ruffle the fresh, blunt cut amidst Krystal's perm.

"I'd want the follicle attached, yes. But—" Close enough to see the cut himself, Mandelet swore. Then he glared at Faith. "Did you do this?"

"No!"

"Of course she didn't," agreed Greg. This time, his hand on her shoulder felt downright comforting. His belief in her innocence felt simple, straightforward. Easy. She found that she could still concentrate on the situation around them, even with this subtle, physical connection to another human. Interesting. "So who would have?"

"Didn't you say the DB was a tarot reader?" asked the M.E.

Faith frowned. "What's that got to do with anything?"

"It matches her hands." Now that he had an audience, Mandelet drew one of Krystal's waxy hands out from beneath the sheet. Faith caught a glimpse of her friend's bare hip beyond it, and felt embarrassed for her. "She's got calluses on the inside joints of her fingers, on the edges of her thumbs. See? Feel here."

Faith shook her head.

Mandelet grinned, clearly thinking Faith's hesitance had to do with the fact that Krystal was dead, not knowing that Faith had hesitated to touch her even when she lived. "Trust me. This young lady knew her way around a deck of cards. So what I'm thinking is, one of her witchy friends snuck in."

"What? No!"

"Faith," cautioned Greg. "We're just theorizing."

"It's happened more than once around here, especially in the funeral homes," Mandelet insisted. "Voodoo practitioners. People pretending to be voodoo practitioners. Pagans. Psychics. Hair and nail clippings are a big deal to those kinds of weirdos."

Faith's roommate Evan, a practicing Wiccan, would call it the Law of Contagion. Having a piece of something, or something that had been in constant contact with your focus, was considered as good as having the actual focus.

"Huh." Greg sounded amused. But he also dropped his hand from Faith's shoulder, so she couldn't tell why he was amused and had to get her information the old-fashioned way—by turning to him. He was taller than he looked.

"I was just thinking about how important hair and nail clippings are to *us,*" he explained. "Maybe this is another case of magic and science being more closely connected than they're given credit for."

Sometimes Faith *really* liked Greg.

"Anyway," said Mandelet, and from the way he eyed Faith, she knew he hadn't completely discounted her as a suspect in the hair theft, "I wouldn't worry about it."

But before he twitched the sheet back over Krystal's face, Faith had to ask. "Wait. How—exactly how did she die? I really need to know."

Mandelet and Greg exchanged a look, and Greg nodded. The M.E. shrugged and pulled the sheet farther down, so that it barely covered Krystal's breasts. "You work here, little lady. How about you tell me?"

"She's a desk clerk," protested Greg, but this time Faith didn't appreciate his protection.

"She was strangled," she said, starting with the obvious. "I don't know what he used—"

"He?" inquired Mandelet.

"Women only account for a tenth of the murder arrests made, right? And then they usually kill lovers or their children. And aren't women more likely to kill from a distance, like with poison, than in a physical attack?"

Both men were nodding. So Faith felt sure enough to ask, "But what did he use?"

"Wire garrote?" suggested Mandelet. "That would be a professional's choice." But he waited for her response.

"That would leave a cleaner line, wouldn't it?" She bent closer to what had, thankfully, been reduced back to evidence. "And a belt would have left a wider mark. I'm thinking some kind of cord or rope?"

"Silk," agreed Mandelet. "Red silk. I removed fibers from the wound. If we can find that rope, her DNA will be all over it. The killer may have left epithelial evidence on it from his own hands as well, so that we can work toward a second DNA match."

"And if we can't find the rope? Did she maybe scratch him, or pull some of his hair, or—"

The M.E. shook his head. "The only tissue under her nails was her own, from when she fought the rope. There was evidence that she'd had sex in the last few days, but not recently enough for us to match the semen. It seems to have been consensual, in any case. The pattern of tearing on the—"

"That's enough," Greg interrupted firmly, and drew the sheet over Krystal's face. "This is getting too personal. Faith, you're taking a few days off, and that's that."

She nodded slowly. *If we can find that rope...*

It was as good a place to start as any, and she couldn't very easily start looking for it if she was at work all day. "You're right. I'll go. Thank you, though. Both of you."

"When you get back, you're welcome to sit in on a few autopsies," offered Mandelet, and as disgusting a thought as it was, Faith recognized the compliment in his offer. "You have a good eye for it. You don't want to stay a clerk forever, do you?"

"Stop poaching my administrative staff," warned Greg, saving Faith the necessity of answering that question. She really didn't know what she wanted, in the long term.

But in the short...

She wanted to find Krystal's killer.

"You should call Detective Chopin," she said, as she and Greg left the examination room. "That's why I came looking for you. He wants to ask you some questions."

About whether anything had been taken. She'd let the detective and the CSU supervisor work that part out, though.

She had her own investigating to do.

Faith hoped she wouldn't be the only one of the roommates to resume work that Monday. She figured their landlord, some British guy who lived with his wife north of the lake, would want his rent whether there were four people or five living in his multiroomed French Quarter apartment.

She found Evan, at least, where she thought she would, a ten-block walk from work.

Jackson Square.

If Bourbon Street was the heart of the nighttime French Quarter, Jackson Square—spread between the spires of the St. Louis Cathedral and the wide Mississippi River—was its daytime heart. Tankers and barges made their slow way down the expansive river, along with riverboats playing bright calliope music. Cab horses with their great, grassy scent pulled open carriages on slow tours of the oldest part of the city. Street performers—balloon clowns, mimes and today, a truly talented saxophone player—plied their talents in exchange for tips from the tourists. Different psychic readers set out chairs or tables in what Faith had learned was a silent hierarchy, the best readers at one end of the Square, the less experienced at another.

Krystal had been one of the best.

And artists, protected from the heat by little more than oversize patio umbrellas, hung their work on the wrought-iron fence that surrounded the Square, hoping for a sale or a commission.

Evan was one of those artists. He did portraits and was particularly skilled with charcoal and pastels, though he could do caricatures for a quick ten bucks as well.

The humid August air smelled of grass, azaleas, coffee and beignets as Faith crossed the sunny square to her friend's purple umbrella. "Hey."

"Hey there!" He stood from the canvas camp-chair where he'd been sitting, sketching on heaven knew what, as he saw her. Evan had been raised an old-fashioned southern gentleman, by a Garden District family that expected him to become a doctor and marry a debutante. His decision against either option had caused something of a rift in his family, though they still invited him for holidays. "Aren't you supposed to be at work?"

"They threw me out," she admitted, sinking onto the cement base of the fence so that he'd feel comfortable sitting as well. "My boss is calling it bereavement leave, but what that really means is, they're uncomfortable having me so close to the evidence."

Evan's eyes widened. "They don't suspect *you*, do they?"

"I doubt it. But most murdered women are killed by someone they know. Since we knew Krystal, we might know her killer. So there's always the chance I might try to cover something up, you know? Why take that risk? Although…"

Evan resumed his seat and turned the page in his sketchbook. "What?"

"Were you aware that Krys was seeing anybody? Even sleeping with them?" Usually, Faith could catch a whiff of other people off her roommates, if they'd gotten close. But not always. She tried to give them their privacy.

"Not that I know of." Evan shrugged. "So are you going home now?"

"No. What I want to do… This may sound weird."

Evan grinned. "No. Not that. Anything but weirdness."

"You know the community better than I do. Are you aware of any readers who are good at finding things that are lost?"

"Like what?"

"Krystal's murder weapon."

Evan gulped, his hand slowing on the page of sketch paper. "Oh."

"The bastard used some sort of cord or rope, and he didn't leave it with her body. When you pull that hard on something, then some of your own tissue is rubbed off. So if I can find the cord, we might be that much closer to finding the killer. Assuming he didn't take it with him, of course. Or wear gloves."

Evan looked kind of green, but he forged on anyway. "I do know of one person who's good at psychometry. She can touch something and tell you all kinds of things about it, like who held it last, and how they were feeling, and where they were. Nose like a bloodhound, too."

Her recognition of his sarcasm had everything to do with the pitch of his voice and the slight change of his body temperature and scent, and nothing to do with paranormal abilities. "I'm not a psychic."

"Sure you are. You're just a different kind of psychic than most of us."

"No! Moonsong's a psychic—she can look at a person's palm and tell all kinds of things that have nothing to do with how their heart's beating or how they smell. And Absinthe, with her horoscopes. Even Krystal. She could shuffle those cards and lay them out and tell you things nobody could have guessed. She could predict—"

She stopped, tilted her head, met Evan's eyes.

"She could predict the future," he said softly, guessing or intuiting or maybe even *reading* what she'd just thought.

"So why couldn't she predict hers?"

"Well, some readers believe they can't see their own destiny, that they're too subjective to have any clarity."

"Or maybe she did predict it," supposed Faith, "and just didn't tell anyone."

"Or maybe she predicted it, and just didn't tell *us*."

"Absinthe," said Faith, standing.

"Absinthe," agreed Evan. Neither of them imagined that a frightened Krystal would go to Moonsong. Moonsong, for all her innocence and kindness, was one of the protectees of their little group, not one of the protectors. But Absinthe took no prisoners. And if she'd known something…

It certainly would help explain some of the extra grief and guilt their usually implacable roommate was feeling.

"I'll go see what she knows. And then I'll try to find someone who can help me find that rope. Are you sure you don't have any suggestions there?"

"Look, I've heard of some things my circle and I could try. Not psychic, but magic. Like maybe using a pendulum over a map to locate an item or a person, that sort of thing. But if it was my killer you were looking for, I'd put my faith in you. So to speak." Evan turned his sketchbook. "Do you mind if I display this?"

He'd done a charcoal sketch of Faith, every line of her face a graceful curve, a stylish edge. Her reaction—surprise, pride, uncertainty—all of it mixed in her chest, and she took an uncertain step backward. "I—"

"I know it's not that good," Evan insisted.

"No! It's—" *Beautiful.* But how could she say that? "My mom would have a cow," she said instead, changing the subject. "Once I got my picture in the paper, when my sixth-grade class sang Christmas carols at a nursing home, and she called the paper to complain about not getting permission. She never liked…"

Never liked the idea of strangers seeing Faith. Never wanted the publicity.

"That's okay," said Evan, with a shrug. "If you want, I could—"

"No. Go ahead and hang it. It shows what a great artist you are. Mom won't know about it, and if she finds out, she can lump it." *Or finally do me the favor of explaining what the hell she's hiding.* "I've got to go talk to Absinthe."

"Between the lot of us, I bet we can find Krystal's killer," said Evan hopefully.

Faith said, "We can at least help."

In more ways than one.

By that evening, she had enough with which to make a call. It was awfully soon after her interview with the detectives the other night. But for Krystal, Faith had to risk it.

The information she'd gotten from Absinthe was too weird—and too pressing—to ignore.

And forty-two hours had passed since Krystal's murder.

It was time to revive Madame Cassandra.

Chapter 4

"The dead woman," Faith said, with the fake Virginia accent she'd adopted for these anonymous public-telephone contacts, "was having nightmares about vampires."

"Vampires?" repeated Detective Sergeant Butch Jefferson, from his mobile.

In his background, Faith heard someone else—his partner, Roy Chopin. "She's gotta be kidding you."

"Y'all clearly don't understand dream interpretation." As soon as she'd decided to pass information from her psychic companions to the New Orleans Police Department months ago, Faith had known she must remain anonymous. For one thing, she'd been raised to keep a low profile, a habit difficult to shed. For another, explaining that she was merely speaking *for* the psychics, instead of *as* a psychic, would lessen her already shaky credibility.

Instead, when she made contact, she pretended to be a

reader herself. She'd pulled the name Cassandra out of the blue, probably because she believed herself to be conveying the truth, as surely as the ancient Greek heroine had, and because, like that mythic Cassandra, Faith honestly doubted anyone in authority would believe her.

"Well then, Miss Cassie," said Butch, his drawl far more real than hers. "Won't you please enlighten us?"

"I would be delighted." She readjusted the black receiver of the pay phone in the Aquarium of the Americas. She never used private numbers to call Butch. "Dreams can't generally be taken at face value. They tend to be symbols."

"Yes ma'am."

"If Miss Tanner feared vampires, that could mean she was afraid of being drained of power, of energy."

She heard Butch say, away from the mouthpiece, "She thinks maybe the dead psychic was worried about being drained of power."

"Could be she just went into withdrawal when Anne Rice moved to the suburbs," said Chopin.

"Could be," insisted Faith, "that she was predicting something about her own death. Being murdered is about as drained as a girl can get, isn't it? Did either of you nice detectives get the impression that the murderer might believe in magic?"

"I fear we've been too short on likely suspects to do that kind of questioning," admitted Butch. Whether or not that part was true.

"Well, y'all should check. All kinds of details could have magical meaning, which could tell you something about your killer. For example, if you found salt at the crime scene." She knew they had. "Salt's a protective substance, magically speaking. Or if there's a chance she was strangled with something made of natural fiber, that would indicate a killer who's concerned with energy transference."

She'd learned of the dreams from Absinthe. Moonsong had explained the significance of salt, and of a silk cord versus, say, nylon.

"You don't say," mused Butch. "Miss Cassie, I do believe you may be on to something here."

Then she had to wait while he repeated the insight to his partner and fielded the usual smart-mouthed responses. Faith shifted her weight, feeling exposed in the bluish light, filtered by displays of wavering water. The Aquarium of the Americas would be closing in half an hour. She hoped to finish this call before they made any kind of announcement that would tell the detectives where she was.

She also wore a black wig and sunglasses, in hopes of skewing anyone's description if the police traced the call and come around asking questions.

It was during long delays like this that she got the most paranoid. She also didn't like having the time to notice that whoever had used this public phone before her had drunk more than one hurricane. It reeked of rum.

"So what's your opinion, Miss Cassie?" asked Butch. "Was Krystal Tanner killed by one of her spiritualist co-workers?"

"No! I mean—most folks who work on, shall we say, the edge of expected reality? They understand the consequences of karma. If this man you're after wanted to take Krystal Tanner's energy, he's likely some kind of untrained wannabe."

"Why is it you think that?"

"Only two things could make him think he can escape the karmic repercussions of murder, Detective Sergeant. Either he's got such strong personal power, psychic shields, that he doesn't have to worry about it—in which case he'd know that someone else's energy wouldn't do him a whole lot of good— or he's too ignorant to know better."

Butch murmured what she'd said to his partner, then asked, "Do you have anything else for us just now, Miss Cassie?"

She heard a slow beeping on his end of the line, like a car door had been opened while the key was still in the ignition. They'd arrived at wherever they were going.

"If this fellow's a wannabe magic user, he might try some kind of crash course," she suggested. "There's a psychic fair Wednesday night at the Biltmore Hotel."

"The one that had those strange fires last year?" Apparently the damage had been almost entirely external. Then again, almost every old building in the Quarter had some strange story to tell.

"That's the one. There won't just be readers there, there'll be experts offering classes. Someone who wants to learn about manipulating energy, chances are he'll show up." That had been *her* first introduction to the magic community of New Orleans, anyway. "And on the chance that he might be looking for more victims, that would be the place."

"I appreciate that advice," said Butch. "But if you don't mind me asking, Miss Cassie…"

Which was when she felt them. Rather, felt *him*.

Roy Chopin was like a walking car alarm of energy—and he was getting closer. They'd traced the damn call!

"Tsk, tsk," said Faith, frowning, and hung up.

Then she headed deeper into the aquarium, mingling with the other visitors, and was around a corner before the detectives ever made it through the entrance, much less to the pay phones.

He loved that they were all frightened of Him.

He was, in fact, the talk of the Crescent City Psychic Fair! For a while He felt happy just sitting outside one of the ballrooms at the Biltmore, watching the people come and go, lis-

tening to their conversations. He could tell some of the psychics by how they dressed—tie-dyed shirts, multiple necklaces with different charms hung on them, gauzy, sparkly skirts. They were the ones who talked the most about Krystal Tanner—that's what the newspapers called the other night's human battery—and their fears about who might be next. He could tell the visitors by their dazed expressions as they scanned the fair's program, and by their uncomfortably loud jokes, pretending that they were here as a lark when, really, each of them wanted to believe. And then there were the ones in-between, the ones He couldn't be sure about.

Like that green-eyed blonde.

She was the same one who'd chased Him away from Krystal Tanner. She'd caused trouble for Him. And she wasn't scared.

He felt stronger, when people were scared. He felt more real. So he didn't like her. But was she a psychic? She didn't seem to be attending any of the workshops, but neither had she paid for tickets—readings cost between five and twenty-five dollars, in five-dollar increments, depending on how skilled one's reader was. She wasn't even carrying a program, and almost everyone carried programs. Instead, she seemed to just be moving from one ballroom to the other, almost...patrolling.

As if someone like her could protect these witches from the likes of Him.

In any case, if she had no abilities, she was beneath His notice. Once He saw the detectives from the other night approach her, He decided it was time to slip into one of the smaller lecture rooms, to hear about "Chakras and Personal Energies."

Maybe then, He'd figure out how to draw more fear out of these people. Soon, if He kept feeding, even the Master wouldn't be able to contain Him.

Then He would be free.

* * *

Faith felt Chopin's approach, but she decided not to turn until he said something. Why advertise that she could hear his footsteps and his strong heartbeat, could smell his unique scent of coffee, aftershave, motor oil and forcefulness on the hotel's Freon-edged air?

"Don't tell me you believe in this junk?" he demanded, as he leaned around her elbow.

Faith blinked at him, his suit coat rumpled, his tie loose, his top two collar buttons undone to show a tanned throat and a thatch of dark chest hair. He needed a shave and a haircut, and—to judge by the shadows under his intense eyes—a good night's sleep. That extra edge of coffee—black, and lots of it—told her he was pushing himself too hard. If it was to solve Krystal's murder, she liked that about him.

If it wasn't, then she was still annoyed about him trying to catch her—as Cassandra—the previous evening, even if he hadn't succeeded.

"I didn't know you were a believer either," she countered, then had to laugh at the face he pulled in reaction. "Hello, Detective Jefferson," she added to Chopin's more easygoing partner. She knew his real title was Detective Sergeant, but since Cassandra called him that, it seemed a good idea if Faith did not.

"Call me Butch, ma'am."

Even better. "Okay, Butch. Are you two here officially?"

"We figured we'd take a look at the kind of folks Miss Krystal knew," explained Butch, while Chopin looked on like a kid dragged to his sister's school concert. His mouth was in threatening mode, and his jaw was definitely a dare. "Maybe track down that missing lover. Ask a few people if they saw anything. Do you know any of the psychics 'round here?"

"Sure. All three of my roommates are reading tonight."

Chopin let his head fall back, relieved. "So that's why you're here. Keeping an eye on them, right?"

Which was true, but she didn't like his tone. "That, and to maybe get a past-life analysis or have my aura cleansed. Were you two looking for someone in particular?"

"Yeah," said Chopin. "The killer. Any suggestions?"

She had to remember that it was Cassandra who'd brought them here, not, as far as they were concerned, Faith. But it was surprisingly easy to hesitate, to glance around. "A few minutes ago I saw the guy who tended bar at DeLoup's the night Krystal died. But I was talking to him at the time of her murder. And none of my roommates know who Krystal was dating. I believe them."

"Here's a thought," suggested Butch. "We need to figure out more about why this fellow targeted a psychic. Why don't I make the rounds, talk to some of these fortune-teller types, while Roy here trades you a cup of coffee for an overview of this little community. How would that work for everybody?"

If *everybody* was Faith and Roy, they just stared at him.

Chopin snapped out of it first, shrugging his rangy shoulders. His suit coat hung open to show the gun and badge on his belt. "Uh, sure. Couldn't hurt, right?"

Yes, it could, thought Faith. But she wasn't sure why. She didn't sense any threat from this man. He was pure cop, and even if she'd been a suspect through her close knowledge of the victim, the evidence couldn't be less incriminating. He wasn't out to arrest her. He was…

Was he interested in her?

She'd smelled that shift of pheromones often enough in her life to know that yes, he was. But she also knew physical interest wasn't exactly an on/off switch for most men, or quite a few women. Sometimes even inappropriate men, like a professor or a doctor, or even her boss, couldn't help their body's reactions. All she could hope was for them to guard their behavior. Most, like Greg the other day, did just fine.

Other than calling her cute on the phone, which could've just been teasing, Chopin was also keeping it cool. Distant. Although as she continued to hesitate, his brows drew together into a foreboding frown, like he was taking it personally.

"Sure," she said. "I'll tell you whatever I can, Detective Chopin."

"You can call him Roy," insisted Butch with a grin and a wave, veering off toward the first ballroom.

"That guy's as subtle as an ax to the head," muttered Roy, forcing an after-you gesture that was hardly sulky at all.

"I'm guessing you don't get out much?" said Faith, preceding him toward the wide, curved stairway. The restaurant's bar, the only place to get coffee, was off the lobby on the ground floor.

His presence, behind her, felt downright tangible. "Not that it's any business of his or yours, but no, I don't. I'm a little busy what with all the murderers and scumbags running around needing to get caught."

"All work and no play…"

"Is exactly the sort of thing Butch would say. So how do you like your coffee, Miss Corbett?"

She didn't bother requesting that he call her *Ms.* Corbett. She let him fetch the drinks, too. That sort of thing mattered to some guys. For her part, she waited at a little bistro table, her chair turned so she could watch the foot traffic to and from the stairway to the ballrooms and the psychic fair.

"So what can I tell you about the psychic community around here?" she asked, turning her back on the passersby when Chopin returned with the coffee. He was not a graceful man. She felt relieved when the drinks were on the table.

"How'd you get involved with this element?"

She blinked, unused to being taken by surprise. "Am I still a suspect, Detective? I was scheduled to go back to work tomorrow, after the memorial service, but if there's any question…"

"No, you're not." Holding her gaze, Chopin leaned over the table, his presence all but enveloping her. "And it's Roy."

Faith considered him and the way his pulse and body temperature belied his cool attitude. "Oh. Well, if you're asking for personal reasons…I mean, if you're asking because you're interested…" She didn't quite have the guts to finish that sentence, unsure as she felt. "Anyway, you really should be clear about that, and not hide it behind official business."

He sat back now, folded his arms, studied her. Then he nodded. "Yeah. Okay. Tomorrow's my night off. Go out with me."

She stared. For someone who telegraphed his emotions that strongly, he'd surprised her twice in just a few minutes!

Maybe he only telegraphed what he wanted to telegraph. The strength. The intensity. The threat. Things that would tell any suspect with a few brain cells to rub together that this wasn't anybody to mess with. The other stuff, the more personal stuff, he hid that pretty well.

She only caught a whiff of regret when something in his intense eyes faded. "Or not," he said, shrugging. "I just wanted to get that out of the way before—"

"Okay." Now she'd been surprised three times. She hadn't expected to be surprised by herself, though.

He blinked at her, then widened his eyes, raised those expressive brows. "Okay?"

"Tomorrow night. It's a date." Faith was so used to reading what other people gave off, it took her a moment to realize that the flip-flopping in her stomach came from her, not anyone or anything else. But that reaction, at least, wasn't surprising.

She didn't date. Being whatever she was—not *knowing*

what she was—made things way too complicated. And now she'd said yes? To a homicide detective? *One she was hiding things from?*

But I'm only hiding Cassandra, she thought grimly. *I'm only hiding that I'm not...normal.*

What was she supposed to do, make every possible date contingent on a confession of her abnormalities? Magazines suggested that a person keep private problems like STDs or past relationships quiet until at least the second date...or before getting naked, whichever came first. Why was her own freakishness any different?

Now she could barely breathe past the butterflies. *What had she done?*

She'd taken a defiant stab at being normal, that's what.

"Good," said Roy, with a decisive nod. She could tell he was pleased, though he hid it well. "Now, could we move on to the important stuff? How long have you known these people? Not because you're a suspect—but how well do you understand them?"

It was easier, talking about impersonal things like the New Orleans occult community. And the Big Easy definitely had a thriving occult community. Of course, Chopin—Roy—knew a lot already. He'd seen the Voodoo Museum and Marie Laveau's tomb. He knew where the vampire bars were—not for true immortals, as far as Faith knew, but for wannabes marginally more Goth than Absinthe. Lord knew Roy couldn't have patrolled Jackson Square without seeing the readers. But he'd never taken the time to learn what really motivated the psychics.

Until now. When in detective mode, he wasn't a lousy listener.

Faith explained that none of them seemed to be cult members—an official cult had to have a leader, and the majority of psychics were self-taught. She clarified the more innocent reasons that readers often chose new names, and how careful most of them were to abide by the vice laws that—hopefully—kept people from being defrauded by cons like the old curse-removal ploy. She thought she did a pretty good job at not focusing too intently on the detective's thick wrists while she talked, or the dark hair on the back of his wrists, or his big hands as he cradled his cup of coffee and stared intently at her, listening. She thought she managed not to breathe in his scent and think about their upcoming date too often.

Would he touch her?

Would he *kiss* her?

Did she want him to?

How ridiculous was it that she was freaking about something this basic at twenty-two years old! It was time to practice Krystal's quiet breathing techniques.

"So upstairs," he said, thankfully oblivious, "some of the *readers* as you call 'em only charge a nickel a pop."

"Nothing that cheap," said Faith. "It starts at five dollars...."

Roy grinned as if she'd said something cute. He looked a lot more approachable when he grinned, even if it was mocking. "Butch was right. You are an innocent. A nickel *is* five dollars, hon. And when I say that for some of those readers, you need a Jackson to get past the door...?"

She didn't like being an innocent. It sounded too close to being stupid. "You mean a twenty? Got it."

"So why the difference? I mean, it's fantasyland either way. Do they actually think there's something there?"

"It's not fantasyland."

He cocked his head as if waiting for the punch line.

"Really," she insisted. "Some of the readers are so good it's uncanny—"

"Look, Corbett, I've read reports. There's all kinds of tricks people use to make it seem like they're reading your mind when they're just telling you what you want to hear. Now if Miss Cleo up there's only charging a Jackson for it, I can live and let live—I mean, it would cost that much for a hand... uh, for, uh, other kinds of happy feelings that are less legal. If you know what I mean."

He paused, examining her. "I honestly don't know if you *do* know what I mean. I think I like that about you."

She was pretty sure she did know what he meant, but it seemed counterproductive to say so. Especially when her tummy was flip-flopping just because he'd said he liked her.

Get a grip. You aren't even sure you *like* him!

"So the amount they charge makes a difference to you?" she asked.

"The clients are asking to be duped. But what I want to know is, do these people honestly not realize they're fleecing anybody?"

"Maybe you should get to know them better." Faith couldn't keep the ice out of her tone, and Roy visibly drew back. "If you did, you'd know that the majority of psychic readers are honest people trying to provide an honest service. They *aren't* fleecing anybody. They decide what to charge based on who's been practicing the longest and who has the best track record."

"Come on. If everyone up there was really psychic, why wouldn't they win the lottery instead of getting paid a few Jacksons at a time?"

"This is a psychic fair. It's community outreach. Personal readings cost a lot more than a few Jacksons."

"Not an argument in their favor."

"And psychic abilities don't necessarily work that way. How's your eyesight?"

Damn, but he had expressive eyebrows. "Come again?"

"You've got pretty good eyesight, right?"

"Sure."

"So tell me who's standing in front of the Eiffel Tower right now."

He snorted. "I couldn't say."

Faith folded her arms, trying to look severe. "I thought you had good eyesight. Were you conning me when you said you had good eyesight?"

"But," he countered, clearly enjoying himself, "if I got on a plane and flew to Paris, I could describe anyone in front of the Eiffel Tower. Why wouldn't one of those psychic types get on their imaginary plane and fly wherever they needed to go to get a good look at tomorrow's lotto numbers?"

Which left Faith with nothing better than, "It doesn't seem to work that way." It sounded lame, even to her ears. "And then there's karma."

They scowled at each other. Then Roy tried a different angle. "So how good a rep did Krystal Tanner have? As a reader, I mean."

"She was one of the best." And she was. *You're so lonely,* she'd told Faith during that first reading, and that without even touching her. *Because you sense so much, you try not to sense anything at all. You haven't found your soul mates yet—or they haven't found you. You're scared to let people know your secrets. So's the woman who raised you...your mother...?*

"Who else is considered good?"

Faith gave him a few names, most of whom were upstairs, several of whom were published. "Then there are some who don't do the public fairs."

"Name one."

"Celeste Deveaux, I guess—she was a lousy fortune-teller, but she's supposed to be an excellent medium. She doesn't like doing readings for people whose grief is still fresh, so she avoids walk-in readings like this. There's a witch who goes by Hecate who's the real deal, but she's out of state right now."

He actually had his notepad out of his pocket, writing these down. "A witch. Great. Give me more."

No, she thought, annoyed with his pushiness as well as his cynicism—and still, damn it, noticing his thick wrists. Then she had a truly bad idea. An unmistakably bad idea.

So why did it appeal so strongly?

You're playing with fire. Don't even think about it.

"Come on," wheedled Roy, turning on the charm. He would never be a model, not with the tired eyes, definitely not with that nose. But something about him... "Someone. Anyone."

By now, the alternative would have been to bite her tongue off. "She's not well known, but I've heard rumors of someone in town who's supposed to be very good. Very, very good. It's a Greek name...Cassiopeia? No, that's not it...."

He sat up. *"Cassandra?"*

She widened her eyes. He liked innocence? Well here was innocence. "That might be it."

Roy was gritting his jaw so tightly as he shook his head that she feared he might break some teeth. Wow. He *really* didn't like Cassandra, did he?

Better to know that now, she guessed. "Not that I've ever seen the woman. Apparently she keeps to herself."

"Yeah, but you've heard something." Like that, he was leaning over the table again, warm and demanding and coffee-scented. Practically leaning over her. Practically touching. "Tell me what you've heard."

Caught now, she would have been glad for almost any interruption.

She still felt a cold horror wash through her as she recognized something—a footstep, a heartbeat—behind her.

The killer was here.

And he was feeding.

Chapter 5

Faith spun in her chair and stared at the red-carpeted lobby, where at least two people had just left the hotel. It had been him. She was sure it had been him!

"And now I'm talking to myself," muttered Roy, behind her.

She didn't bother stopping to explain. She slid off her bistro chair and took off out of the bar.

"Hey!" Roy yelled. But Faith was busy racing across the oriental rug of the lobby, putting her shoulder into the revolving door, stepping out into the spattering rainfall that was New Orleans in August. She looked one way.

Nothing.

She looked the other.

Nothing. Rather, there were plenty of people heading in both directions, umbrellas hiding their faces or heads bent against the rain. This was the French Quarter! Tourists wandered, enjoying the rain like they might a special effect in a theme park.

Partygoers hustled, trying to keep their good clothes dry. A trumpet player on the corner ignored the rain to wail out a tune reminiscent of Al Hirt, with a hat by his feet for wet tips. The air was thick with the perfume of plopping raindrops on hot concrete, underscored by the scent of the nearby river, of ice cream and soft pretzels, of wisteria from a nearby courtyard. But whatever Faith had sensed inside had faded.

It didn't make any sense.

She'd felt him going in this direction! It wasn't like he could suddenly ditch his unique heartbeat, like someone pulling off a mask…was it?

"What the hell was that?" The words, immediately behind her, didn't startle her anywhere near the way Roy Chopin's hands, catching her damp arms, did.

Oh, God! Like an exposed power line.

Faith stiffened, but not in time to escape the sudden burst of energy that sizzled through her, the emotions, the images. *Someone fed him home cooking on a weekly basis. He liked beer. He spent too much time around the jail and the station and on the streets. His underlying edge of violence was a constant problem for him. He'd had sex sometime in the last month but that's all it had been, sex, he didn't love the woman—*

With a mew of protest, she wrenched away from him, spun to face him.

Then she saw how his eyes widened, how he raised his spread hands and took a step back as if to show her he was unarmed despite the belt holster. She smelled his sudden guilt and confusion. That's when she realized how she'd hunched down into herself at his touch. Like some kind of frightened victim.

Deliberately she squared her shoulders, raised her chin, even if it felt like she'd snap something, forcing herself back into a posture she didn't yet feel. So much for being normal.

Roy Chopin kept his distance, lowering his hands slowly, clearly meaning to convey how harmless he thought he was. He squinted against raindrops in his eyes. "You okay there, Corbett?"

But he was looking at her as if she wasn't okay at all.

"I...I don't like being touched," she said, blinking back against the wet. Her voice sounded only a little husky from sheer mortification. *There* was a statement that would win dates, for sure. "You startled me."

"I'm sorry." The hands were by his sides again. He was starting to relax, to breathe again, hair dripping across his forehead. She'd scared him.

"No, I'm sorry. I know it's weird."

"I didn't touch you till you were already out here," he said. For a minute, she was confused. Then he said, "You just ran off. What's up?"

He wasn't just confused about her reaction to his touch. He was confused about how she'd bolted.

I sensed the killer. Then I didn't.

"I thought I heard something," she said, which was at least true, if lame.

He was feeding. The thought came to her again—but what had it meant?

The fear, when it hit, hit hard. Absinthe! Moonsong! Evan!

She spun for the hotel again—but luckily, before she could put the icing on her embarrassment cake, Butch Jefferson came through the revolving door. "Now what are you two doing out here in the wet?" he demanded, the seriousness in his gaze contradicting his friendly tone. "Son, I got something upstairs you should see."

Chopin gave her an after-you gesture, so they headed inside in detective-Faith-detective order.

It was a handwritten note. Someone had found it at the empty table where Krystal would have "read." Their shout of alarm had drawn the attention of others.

Now too many bystanders clustered and whispered, while Butch and Roy studied the piece of Biltmore stationary without touching it.

"'She was delicious,'" read Roy, frowning. "'The next one will be even tastier.'"

The whispering of the psychics and guests and hotel staff became something closer to a group moan—a noise with too many words to retain any individuality, merely distress. But they were communicating the same fear, something Faith had already half guessed herself.

Hadn't she suggested the killer might come here to scope out more victims?

"He's a serial killer," she whispered, giving voice to what the others were murmuring amongst themselves…kind of like she did with her informative calls as Cassandra.

"No," said Roy firmly, standing. "There's no proof of that. He's just trying to get as much mileage as he can off of the one killing we do know about."

"But—"

"This is a note, not a body," he insisted, while Butch used tweezers to lift the page into a Ziploc bag from his pocket. These detectives came prepared. "Don't buy into his game, Corbett. It's what he wants folks to do."

He was feeding, thought Faith again—and now it made sense. The killer had been high on the fear he'd created. That's why he'd left the note—to create fear. That's what she'd heard in his pulse, in his heartbeat.

She shivered.

Roy made a disgusted sound. "You're wet. You want my jacket?"

"No." She managed to stop him before he could shrug it off. "I should probably get my roommates home. It looks like things are closing up early, after this."

"They were in the main ballroom the whole time, right? As long as they didn't see anything suspicious, head 'em out."

"Thank you for the coffee."

Roy was frowning at the now-bagged note, holding it up to the light. He wasn't even looking at her. But he said, "Seven okay?"

That took Faith by surprise. "What?"

He slid his gaze from the missive to her, mouth threatening again. "Tomorrow night. Date. Seven?"

Despite her attack of the heebie-jeebies out front? The only thing more embarrassing than the idea that this was now a pity date was the idea of him knowing she knew it was a pity date. "Okay," she said, as they both turned to their own particular duties.

Butch looked immensely pleased with himself.

Faith had never been to a funeral before. She had no family besides her mother—no grandparents, no great-aunts or uncles, nobody whose passing would have required she attend their services. Since she and her mother tended to move every few years, she rarely made friends long enough to see one of them die. So she wasn't sure how Krystal's memorial service compared to other funerals.

But she knew she hated it.

The grief was palpable—grief from Krystal's parents, who'd come to collect the body; grief from all her friends; grief from some members of the community who'd shown up without even knowing Krystal, just as a way of expressing their anguish and outrage over this murder in their city.

That last group made Faith wonder if perhaps moving

every few years hadn't been a good enough excuse for not attending funerals in the past, after all.

Butch Jefferson and Roy Chopin were there, too, though they stayed in back. Faith supposed they were taking note of who attended. She remembered from a criminal psychology class that some killers liked to see the results of what they'd done.

In any case, the detectives' solemn distance seemed respectful, and Faith knew she could count on them to notice anything suspicious. She kept her focus on the people who needed her more. Her roommates. The family.

Once the last songs had been sung and the casket had been carried to a waiting hearse for its drive to Texas, Faith had to go home and shower before she could bear to go back to work.

"Welcome back," greeted Greg with his characteristically vague smile, once he noticed she was there. "I'm afraid there's a pretty good backlog of forms for inputting."

"Gee, thanks. You need to make me take time off more often," Faith teased weakly. But it felt good to settle in at her desk and take care of a good chunk of the work, her fingers clattering softly over the keyboard. It felt good to make progress on something and, more important, it felt normal.

As close to normal as her life got, anyway.

Not that it would ever stay that way.

"I thought you'd want to know," Greg announced, after a lunch break that Faith had worked through. He sat on the corner of her desk, like he had before, and smiled at her over his wire rims. "We didn't get any full prints off last night's letter. Other than the prints of the woman who found it, that is. It goes to graphology next."

He held up the see-through bag with the Biltmore note inside.

She was delicious....

"Can I see it?" When he handed the bag to her, Faith knew she'd have to stall in order to figure out how to do this as subtly as possible. "What do you suppose the handwriting analyst will find?"

Even forensic scientists who specialized tended to dabble in other areas of the job.

"Chances are it's a man's handwriting," said Greg. "Although that's never a hundred percent. The left slant could indicate low self-esteem, maybe a personality that's trying to hide the truth about himself. The lower the t-bar, the lower the goals this guy sets for him—what are you doing?"

Faith had used his distraction to unseal the bag the slightest bit and take a whiff of the note. *It was him.* She was almost sure of it. She suspected that if she touched the note, she could be positive, but that would be far too suspicious.

Evidence, around here, was sacred.

"I was wondering if he used one of those smelly inks," she lied.

Greg took the bag back from her and resealed it, but he smiled with bemused patience as he did. "The labs will also give us that, don't worry."

Faith returned his smile, glad he was so easy about things, and turned back to the computer—but Greg didn't stand up. "Faith," he said.

She turned back to him, surprised at this break from their usual patterns of conversation. "Yes?"

"I was wondering…would you let me take you out to dinner? We could discuss everything you've been through lately, make sure you're in a good place…."

She stared at him. Her mother sometimes said that when it rained, it poured, and she'd just run into the perfect illustration. Two invitations for dates in less than twenty-four hours.

And one from *Greg?*

He was even older than Roy Chopin—by almost another decade!

"Never mind," he said quickly, standing. "It was a bad idea."

But was it? She'd liked how it felt when he touched her face the other day, the edge taken off his energy by his latex gloves. She liked how his hands always smelled of balloons.

On the other hand, it wasn't like she could ask him to wear latex gloves on a date. And he really was old enough to be her dad. She may have desperately missed having a father figure growing up, but that didn't mean she should date one.

"I'm sorry," she started, past the uncertain ache in her throat.

"Forget I asked. Really."

"It's just that—we work together. It would be awkward."

He nodded. "And I've kept you from work long enough. Will you come find me if the detectives working the Tanner case call? I want to give them an update on the prints we lifted."

"Will do." She wanted to say more—mostly, she wanted to apologize again. But she suspected that would only make it worse, so she went back to work, as if nothing was wrong. This was by no means the first date she'd ever turned down.

Just the first date she'd ever turned down with someone she genuinely cared about.

And instead she'd agreed to a date with Roy Chopin?

The minute she thought about it, butterflies started again. Was she an idiot? She might say something that told him she was less than normal. She might say something that told him she was Cassandra! Even if neither of those minor disasters took place, she had to worry about what would happen if he tried to touch her and she shrank from him like a beaten dog. Or what if he didn't try to touch her? This was a date, wasn't it? Shouldn't there be at least minimal touching?

Faith had tried to date, in high school. It had been a disaster. Teenage boys were all about sex, and unlike most teenage girls, she'd been able to tell that from their scent, their temperature. She was intrigued by the idea of sex, but she'd barely managed the few kisses she'd tried without recoiling from heavy doses of Too Much Information. How could she ever manage more? By the time she'd started college, she'd pretty much given up.

Last year, her junior year at Tulane, she'd met a nice guy named Jesse. Jesse seemed to really like her, not just the idea of sex with her. He'd said they would go as slowly as she needed. They started just by holding hands. Once she got used to his presence, the contact didn't open up a new screen in her head every time they touched. Then they moved onto a few careful kisses. She'd thought she was falling in love. For a few weeks it was as if the whole world had a glitter about it, as if she had a chance at normalcy, at human contact, at last. She'd even started looking forward to doing more than kissing....

Then he'd shown up for a date smelling like his study partner, smelling like fresh sex. When she'd accused him of cheating on her, then challenged his denial, he'd said there was no way she could tell that. He'd called her a freak....

It wasn't long after that ugly breakup that she'd sought out the local psychics, hoping they might have some answers. Why was she the way she was? They hadn't known. But at least they'd had a place for her. She'd dropped out of school after that semester—she could always finish her degree when she was sure what she wanted. And she hadn't gone out with a man since.

Was she honestly going to end her drought with an example of walking attitude like *Roy Chopin*? Especially when she was hiding things from him? When she was turning down a perfectly nice, gentle Greg Boulanger?

And hadn't she just told Greg she didn't date people from work?

Faith took the coward's way out. She called Roy at the station and left a message. *Can't make it. Thanks anyway. Faith.*

Afterward, for the rest of the afternoon, she felt lonely. But she was used to feeling lonely.

Feeling like a freak of nature, though…when had that begun to matter? Either way, she didn't want to go through it just now. Not this soon after Krystal's funeral. The week had been hard enough.

After hanging up with the station, she phoned the apartment and suggested they all go to the movies to forget their troubles.

The movie wasn't great, but it proved a decent enough distraction. When Faith and her roommates got back to the apartment, Evan said he'd come upstairs after he grabbed a smoke.

The apartment was a steal, for what they paid in rent. It had a second-story entrance off a cobblestone courtyard, French doors, plantation shutters and wrought-iron railings. Faith sometimes imagined that the rooms held memories, trapped energy and emotions from its previous tenants—a mother who had taken on surprising responsibilities, a son whose morality could have gone either way. Rumor had it the owner had a soft spot for the magical community, which was why he'd initially rented it to Krystal. He'd been at the funeral, a solemn Englishman with a dusky-skinned Creole wife, and Faith hadn't sensed anything in particular off him, but she hadn't gotten that close, either. Whatever his reasons for renting, Faith was glad for it. She loved the place. Inside was just as nice—marble floors, ornate moldings. There were two bedrooms and an office, which they used as a third bedroom, Evan's. Absinthe and Krystal had shared a room. Moonsong and Faith had the other.

Like a boarding school. Like a dorm room at college—
which Faith had never had, having commuted to school from
her mother's house.

Now Moonsong had decided to move in with Absinthe,
where Krystal had stayed, and Faith wasn't sure how she felt
about that. It really had been an awful week, and as she fell
back into the overstuffed sofa in their living room, she was
aware of a dull ache deep in her chest. Was it guilt, for can-
celing her date? Was it maybe disgust at her cowardice?

Or maybe it was just disappointment for losing a chance
at something so normal.

But you're not normal, so how could the date have been?

It didn't help when Moonsong pressed the play button on
their blinking answering machine.

"So here's the thing," announced Chopin's deep voice, and
Faith sat up. "You say no, I gotta take no—I mean, I'm not a
stalker or anything. But could I maybe ask why? Is this a let's-
reschedule can't make it or a leave-me-alone can't make it?
Call me. Unless it's the second one. Then, I guess, don't. I'll
try your other number."

But if he meant her last, lost cell phone, he would be out
of luck. He recited what must be his cell phone number.

Then he said, "Oh. Uh, this is for Corbett."

The machine beeped, and Faith was conscious of both Absinthe and Moonsong's intrigued stares. What a difference
there was between the two women—Absinthe's eyes darkly
lined and cryptic, Moonsong's large and lustrous and hopeful despite wearing no makeup.

Before she could say, or even *think* to say "I can explain
that," the next message came on.

"Faith? Faith, baby, are you there? Pick up."

It was Faith's mother, Tamara. Her voice shook. She was
crying.

Faith stood and moved dumbly closer to the machine, as if she couldn't already hear every stuttering gasp in her mother's breathing, every crackle on the recorder's old tape.

"We need to talk, baby," said Tamara. "Please."

Faith had snatched up and was dialing the telephone before the machine beeped to indicate the end of messages.

"She sounded awful," marveled Absinthe.

"Something's wrong," whispered Moonsong, thankfully not claiming that bit of blinding obviousness as a psychic impression.

"Shhh," hissed Faith. She'd gotten her mother's machine. It wasn't her mother's voice but that of her employer, Mr. Manning, but Faith already knew about that. Her super cautious mother had read somewhere that it was better to have a man's voice on the answering machine.

"Mom?" she said, as soon as the message ended. "It's Faith. Pick up. What's wrong?"

The line clicked and Tamara said, "Faith?"

Taking a deep, openmouthed breath, Faith leaned back against the wall. Her friends exchanged thankful looks as well, at this obvious sign of Faith's relief.

"Yes, Mom. That's why I said 'It's Faith.' *What's wrong?*"

"Everything," whispered Tamara. "Everything's wrong. First the e-mails. Now phone calls. I need to talk to you, baby. I need to talk to you before they do."

"What do you mean? Is someone harassing you?"

"We need to talk, Faith."

"Mom, I'm right here. We're talking."

"No…alone. Face-to-face." Faith was accustomed to her mother's occasional hysterics, but this seemed legitimate. Probably. Maybe.

"Okay. I'm on my way."

"Take a cab, baby."

"I'll take the streetcar, Mom. It runs twenty-four hours."

"I wish you wouldn't risk yourself like that…."

"See you soon," said Faith, and hung up. She was twenty-two, for heaven's sake. Her mother didn't want her living away from home, and now she wanted to dictate Faith's transportation choices? The streetcar was eminently safe. New Orleans couldn't risk its tourist business by letting it be otherwise.

She didn't realize she was scowling until Moonsong said, "You weren't very nice."

"Sometimes my mom drives me crazy."

"As opposed to everyone else's mom," scoffed Absinthe, while Faith grabbed a lightweight rain jacket, just in case.

Chances were, Tamara had been frightened by shadows. A wrong number on the telephone. Misdirected mail. Someone watching her at the supermarket. She'd once quit a job and moved herself and Faith across the country because of some man who'd been staring intently at them every time they went to the supermarket. But there was still the chance that her fears, whatever they were, were legitimate this time.

Just as important, there was the chance Tamara was ready to confess whatever guilty secret Faith had begun to sense more and more over these past few years.

We need to talk, Tamara had said. *Face-to-face.*

Faith felt a sickening dread at whatever her mother might confess. But she also felt a certain excitement. Maybe now, finally, she'd know the answer. Maybe she'd understand.

"Don't wait up for me," she instructed her roommates, heading out.

"Don't get killed," countered Moonsong, her dark eyes big. "Couldn't someone go with you? Evan maybe?"

"I'll ask." Faith shut the door behind her, turned on the stoop—

She realized they were there—heard them, smelled them—even before she saw who waited downstairs in the courtyard.

Evan was there, yes.

He was also surrounded by five menacing young men.

Chapter 6

Had someone mentioned gang activity in Storyville?

Several of the men looked up at the sound of Faith shutting the door. Their smiles gleamed into the night.

Evan looked up, too. To judge by the whites of his eyes as well as the rush of adrenaline she smelled, he was frightened.

"Go back in," he pleaded quickly, loudly. "Call the—"

His words ended in a grunt as one of the boys drove a fist into his gut. Evan doubled over with a cry, crumpled to his knees.

Before she'd considered what she was doing, Faith vaulted the railing and landed into a crouch on the cobblestones of the courtyard, maybe ten feet below.

"You don't want to do this," she warned the intruders as she straightened. Now... how was she going to persuade them without touching anyone? "Get out while you can."

The boys grinned. They seemed to be teens, but big teens with facial hair. A couple of them actually laughed. One swore in that way boys do, trying to sound tough. They were all wearing something green, like some desecration of St. Patrick's Day, and they were a surprising mixture of races, like an old Benetton advertisement gone violently bad.

"Now her," said a scraggly, tattooed white boy, the one who'd punched Evan. "Her, I could like."

She could smell lust off him and several others, an ugly, dominating smell. They weren't about to get out while they could. In fact, she sensed violent promise in the tightening of their muscles, the faint increase in their temperatures, the quick inhalations as they made the decision to attack.

Chances were, they would do more than touch her.

So Faith attacked first. She leaped and kicked the scraggly bastard right in the solar plexus. Between the sole of her shoe and his shirt there was no real contact—well, none except the blunt impact that shot up her leg, but that she could handle. She felt something give under her heel as the boy staggered backward.

He looked almost as surprised as she felt. Wow!

She'd taken kickboxing for one of her P.E. credits at Tulane, but only for one semester. She'd taken archery the semester before that, but that hadn't made her Robin Hood either. How had she…?

Two others surged at her. She felt their heat behind her, heard their heartbeats. She knew where to strike and gave up wondering how. She drove the hard angle of her elbow into someone's shirted gut. She barely felt it. Following through on that spin, she struck out again with a closed fist—

Right into someone's nose. Skin to skin.

He was scared of looking weak, scared of being embarrassed by a girl. He thought Evan was strangely attractive, and for that Evan would have to die. He'd done something, crack maybe, not half an hour ago—

Luckily, the contact was brief. It hurt her hand, the pain in her wrist mingling with the backlash of his pain. Amazingly, the sensations somehow canceled each other out. The cracking sensation beneath her knuckles, his bellow—they washed away the unwanted images she'd gotten from that moment of touch.

It felt…freeing.

One of the intruders was backing away, eyes wide as if staring at a ghost. One stumbled with a cry. Evan, who'd tripped him while still on his knees, gasping for breath, said, "Hah!"

The other three fell on Faith.

Arms circled her from behind. Hands grabbed at her waist. A face thrust into her bare neck, too close, too intimate. Three at once. Contact everywhere. For a moment she was dizzy, overwhelmed. *One had been molested as a child. One had recently forced himself on his little sister's friend and her crying had pissed him off. One had already decided to kill her and Evan rather than leave witnesses—*

Oh, God!

But when she struck out, as randomly as a blindfolded child swinging for a piñata, the images stopped.

The momentary overload stopped.

Suddenly she could focus on where they stood in relation to her, on what they were doing, on how they were moving—and how best to defeat them.

As if following a choreographed routine, Faith moved. The face pressed against her neck gave her an ear to bite into. She did that, hard, and felt her teeth break through skin. She tasted blood.

The boy reared back, screaming. Even as she spat out his blood she was already leaning forward, away from someone else's bear hug. Her captor bent with her. When she quickly straightened and snapped her head back, her skull impacted his face with a crack that reverberated through her. It made her see stars—but he slumped.

Especially since she'd swung her fist down and backward too, at hip level. He'd been hard—she couldn't think about that. But the way she drove his privates up into his groin, he wouldn't be for long.

The Asian boy in front of her had the collar of her shirt and a handful of her hair. Now that Bear Hug had let go, she clasped her hands above this one's arms and drew all her weight down, inside his bent elbows. As he was jerked forward by her weight, she head-butted his face.

Again, she saw stars. She didn't care. It was as exhilarating as hurricane-force winds. Wild. Stupid. Wonderful.

Someone else came at her from the side—she heard his footsteps, his breathing, his heart, and knew exactly where he was. She spun and clapped her hands against both of his ears at the same time. A self-defense instructor had once said the move could break eardrums.

She thought she heard a muffled *pop*. She didn't imagine his scream, or the wet smear on her palm. He was the one she'd already bitten.

She spat again at the memory, and looked for her next victim.

They were backing away from her now. At least one was crawling.

Evan rose to an unsteady crouch, then to his feet, so that the two of them could stand shoulder to shoulder and present a united front.

Most of the teenagers were muttering profane insults, which didn't carry as much weight when someone backed away while saying them. But one guy, the Latino who hadn't fought, just breathed out three stunned words.

"What *are* you?"

His words shuddered through Faith, more powerfully even than her own gasps for breath. Because she really didn't know.

She didn't know how she'd managed to fight like that. Not from just a semester of kickboxing, she didn't. Not from an evening workshop on self-defense for women. And she sure as hell hadn't inherited the skill from her mother.

Then the boys turned and ran, helping the one she'd hit in the balls and the one she'd kicked in the kneecap. Then the courtyard was empty again except for her, Evan…

And the sound of approaching sirens.

"You aren't coming?" repeated Tamara Corbett, outrage in every shaking word. Her voice got softer, accusing. "You said you were coming, baby."

From the sofa, Absinthe was saying, "They're targeting us. First Krystal, now Evan and Faith."

From the doorway, Evan was telling one of the patrolmen, "They said they were playing a new game. Bag the fag. If Faith hadn't come out when she did—"

The second officer, a black woman, was asking Moonsong, "And that's when you called 9-1-1?"

"I kind of got delayed," said Faith into the phone.

"What could be more important than your mother?"

She went with the truth. "Some guys jumped Evan. I helped fight them off." *And I was really good at it!* "We have to make official reports. Tomorrow we get to go look at mug shots."

"Oh my God," breathed Tamara.

"I'm fine," Faith hurried to assure her. And she was. Sort of. Her head hurt from where she'd butted into people. Her hands were swelling, especially on the knuckles and the edge where she'd whacked that guy's neck. One of her ankles felt sore, and one of her wrists throbbed. And yet…

She barely noticed. It was a clean pain.

Normal.

"You're moving home," announced Tamara. "Now. I'm calling a cab, right now, so you pack up your things—"

"No."

"I won't take no for an answer," warned her mother.

"You'll have to." Even the cops looked at Faith when she said that. She smiled, shrugged, turned her back and lowered her voice. "I'm not moving home with you, Mom. I'm perfectly safe here."

"Your roommate's dead and you were attacked in your own courtyard!"

"I doubt they're related." No matter what Absinthe said. "The MOs are completely different."

"Don't talk as if you're some expert on law enforcement. You're a desk clerk!"

"Don't minimize what I do." Maybe it wasn't what Faith hoped to be doing in five years, but it was a start. "And don't pretend I'm a child anymore. I'm staying here, and that's final. The two attacks aren't related. Really. And the police said they'll make more frequent patrols near us. We're locking the courtyard gate when they leave. Anyway, that's why I'm running late and why I wanted to know how important it is that we talk tonight. If it's really that immediate, I'll take a cab."

Tamara snapped at the chance. "Bring a suitcase."

"And once we've talked I'll come right back, no matter how late it is. But if it *will* wait until tomorrow, why don't I come over after work? In the daylight?"

For a long time her mother was silent. "Tomorrow will be fine."

Faith wasn't that surprised. Tamara had her faults, but not caring about Faith's safety was hardly one of them. "You sure?"

"Yes, you come tomorrow evening, while it's light. I'll make pork chops."

"Thanks." Faith turned to see another man and woman appear in their doorway. These were NOPD detectives—she could tell by the world-weary looks and plain clothes. Not Roy or Butch. This was their night off. "I should probably go."

"Wait. I won't keep you, baby, I promise," Tamara insisted. "But…do you think there's even a chance someone could have *hired* these men to attack you?"

The question came from so far out in left field, Faith had trouble processing it. "They attacked Evan. I just got in the way."

"Never mind," said Tamara quickly. "We'll talk tomorrow night, then. You take care of yourself, promise?"

"Yes."

"You *promise*."

"Cross my heart," Faith insisted. Then, after the requisite I-love-you's, she turned to the detectives.

Roy's presence hit the office like a storm front. As soon as he pushed through the doors, Faith's head came up from where she'd been reading a poorly written form—some cops had handwriting second only to doctors. She was almost surprised that the other papers weren't blowing off her desk.

"So I go by the department gym to lift some weights before shift," announced Detective Chopin to her, as if they'd been in the middle of a conversation. He grabbed someone's desk chair as he stalked by, whirled it in a circle, planted it in front of Faith's desk and straddled it from behind. He braced his forearms across the chair back, leaned over them and fixed Faith with that deep gaze of his. "This beat cop from third shift's working off his night. He says, 'Wait till you hear this one. This little blond number, she takes down five gangbangers.' He describes the whole thing. We're both laughing, ha ha, at the idea of some cutie wiping the floor with these delinquents."

Faith knew he was describing her, but she waited for the punch line, watching those eyes. And those wrists. And those fresh-from-the-gym arms. He'd showered after his workout; she could smell his fresh deodorant soap along with the coffee. His hair was still damp. She felt an internal fluttering again, half-push, half-pull. He made her uncomfortable, and she still wasn't sure what to do with that.

Roy's fake expression of amusement sobered, just like that. "Then he tells me the address," he growled.

She shrugged.

"I say, 'Hey, I think she's the one who stood me up last night.' He says, 'That should be a relief.'"

"I didn't stand you up," Faith pointed out. "I called first."

"Yeah, that makes it all better. You took down five gangbangers?"

"No, I took down three gangbangers. One of them wasn't fighting us, and Evan knocked another one over."

"Oh." His taut nod radiated sarcasm. "Well, that's different."

"Why are you angry at me?"

"'Cause the way I read the report, you could've just stepped back inside and called 9-1-1."

"And left Evan alone with them? That's no alternative at all. He's the one they were after."

"I'm thinking not for long they weren't."

"You're interrupting my work," Faith announced, and turned back to her data entry.

"Bernie." By thigh power alone, ignoring her rolled eyes at the strange nickname, Roy propelled the chair he straddled, a chair without wheels, against her desk. A metallic clang sounded, and a pen rolled off from the impact. "Appearance is everything to those guys. They aren't going to like it that a girl beat them up."

"Not my problem."

"It will be when they try to even the score."

She looked up at that. "Are you trying to scare me?"

He widened his eyes, like, *duh*. "Is it working?"

"No. Go away now."

"I'm here to see Boulanger."

"I could tell." She gestured to her desk, the only thing separating her from his intensity and the corded arms under his T-shirt. "He doesn't seem to be on my desk right now. Maybe you should try his office."

"You're cute when you're a smart-ass, but I'm not sure I need the agony of dating someone who's gonna end up on that slab back there."

"Then it's a good thing I stood you up, isn't it?"

"You still haven't told me why." He spread his arms. "What's not to like?" His mix of arrogance and self-deprecation made her smile, despite herself.

"Maybe you're too pushy. Maybe you scare me."

She'd meant the second comment to be teasing, but the truth of it struck her uncomfortably. The way Roy scowled, it didn't strike him so well either. She remembered how she'd acted when he'd grabbed her in the rain. *Damn.*

"I don't know what to do about that," he said, leaning back in the chair, studying her. "It's not like you can't take me, right?"

She couldn't help it. She eyed his broad shoulders, his pumped biceps, his big hands. Just thinking about trying to fight him off gave her the shakes.

But not in the same way fighting off gang members had. Not even necessarily in a bad way.

"I wouldn't count on it," she said, hiding her gaze by looking down at her paperwork.

"Looks like you did a job on your knuckles. So where'd you learn to fight like that, anyway?"

"Tulane." *And maybe from my Dad.* She'd been thinking about it a lot, since the previous night. Could a person inherit her father's fighting skills, without ever having met him? *If* her father could fight, why hadn't her mom mentioned it before?

Luckily, Greg arrived. "Hey, Roy. What's up? I didn't know you were on this early."

"I'm here to ask you about the note." Roy stood. "And I heard Faith here was heading to the station on her lunch hour to ID the mug shots of a few of her victims. I thought I might walk with her."

"And what," challenged Faith, amused that he was telling this to Greg before he mentioned it to her. "Carry my books?"

"Yeah, and if my newspaper route pays off, maybe I'll even buy you a soda. Grow up. It's damage control because you're a magnet for bad guys, is what it is." He talked big, but she sensed his concern was real. That had to concern her, too.

"Do you mean just the gangbangers?" she asked. "Or do you know something else about the serial killer?"

Roy planted both hands on her desk and bent over them, his face uncomfortably close to hers. Coffee. Soap. "There's no proof he's a serial killer. If he were, we'd have to bring in the feebies, and I'm not going there without more than one body."

Feebies were the FBI, whose jurisdiction included serial killers. Cops and the FBI weren't exactly a model for inter-agency cooperation.

"He may have been at the psychic fair to scout victims," Faith insisted. "He says he'll kill again."

"Which makes him a *potential*—" Instead of finishing, he rolled his eyes in defeat, straightened and nodded at Greg. "Tell her, will you? The chance of this one whack-job going after her is a lot lower than the chance of an entire gang try-ing to recover their lost dignity."

Greg, looking from one of them to the other, said, "Faith told me about the attack last night. You don't think it's con-nected to her dead roommate?"

"No, but I'm not above using it as an excuse to talk her into dating me." Waving her away, Roy headed for Greg's office. "All likely agony aside."

"She doesn't date co-workers," Greg said.

"Are we co-workers?"

But then Greg shut the door. Not that it kept Faith from hearing, if she made the least effort. But since the only rea-son Roy was talking about her was to annoy her, he immedi-ately changed subjects to something more important.

The killer's note.

Faith went back to her data entry, but she worked slowly, quieting the sound of her fingers on the keys to better follow snatches of what was going on in Greg's office. Apparently the handwriting analysis had shown that the writer might be mentally disturbed, but he hid it well. Roy said that was good news, but he was being sarcastic. He admitted that they'd questioned Krystal's boyfriend from the previous year but had to let him go; he wasn't the killer. They had no idea who the killer was.

"We got nothing," Faith heard him admit. "Butch has re-sorted to listening to some psychic contact he's got."

"What, Cassandra?" Greg laughed. "I talk to Butch, too."

"An anonymous contact is bad enough, but an anonymous *psychic* contact?" Roy swore crudely. "I say if they aren't will-ing to meet you face-to-face, they aren't worth it."

"When you've exhausted all the possibilities…" Greg re-minded him, a shrug in his voice.

"And in the meantime we've got a bunch of so-called *read-*

ers who are either scared out of their wits or not scared enough, and a few hangers-on like that assistant of yours who swings either direction. Hey. Tell me something."

As Roy lowered his voice, Faith's fingers slowed to a stop on her computer keyboard.

Then he asked, "You ever talk to her mom? What's up with that one?"

Greg said something about only speaking to Mrs. Corbett once, when Faith was out, but Faith couldn't hear clearly anymore, not through the buzz of understanding that filled her head. Roy thought her mother was crazy? *When had he talked to her mom?*

But the answer to that was suddenly obvious. It must have been last night, when Faith cancelled the date. That must be why Tamara, in a panic, had called Faith.

Faith stood, torn in two directions. On the one hand, she couldn't call Roy out on this without letting him and Greg know she'd overheard. So much for banter, bulging biceps and the possibility of him carrying her imaginary books.

On the other hand...

Damn. The only other alternative was to pretend she didn't know about it, and that was no alternative at all.

She stalked to Greg's office and hurled the door open, not bothering to knock, startling the hell out of the two men inside.

"You called my *mother?*"

Chapter 7

By the time Faith stepped off the St. Charles streetcar a few blocks from her mother's Garden District residence that afternoon, she felt physically ill.

Not just because of the shouting match she'd had with Roy Chopin, one that had ended with them writing each other off for good. Not just because of how bad her behavior had made her look in front of Greg, who wasn't just her boss but someone whose opinion she very much valued.

Not even because of the time she'd spent in the horrible atmosphere of the police station, turning pages of mug shots that carried energy of countless victims before her—though that had been its own ordeal.

She felt sick because, without knowing what her mother would confess, Faith had apparently read enough, subconsciously, to know she wouldn't like it. She'd suspected that, avoided that, for far too long. Her increasing awareness of Tamara's secrets was partly why she'd moved out.

And now it was time to face them.

The Garden District was the most elegant representation of old New Orleans, a showcase for mansions and arching oak trees. Moving there from Kansas City had been like stepping into a version of *Gone With the Wind* in which the north had lost. From the streetcar stop, Faith passed several stately homes—the Deveaux Villa, the Bernard House—before she reached the Manning Mansion, a showplace surrounded by iron fencing, fronted with Doric columns and accompanied by a cluster of historic outbuildings. One, which used to be the white-bricked carriage house, had been adapted to a separate residence at about the same time the Mannings had traded their four-footed horsepower for the kind that took gasoline.

That's where Faith's mother lived, where Faith had lived during her college years. Mr. Manning had old money and political clout, but he wanted to be an author…except, he had no interest in actually writing. Tamara was a talented writer. She sometimes wrote as Tammy Betts, but her favorite job was ghosting for clients such as Manning. When her agent hooked the two of them up, room and board in such a prestigious neighborhood had been one of Tamara's main reasons for taking the job.

As long as Michael Manning's historic murder mysteries kept selling, Tamara had one hell of a zip code. She still couldn't understand why Faith didn't value locale the way she did. But there were some things Faith had never understood, either.

Such as why her mother, clearly a talented writer, never took her own byline. And now, why a simple phone call from a police detective, on personal business, had thrown her into a panic.

"I told her who I was," Roy had insisted, annoyance at her accusations turning into temper. *"I asked if you were there. She said 'no,' I said 'thanks for your time.' What's the big deal?"*

"The big deal is, you scared her half to death!"

"I noticed. And I gotta tell you, someone who scares that easy is guilty of something."

Which was exactly what Faith hadn't wanted to hear, exactly why she couldn't be reasonable with him, exactly why she'd pushed him into giving up on her.

Because she knew, in her heart, that it was true. Her mother was guilty of something—worse, something concerning Faith. She didn't want to hear it. Not from anybody. The consequences…

Was it wrong to *not* want to know certain things?

"Consider that and the way you are," Roy had said.

"What do you mean, 'the way I am?'"

"That not-liking-to-be-touched business. Makes me wonder what happened to you, if maybe you got touched wrong. Makes me wonder if you even know it, or if you were so young, you forgot. Makes me wonder if your mom hasn't forgotten squat, so she gets freaky when a cop calls. And that makes me wonder if she's the sort of woman who brings home guys who don't just abuse her but spread the joy. That's what I mean. But hey, what do I know? I just do this for a living."

And this from a man who'd never even met her mother! Faith had told him exactly what he could do with what he did for a living, and that had been the end of that.

Except for the fact that she couldn't dismiss his accusations as easily as she could dismiss him.

"Mom?" she called, after unlocking the two dead bolts with her keys and opening the door. "It's me, Faith."

"You're here early." Tamara came out from the back office, looking relieved. She was a small woman with dark, curly brown hair and startlingly pale-blue eyes. The carriage house apartment was charming—exposed brick interiors, copper pipes running across the ceiling like some kind of modern art, regular panes alternating with stained glass in the windows. Tamara, who'd always had the skill of seeming to fit in anywhere, matched the home beautifully. "Is everything all right?"

Faith meant to say that sure, everything was great. But when her mother enveloped her in a soft hug, a *mom* hug, no way could she lie. Her mom was one of the few people in her life that Faith could touch easily, probably because she'd done it so often that she'd adapted to the sensations, like a person learns to tune out a permanent smell or a continuous noise. That made her Faith's sole source for easy contact. Faith didn't want to lose that.

"No," she mumbled into Tamara's shoulder. "I mean, I'm okay," she hurried to add, when her mother drew back in alarm. "But everything else…"

"Your murdered roommate," guessed Tamara. "And that horrible attack last night."

Faith laughed. "Mom, I haven't told you anything about the attack except that it happened. Why would you describe it as horrible?"

"Because anybody who would dare hurt my baby is by definition horrible." Which was exactly why Roy's accusations were so crazy…. Well, some of them. "Come into the kitchen with me. I'll start dinner."

"The detective who called you last night…" Faith hated even mentioning Roy, but she had to know. "Is he what scared you?"

Tamara, who'd been unhooking pans from the hanging rack, paused. Although Faith had long ago gotten in the habit of ignoring her mother's vital signs, if only from courtesy, she now made a point to notice. Tamara's pulse sped up. Her pale eyes darted to the left. "You know that a detective called?"

"Yes, Mom. He said his name was Roy Chopin, right?"

Tamara nodded, tightly, and continued to get out the makings for pork chops. "But he said you broke a date with him. He had to be mistaken. You wouldn't date a—"

"A cop?" supplied Faith. "Why wouldn't I? I work with them every day."

"Which I still hate. You know their reputation around here."

Faith had heard the rumors from the mid-90s. *Better to be pulled over by a carjacker than a New Orleans cop,* people had once joked. But she and her mother had lived halfway across the country back then. "The city's been working to change that for a decade, Mother."

Tamara turned to her, sweating slightly now. Not enough so that anybody without a hound-dog nose would notice, but still… "Faith! You know what those authority types are like, always asking questions, always prying into our business, always jumping to rude conclusions…."

"Like the conclusion that you're hiding something?"

"Exactly!"

Why was it so hard to force the question out? Maybe because it was her mother. Maybe because Tamara was all Faith had left. No dad; he'd walked out when she was still an infant—walked out and then died. Not a single sister, brother or cousin. No grandparents, or aunts, or uncles. Without her mother… "*Are* you hiding something, Mom?"

"Faith!"

"Then why have you never told me more about my father?"

Tamara looked down. "Because he chose not to be part of our lives. He's dead now. It would only hurt you to dwell on him."

But instead of seeking safety in denial, as she had for most of her life, Faith was watching this time. Listening. Scenting her mother's lies. And somewhere amidst those justifications, Tamara was definitely lying.

"Why did we move so often?" Faith asked.

Tamara clasped her hands together, shook her head. "This isn't what I meant when I said we had to talk."

"Were we running from someone?"

Now her mother said nothing. But her pulse, her temperature, her breathing…those spoke for her. Faith wasn't sure she could stand what they were saying. But she couldn't pretend them away, either.

"Is that why you never wanted my picture in the paper? Is that why you never published under your own name?"

"I was trying to protect you," murmured Tamara as she stood, lost, by the still-cold stove. "Because you're so…different."

It was an excuse she'd used before. It had always sounded like a good one. Faith knew firsthand how people could react, when they recognized her strange abilities.

But now she heard that this, too, was a lie.

"No you weren't," she whispered. "Oh my God. You're some kind of fugitive, and you made me a fugitive, and I want to know why. Mom, if you committed some kind of crime, maybe the statute of limitations is up. Or maybe we could find you a good lawyer." But that wasn't it—or it wasn't all of it. Some of this led back to her father. "Did you kidnap me?"

"What?" But the guilt behind that protest was palpable.

"Maybe because my father abused me?" That would be an understandable reason, anyway, no matter how mistaken it felt.

"Nobody abused you, baby!" Tamara's denial sounded honest, which was a mixed relief. But she'd only denied the abuse. The rest…?

"I can't tell you the number of noncustodial kidnappings that come across my desk, Mom. Did you do that?"

"I— No!" Her truth there seemed more cloudy. As if the issue were more complicated than that.

"Oh my God. Am I even really your daughter?"

"Of *course* you are! I carried you for nine months. I was in labor for fourteen hours. I've told you about your birth—7:03 a.m., County Hospital in Chicago. You can't possibly believe— Why are you even asking these things?"

Faith shut her eyes, shook her head. Some of her mother's answers sounded true, heartfelt, but some of them were lies, and she couldn't tell where the line lay. What good did it do to ask the questions when she couldn't trust even her perception of the answers? This wasn't why she'd come. This wasn't accomplishing anything.

"Why are you acting this way?" demanded Tamara, her hands—smaller hands than Faith's—fisted. "Why are you looking at me like that? You're acting as if I'm some kind of criminal. I'm not! I gave you the best life I knew how."

That, at least, was the truth. Faith worked to make her voice more gentle. "You said you wanted to talk. Why don't you tell me what it is you wanted to say?"

But her mother—surely Tamara really was her mother, even if they didn't look at all alike—her mother was too upset by now. The shrill edge to her voice showed no sign of softening. "I wanted to ask if you really knew that detective who called. If you really had a date with him. I thought he had to be lying, but clearly I don't even know my own daughter anymore."

That makes two of us. I don't know my own mother.

"And the e-mail?" asked Faith.

Tamara scowled at the floor.

"You said last night, 'first the e-mail, now the phone calls.' You said you had to talk to me before they did. Who are 'they'?"

Tamara looked up, blinked, and lied again. Blatantly. Deliberately. "I was upset about the detective's phone call. I didn't know what I was saying."

And that was that. "Goodbye, Mom."

Faith turned and headed for the front door.

After a pause, her mother came after her. "Baby, no! Stay for dinner. I'm sorry I upset you over nothing—you know how nervous I can get, but it doesn't mean anything. Let's have a nice evening together, catch up, maybe you can spend the night in your old room—"

Faith spun on her. "No!"

Tamara's eyes widened.

"No, Mother. I'm not spending the night in my old room. I stayed there too long already. And I'm not sitting across a dinner table from you making small talk when this, maybe the most important thing in my life—"

"You're exaggerating, baby."

"Tell me why my father left us!"

And Tamara said, "I can't."

So Faith left. As she headed down the walk, she heard her mother weeping. She felt as if someone had reached inside her and torn her in half, as if she might never patch those two halves together. Half of her came from a father whose first name she didn't even know. A man her mother would tell her nothing about except that he was dead. And the other half…

Was she even Tamara's daughter? Or was it possible she was one of those children you heard about, snatched out of their baby carriage, stolen from a day care, grabbed off the street?

She practically ran to the streetcar stop, barely aware that the sun was still out, too upset to care about such mundane safety concerns. Not with her whole identity in tatters.

If she couldn't get that information from Tamara, then Faith would have to find it the old-fashioned way. She would try to get a copy of her birth certificate, maybe her mother's marriage certificate, assuming Tamara and her father had even been married. And maybe…

Faith climbed onto the streetcar and settled into one of the wooden seats, staring blankly at the mansions and estates and trees that lined St. Charles Avenue, and a name struck her. *Deveaux*. The old Deveaux villa.

Whether or not there was any relationship to the French Quarter medium didn't really matter. What did matter was, Faith had a few resources that "the old-fashioned way" had never included. She might just be able to contact her father, even if he was dead. *Because* he was dead.

At least, she could try. If she knew a good enough medium. And she was pretty sure she did.

Celeste Deveaux was a tall, mixed-race woman with café-au-lait skin, wavy black hair and warm brown eyes. When Faith first met her, a year ago, Celeste had been working as a psychic reader. She'd been lousy at it. Only after one of her clients died—shortly after Celeste had promised him a long and happy life—did Celeste eventually come to realize her skills lay in speaking to the dead.

Since then, she'd gotten such a good reputation that she could afford her own two-room parlor only three blocks off of Jackson Square. The back room, her "reading room," was used for nothing except her one-on-one séances.

When she went in for a reading on Saturday afternoon, Faith had expected blue velvet or glittery stars or crystal balls. What she got was tasteful dark paneling, rich carpeting, three upholstered chairs and artistic black-and-white photography of angelic sculptures.

More importantly, she got a *feeling*.

The air in here practically vibrated. Faith had no doubt that something otherworldly happened here on a regular basis, anymore than she'd doubt the sun rose while watching it with her own eyes. Celeste was a legitimate medium.

So why weren't her skills kicking in for Faith?

"Talk to me," the older woman whispered into the ether, her dark eyes half-closed, unfocused. She swayed in her chair, her hands spread. "This here little girl wants to meet her daddy. She's got some questions she deserves to have answered."

Faith held her breath. She could tell Celeste was in a legitimate trance—her heartbeat had slowed significantly, as had her breathing and something harder to pinpoint...her brain waves? But that was insane. Even a freak couldn't hear or smell or see brain waves...could she?

"I'm calling on Faith's father to come talk with us, now," insisted Celeste, sounding vaguely annoyed. "No, not you, *chère*. No, not you either. I'm looking for Faith's daddy."

Finally, Faith had to breathe. It felt like inhaling past a hole in her chest. So much for her brilliant idea.

Celeste's heartbeat picked up, returning toward normal. Her own breathing deepened. She opened her dark eyes. "I'm sorry."

Faith shrugged. "That's the chance you take with psychic abilities, right? Sometimes they work, sometimes they don't?"

Unlike her own abilities, which seemed surprisingly consistent, another reason she thought she wasn't psychic.

"For me, they usually work better than *that*." Celeste stood and offered her brown hand. She wore many rings, some crystal, some silver, some copper, but the one she seemed proudest of was a simple gold wedding band. "I try not to use this room for anything but readings...don't want to dispel the energy. How about we go out front while we try to figure this out?"

Faith didn't take her hand. Between the fight with Roy, having to look at mug shots in the sludge-for-energy police station and the blowup with her mother, and now her disappointment with Celeste's help, she felt too emotionally vulnerable.

But she followed to the front room, nevertheless, and sat where Celeste gestured, at a small consulting table.

"It's a skill I inherited from my great-grandmother, So-lange," explained Celeste, getting them some iced tea. "That witch was something—all my cousins and I inherited power from her. She's the one who first lived in that house you mentioned, in the Garden District. My folks live there now."

"So if it normally works," said Faith, "why not this time? Can you think of any particular reason you wouldn't be able to contact my father?"

"If he weren't dead, for one," suggested Celeste jokingly. Considering that Faith didn't know anything about the man, though, even that was possible. "Or it could be us not having his name. Having a name, or an item that once belonged to him, that really helps."

"*I'm* an item that once belonged to him." God, but she sounded pitiful.

"Now none of that! There's other reasons, too, good reasons. You're what—twenty-two? That means the man could've been dead as many as twenty-three years. Most folks take longer than that to reincarnate, but you never know. If his soul's busy elsewhere, I doubt even my great-grandmother could've found him."

Celeste's reasons made sense, but Faith could only imagine what kind of skeptical spin someone like Roy Chopin would put on them.

"Wait a minute, there," challenged Celeste. "What's with that face? You don't believe me? I wasn't going to charge you, girl, but if you start pulling an attitude on me…"

That, and the scolding expression Celeste wore, was enough to drag a smile out of Faith. "I was just thinking how easy it is for other people who don't believe to dismiss what you do. Baseball players don't always hit the ball, do they? And yet they're still called baseball players. And sometimes a doctor's patient dies—"

"Don't I know it," agreed Celeste.

"—but he's still a doctor. It's as if some people *want* to disbelieve."

"Mmm-hmm." Celeste took a sip from her tall glass of tea. "Does this 'some people' have a name?"

"He's just some man I decided not to go out with."

"I hope you didn't pull away just because the poor boy doesn't believe you're psychic."

"*I* don't believe I'm psychic."

Celeste considered that, as if weighing several items, then shifted in her chair. "First of all, don't you make the mistake of tuning out anyone who can't see what we see. I've been there and done that, girl, and it's no good. My husband, he didn't believe in my abilities when we started dating, but it was my pride got in the way, not his disbelief. Love's the real power, not anyone's ability to read thoughts or speak to the dead or see the future. Love's the ultimate good."

Love? That sounded so…gushy. "This isn't the same thing. At most, maybe it's chemistry. Or maybe just masochism. It's done with, anyway."

Celeste folded her arms. "Mmm-hmm."

When in doubt, turn the subject back to the other person. "So, did your husband ever change his mind? About your abilities, I mean?"

"Sure he did, eventually. After we were already engaged. But what's important is that he believed in *me,* and *I* believed in my abilities."

"I don't believe in mine. I mean, I don't believe they're psychic. I can feel things, hear things, smell things…."

"Sweetie, you're the best natural psychic I know."

"This from as bad a reader as you were?"

"Fake it till you make it, girl." Celeste's eyes brightened as she lit on an idea. "In fact—why not let yourself *pretend* you're psychic, just for a while? You might be surprised by what falls into place. If you don't want to out yourself, then let your inner psychic be someone else. Give her a different face. A different name."

"Madame Cassandra?" suggested Faith, with a laugh.

"There you go, M.C.," agreed Celeste, who'd heard Faith use the name at least once before. "For all you know—"

The door opened and another client came in from the shimmering August heat. He was a young man. Brown hair. Quiet eyes. Faith looked up at him, strangely drawn, as Celeste finished.

"—Madame Cassandra could turn out to be one of the most powerful forces in New Orleans."

Then Celeste looked up at her visitor—and blanched.

Faith looked from the man to her friend, then back. There was nothing about him to warrant Celeste's reaction or Faith's discomfort. He seemed like the type the words "mild mannered" had been invented for. Sure, she sensed an edge of interest, of expectancy about him, but if this was his first visit to a medium, that would explain it. Right?

So what was niggling at her? What was she noticing without yet understanding?

"I'm sorry to interrupt," he said softly. "I can come back when you're done."

"Get out," commanded Celeste.

The client blinked, surprised. His heartbeat began to pick up, a normal reaction to her rudeness and yet…

"What is it?" he asked.

Celeste stood, pointed a ringed finger at the man. "Get the hell out of here!"

Then she swayed, not so much dizzy as…as altered. *She'd just gone into an instant trance.*

Watching, probably unable to tell the difference, the man took

a deep, unnervingly satisfied breath. His pulse was beginning
to race now, speeding with something close to pleasure—

And then Faith heard it.

Something strange about his heartbeat. Something that
hadn't been there seconds ago. Something she'd heard before.

In the bar. In the morgue. In the hotel lobby.

All that, and a scent she didn't even *want* to identify.

"Your victims," moaned Celeste, clearly channeling now.
"Can't you sense them, thronging around you? They're crying for vengeance. They will have it, boy. Don't you bring that
shit into my place of business."

Then her eyes snapped open, wide and ferocious. *"They're
gonna take you down!"*

The man took a quick step back, clearly startled to realize
that Celeste wasn't the least bit scared.

Faith, on the other hand—Faith was scared. Even before
she recognized what she'd smelled as blood.

The faintest whiff of week-old blood. Krystal's blood.

Even before that, Faith knew.

She was face-to-face with the killer.

Chapter 8

Faith leaped to her feet, sending her chair skittering wildly out behind her. Startled, the killer looked at her—and recognized her. The way his eyes widened, his breath caught, he might as well have announced it.

Then he spun and raced into the street. And there was no alternative.

She went after him.

The streets of the French Quarter were thick with tourists and vendors and performers this early in the evening, when there was still sunlight, but marginally less heat. The killer plowed through them, knocking over a woman in a sundress, pushing a man in a ball cap against a wrought-iron gate. In a flash, he'd vanished around the corner onto Chartres Street.

Faith dove through the holes he'd created. As she skidded around the corner, she caught sight of him again and ran faster. She also tried to memorize everything she could from the back. *Caramel-brown hair. Green shirt.* They pounded past a pretzel vendor. Past Toulouse, heading for Jackson Square. *Maybe six feet tall,* she thought. *Wiry build.*

Faith's feet and her heartbeat created a percussive background to her sprint. But that wasn't all she heard, and she could definitely recognize him now. That distinctive extra skip in his heartbeat. That scent—

Past St. Peters. She was already breathing hard, sweating. God, but it was hot out!

His scent was the same smell she'd first caught in the ceiling of the DeLoup bar, a scent of fear. He didn't want to be caught. Go figure.

But if he really had something on him with Krystal's DNA still present—something like Krystal's hair, or the murder weapon—Faith would sell years off her life to catch him. When an old man taking a picture stepped inadvertently in front of her and she had to dodge around him, she grunted out a curse for those lost seconds. What she wouldn't give for superspeed, instead of supersenses!

The killer shoved past a mime, sent balloons flying from a balloon-animal clown, and tore through the square. So did Faith, right past the statue of Andrew Jackson on rearing horseback.

She thought she might be gaining on him. But at the other side, her quarry dove under an open-top horse carriage, right between the front and back wheels. Faith wasn't quite that foolhardy. She went over the carriage, past a couple who looked to be on a date.

"Hey!" protested the man.

"Sorry!" gasped Faith as she launched herself off the other side, landed running and dodged traffic across Decatur. Past that lay a wide bank of stairs up to the levee. Her quarry was already halfway up by the time she hit them. Beyond those, two separate stairways created a vee against the stone wall. The killer took the right set of stairs. Swinging around with the help of the railing, gulping mouthfuls of August air, Faith pummeled after him. She might be in good shape, but she was gasping for breath as she hit the top. There lay Washington Artillery Park and, past that, the Moonwalk overlooking the Mississippi.

And no killer.

Following her instincts, Faith hurried across the bricked walking path, her head pivoting in both directions, her keen senses alert. She knew this view pretty well. The iron benches. The old-fashioned lampposts. And beyond the walk, lapping at the levee's tumble of stone blocks, stretched the wide expanse of the river, exuding its own impersonal power. The Mississippi spread out like a lake, barges and tankers making their slow way along her depths. Just to the south, calliope music danced from one of the riverboats at the Toulouse Street Warf.

But no killer.

"Damn!" she exclaimed, and kicked a beer can someone had left lying on the ground. It bounced down the levee and into the river, which wasn't what she'd meant to happen. "*Damn* it!"

Somehow, he'd gotten away.

Faith got back to Celeste's just in time to hear her friend say, "One other person. But she left, after he did. She, uh, goes by the name of Cassandra."

Celeste was talking to a pair of street cops.

Oh, great! Faith quickly faded back onto the street, but not before she saw the officers exchange significant glances. Luckily, with her hearing, she was able to wander to a stand selling T-shirts and pretend to examine those while still listening. *Allons Danse,* read the first one she picked up, a zy-deco shirt. *Let's go dance.*

"Cassandra, huh?" asked one of the patrolmen, just as Faith could have predicted he would. "Would you mind describing her?"

Celeste said, "I would rather describe the killer, if you don't mind." And she said it with the kind of attitude that spoke at growing frustration.

"Like we explained to you," said the other officer, "we'll file your statement, but it's not going to carry a lot of weight. You didn't see this man commit any crime. He didn't confess to anything."

"He didn't have to. His victims were right there with him!"

Still listening, Faith exchanged the first shirt for one with a cartoon crawfish on it. It read, *Suck WHAT?*

"Uh…yeah." Now the first cop was clearly humoring her. "We'll make sure to mention that in our report. You have yourself a nice day, Ms. Deveaux."

He barely waited until the door closed behind the pair of them to burst out laughing. Putting down the shirt, Faith got the feeling there'd be another funny, ha-ha story to tell over free weights in the gym. Once the patrolmen rounded the corner, she went into Celeste's shop.

"Oh, *my!*" Celeste flew to her feet as if levitated. "Are you all right? Did you catch the bastard? New Orleans' finest is about as useful as a screen-bottomed bucket."

"You *told* them Cassandra was *with* you?"

Celeste blinked, surprised by Faith's vehemence. "I don't know about you, but there's plenty of folks around here who wouldn't want their real names given to the police. If you heard, you could have come in and corrected me—"

"No!" Faith took a deep breath to calm herself down. The footrace through the heat and the crowd had tired her, and now this. "No, then I'd have to explain why you called me Cassandra, and then they'd know… It's a secret. But I can't let them connect Cassandra to me, not if I can avoid it."

She paced across the room, turned around and paced back. The part of her that had always been drawn to the law hated this, hated not giving the police every bit of information she could, including the fact that she'd chased someone they wouldn't believe was the killer in the first place. But to the part of her that had grown up with her mom, moving every few years and keeping a low profile, this came too easily. "Whatever you do, don't describe me."

"So what does Cassandra look like?"

"I'm not asking you to lie."

"And I'm not saying I will. So what's she look like?"

Faith considered it. "Black hair," she admitted—that was a given, considering the wig she sometimes wore as a failsafe during her anonymous calls. "I like to pretend she's a little shorter than me. She dresses like…like a gypsy, I guess."

"You do have her down, don't you?"

Faith considered her alternatives, then sank into one of Celeste's chairs and leaned closer. "Do you remember last year, when the city manager's assistant went missing?"

"That little redhead." Celeste nodded.

"Krystal told me that she'd done a reading for her, not a week before she vanished, and warned her that her boss was dangerous. I said for her to go to the police, but she said a beat cop had been hassling her, acting like he'd take her in on vice charges. She didn't trust any of them. So I asked around, checked out the different detectives, and called Butch Jefferson. I told him I had a psychic tip—which I did, it just wasn't *mine*. And when he asked for my name, I said—"

"Madame Cassandra," guessed Celeste, sitting back. Now she understood. "But they never convicted the city manager."

Faith hadn't realized how freeing it would feel, to have someone know all this. "Yeah, but he's not the city manager anymore, either. There may be an old boy's network around here, but it doesn't mean a free ride. Once the detectives got close, he was finished. And Krystal and I were the ones who put them close."

"So you've been a police contact for a year? Even before you started working in evidence?"

"Cassandra can point them in the right direction, but nothing she says is admissible in court. They can't even get a search warrant based on it. I started wanting to do something legitimate, something as Faith. Now that I work so closely with the police, Detective Jefferson knows Faith, too. And I'd rather he not know we're the same person."

"And why is that? Would he be the 'some people' who wants to disbelieve in psychic abilities?"

"No, that's his partner. But if anyone connects me to Cassandra, my credibility is shot. So's hers. Especially since they think Cassandra's getting this psychic information herself. I've kind of…well…"

"Oh, sweetie. Don't stop now."

"I might have told the partner that Cassandra was one of the most powerful readers in the city."

Celeste's smile widened. "And you thought you were lying?"

But Faith didn't want to go there again. "So you'll keep my secret?"

"I told 'em Cassandra was with me. As far as I'm concerned, that's who it was. It's not like they believe I saw the killer anyway. Or that I could know it was him."

"How *did* you know? What did you see?"

"I didn't see anybody—except him, I mean. That's not how it works. I heard them. The loudest voice was Krystal's."

Faith hadn't expected her breath to catch in her throat like that, her heart to squeeze quite that tightly. Krystal dead was bad enough. Krystal haunting her murderer…

Then something else distracted her. "But not *just* Krystal? Oh, my God. Who else?"

Celeste hesitated, studying her rings, then looked up with a new determination in her dark gaze. "Madame Cassandra, how about you and me go ask Krystal ourselves?"

Butch picked up on the second ring. "Jefferson here."

"Hello there, Detective Sergeant," drawled Faith.

Celeste widened her eyes, surprised by the fake Virginian accent. Standing across the counter from her, using her shop's phone, Faith shrugged. She had to disguise her voice somehow, didn't she?

"Well if it isn't Miss Cassie!" greeted Butch, sounding as delighted as ever. "How're you doing? I hear you had some excitement this evening."

So Faith hadn't imagined the patrolmen's reaction to her fake name. "Not enough excitement for you and that partner of yours to bother with now, was it? Don't you think my friend Celeste is important enough to rate detectives?"

Roy was saying something at the same time—something about "again?" and "feeding you now?"

After an echoing rustle—covering the phone—Butch whispered, "I'll tell you if you give her a chance." Then his voice got clearer. He was addressing her again. "We meant no disrespect to your medium friend, Miss Cassie."

In the background she heard, "You've got to be shitting me."

"It's just that sometimes we have to, you know, delegate."

"The problem with delegating is, sometimes you don't get the whole message passed on," Faith warned. "Did those nice officers tell you what a close look Celeste got at the killer?"

"The alleged killer," Butch corrected her.

"They didn't offer to have her see a composite sketch artist or anything."

"The sketch artists cost money, Miss Cassie."

Faith ignored the bark of laughter—not Butch's—that followed his statement. Had she really considered dating that jerk?

"Here's what she's going to do, being such a good citizen and all," she drawled, glancing back at Celeste. "She's going to get one of the street artists to draw the man she saw, off her description. Then she'll get that picture to you, just in case. Then when you catch the man, you can owe her a big apology. How's that?"

"We appreciate any help," Butch assured her. "If we catch the fellow, and it's the man in her picture, then we'll be happy to apologize."

In the background: "Or arrest her as an accomplice."

"Since you're so appreciative, I've got more information," Faith said. "You're dealing with a serial killer."

There was a long pause while Butch mumbled that announcement. Then he said, "I reckon you've heard tell of that note from the Biltmore, Miss Cassie, but that's not enough—"

"He's killed three people," she insisted. "Krystal Tanner, and two others before her. The first one doesn't seem to have been premeditated, but he liked the taste. That's when he went after the second one. All three were women, Detective Sergeant. And all three may have been psychics."

"It would surely help if you could provide their names."

This was where psychic information so often fell short. Krystal hadn't been sure. The first girl had died ten, even fifteen years before, and had been reduced to a bare wisp of lingering anguish. But the second... "The second woman's name started with a *P.* Pamela, or maybe Patricia."

Again, Butch passed on the information. Roy tried to whisper, but Faith didn't need her keen hearing to hear him say, "Or Prudence or Peppermint Patty. Does she expect—"

"Tell your partner," she drawled, finding a certain amount of freedom in her Cassandra persona, "that he's a horse's ass."

Celeste covered her mouth with a ringed hand to stifle a laugh, and Faith pressed her lips together. This anonymity thing was more fun than she'd expected.

"Well tell your psychic friend," called Roy at the phone, after Butch passed on the message, "that she's a fake and a coward. If she really had information, she'd bring it to us in person so we could see if she's legitimate. Instead, she's just wasting our time."

Faith gritted her teeth. "Two other women, Detective Sergeant. Both psychics. Both strangled. That shouldn't be so hard to find. You take care now, all right?"

"You, too, Miss Cassie. And thank you kindly."

She hung up. She didn't think they'd been trying to track her this time—the noise in the background had been the bustle of the police station, not the drone of a car. Still, she meant to go out the back way, just in case.

"You've got a ride home, right?" she asked Celeste, glad to return to her usual voice. "He knows where you work, now."

"I don't think he'll be coming back any time soon. He knows I can tell him what he doesn't want to hear," Celeste said. "What he killed some girls to keep quiet. But yes, I'll have Ben pick me up. How 'bout you?"

"Supposedly I'm in greater danger from a gang from Storyville than I am from him," said Faith. "But the sun isn't down yet. I'll hurry."

"I'll go by Evan's stall and look at the picture you describe to him," Celeste promised. "Then I'll take it to the precinct."

"Thanks." Faith knew she should leave—she was fighting daylight and, just as important, the possibility that even now

Butch and Roy were heading for Celeste's shop. But a one-word thank-you seemed so…insignificant.

Maybe Celeste hadn't been able to connect with Faith's father. But she'd done something almost as magical. She'd connected with Faith.

"Get on with it," insisted her new friend, seeming to understand.

So Faith slipped out the back, glad to hear the lock turn behind her.

Damn it. Damn it. DAMN IT!

He hadn't enjoyed His run-in with the medium, even before that troublesome blonde had come after Him. Like those other psychics whose power He'd taken could be any threat to Him. Crying for vengeance? They should be crying for mercy!

And what was that about the powerful Madame Cassandra? If there was someone that powerful in the city, He meant to have her.

The Master had mentioned Cassandra, too. He said that she was the one He had to go after. But neither of them knew how to find her. And He needed more power first. He needed to drink more pain….

After a day of planning, calming down from the disturbing encounter, He went about doing just that.

The victim He chose had returned to the Moonwalk. That popular spot that had nothing to do with the moon, despite the fine view when it was full, and everything to do with former mayor Moon Landrieu. Some people thought that was power, having landmarks named after you. He and the Master both knew better. Power came down to making people do what you wanted them to do.

And right now, He wanted someone to die.

No matter who else this one was, she was a psychic. Hadn't

He seen her at the psychic fair? The fact that she'd been drawn to the river, where He felt the safest, just made His success all the more fated. At several places along the levee, wooden stairways angled right down into the water. That's where she went, like a deer drawn to a salt lick. She wandered to the edge of the mighty Mississippi, sat on the wooden steps and stared out at the seemingly tiny buildings far across the river, the maritime traffic in between, the lit expanse of the Huey P. Long Bridge.

She didn't seem to notice that He'd already broken the bulb of the street lamp nearest the head of the stairs. Maybe she thought it being Sunday night would protect her. Saxophone music from the Moonwalk and jazz from Jackson Square beyond filtered through the sultry, humid August night.

He crept down the stairs behind her.

If she heard Him, she didn't react. Perhaps her thoughts were that heavy, this night. More likely, it was His magical protection, being in this safe place. He was barely a foot behind her when her head came up—

Which was all He needed.

He looped the red silk cord around the blonde's throat and yanked, hard, upward, backward. She cried out, but not loudly enough to be heard over the saxophone and the jazz. People didn't ever die as easily as He would like. Her feet kicked, one of them splashing into the lapping edge of the Mississippi. Her ringed hands clawed back, not at her throat—not like that fool the previous week—but toward His hands. It wouldn't do her any good. He wore leather gloves with high cuffs. Her fingernails scrabbled uselessly, increasingly frantic.

He pulled harder, tighter, His forearms trembling. In the tension of the cord, He could feel the inexorable damage to her throat. And then—

Oh, God, yes! *Amplification.*

As she died, all her powers, all her abilities rushed into Him. It felt the way sex was supposed to feel. It felt like strength. It felt like control.

Yes! Yes, yes, yes…

Yes.

He sprawled backward onto the step, panting, physically and literally drained. If she could see Him now, she would probably say He was glowing, pulsing with energy, with dominance. That's what she'd been good at, according to the program at the psychic fair. She read auras.

But that's why He couldn't stay, now—someone else might see the light He gave off! There were, after all, too many witches around here.

He quickly threw a handful of protective salt down, and sliced off a long hank of her hair, to add to His collection. He pocketed both the hair and the cord, in which He had captured her excess energy.

He considered rolling her body into the river…it would be so easy, and the Mississippi rarely gave up her dead. But no. If He left her, then the other psychics would know about it. They'd fear Him even more. And that's what He wanted.

He was perfectly safe. There was a huge expanse of running water right beside her, to contain her, to protect Him.

Sated, satisfied, He climbed the steps back to the Moonwalk, made sure nobody was watching, then headed toward the riverboat landing. He could choose His own prey, now. That's how strong He'd become.

Even the Master couldn't control Him, now.

Nobody could. He could do anything He wanted.

And that's how He liked it.

Chapter 9

The phone in the den screamed through the dark apartment.

Faith switched on her bedside lamp. She never fumbled for it; she could feel where it was, which Moonsong used to say was odd.

Light blossomed in her room as the phone rang a second time. Even as Faith padded into the hallway, then the den, she saw lights come on in Evan's room and saw light spilling out of Absinthe and Krystal's—rather, *Moonsong's*—open door. They had only the one phone, which Absinthe was reaching for as it rang a third time.

At least Absinthe had pulled on a shorty robe; she tended to sleep nude. Faith wore boxers and a tank top. Moonsong, in a filmy white nightgown that contrasted mistily against her dark skin, hugged herself. Her eyes were as big as a heroine's in an anime cartoon.

"Something awful has happened," she whispered.

Absinthe looked strange, even vulnerable, without her heavy makeup. She broke that impression when she picked up the phone with the words, "It's three in the fucking morning. What the hell do you want?"

"'Sup?" murmured Evan, arriving last in a pair of pj bottoms. He usually woke up faster than that. Then again, Faith had kept him up late the past two nights sketching a passing likeness of the killer, based on her keen observations.

Absinthe thrust the phone, stiff-armed, in their direction. "It's for Faith."

Faith's first step was hesitant, then she hurried. You didn't have to be psychic to fear phone calls this late at night. "Is it my mom?"

"No, it's that anthropoid detective." Absinthe passed over the phone and shuffled back toward her room, black-dyed hair spiking in strange directions. "Teach him how to tell time, will you? I've heard some simians are clever that way."

Faith pressed the receiver to her ear. "Roy?"

It seemed too dark, too soon since she'd been dreaming, to call him Detective Chopin.

"You've got some sweet friends there," he said. But surely he hadn't called to gripe about Absinthe.

"Is something wrong?"

"No. Sort of. I shouldn't have called." He seemed to be overthinking each set of words, as if he were drunk or very tired. Or both.

Faith sank into the overstuffed sofa, waving the others away. Waving Evan and Moonsong away, at least. Absinthe had already given up on the lot of them.

At least, if he shouldn't have called, this couldn't have been an emergency. Right?

"Well, you *did* call," said Faith. "And I'm awake now. So talk to me. What's up?"

"I just…uh…" More hesitation on his end made her distinctly uncomfortable. She hadn't thought of Roy Chopin as the kind of guy who hesitated so much. "I wanted to apologize, okay? For contacting your mother after you broke the date. For being a jerk when you called me on it."

Faith pulled her feet up onto the sofa, drew her bare knees to her chest. Whatever had happened, it had upset him. "I was less than nice when I called you on it."

"Yeah." He snorted, but his amusement seemed short-lived. "It's just…it comes with the job," he admitted then. "Suspecting people. We call it the asshole theory. The longer you do the work, the more assholes you think are out there. Bad enough when I was in uniform, but now, working homicide—nothing shocks you. It twists how you look at the world. That's why Butch thinks…"

Faith wasn't sure what to say about something that sad—especially since he may have been right to suspect her mother. "What does Butch think?"

"It's stupid. It's about personal lives and balance. It doesn't matter."

Oookay. "So…you're apologizing?"

"The words *I wanted to apologize* mean something else to you?"

Now that sounded more like Roy. "Then I forgive you."

"Don't dip too deep into your generosity fund there, Corbett."

"Why'd you decide to apologize at three in the freakin' morning?"

His heavy exhalation of breath was his only response. Again she thought drunk or exhausted. Or both.

Oh, god. This couldn't be good. "Roy?"

"Don't change, hon. And tell your roommates to be extra careful, okay?"

"Roy?"

"I can't talk about the rest just now. Business as usual. You'll catch the highlights at work tomorrow. By which I mean, today. Damn. I shouldn't—"

"I'm glad you called," Faith insisted, before he could dig himself in deeper. She'd worked with cops long enough to know that sometimes, they really couldn't give more specifics. If it involved her personally, he could have said more. Since it didn't... She would know soon enough.

"Sleep tight, okay?" he asked, his voice thick. "Be safe?"

"Sure. You too. Be safe."

"As much as the job allows." He hung up.

Faith settled the receiver into the cradle more slowly, more than a little unnerved, and not just because she didn't know what to make of Detective Roy Chopin anymore.

Moonsong was right.

Something awful must have happened.

Roy had been right. Faith "caught the highlights" almost as soon as she arrived at work—the fact that some of the night shift were still milling around, running tests and going over clues from something that had gone down the previous night, was her first hint. Then Greg called her into his office as she passed, to break the news more gently than an excited tech might have.

"Your roommate may have been murdered by a serial killer." He came out from around a cluttered desk and gestured to one of a pair of chairs. As they both sat, Faith was strangely reminded of her reading with Celeste. "Either that, or one skillful copycat. A second woman was strangled last night— her body's in back right now, and night shift is still running the evidence. She was blond, like your roommate. And she was a psychic. Did you know someone named Nessa French?"

Nessa? Oh, God. *Nessa.* "Enough for us to say hi at parties," Faith admitted, stunned. "We weren't close."

"At least there's that." Greg leaned nearer, his elbows on his knees, his posture carefully nonthreatening. His even breathing and casual heartbeat were remarkably comforting. For a science geek, he seemed surprisingly focused, for once.

On her.

"Are there any details you would like to ask about, before you start pretending it's just another case?" he asked gently.

"She was strangled?"

"Yes. The weapon left similar marks to the one used on Krystal. We're running tests to confirm if it was the same cord."

Faith wondered if he realized it might be the exact same cord, complete with Krystal's blood still on it. Probably. Greg had been doing this for a long time. Not much surprised him.

She tried to swallow past a rush of nausea and focused on the soothing regularity of his pulse, his breathing. "Did he take some of her hair?"

Greg's pale eyes blinked from behind his spectacles. "Why would you—? Faith, when your roommate's hair was taken, she was already in the morgue. That was some kind of souvenir collector, not a killer's organ trophy."

"But was some of this woman's hair missing?"

After staring a moment, his brow furrowing as he considered the consequences, Greg nodded. "Yes. Some of her hair was gone."

She considered it. "Has the FBI been called in?"

"They're aware of the situation, but with only two vics, they're just going to monitor for now." He didn't have to add that the vics were members of a subculture that didn't carry a lot of political clout. As if, just by being psychics, Krystal and Nessa had been asking for trouble. "It's still New Orleans' jurisdiction."

Which meant New Orleans would just have to solve it. "Did the killer leave a faucet on, near her?"

"No, she wasn't found indoors. She was on the edge of the levee, beside the river. Rotten luck—you know how hard outdoor scenes are to clear. The detectives were there halfway through the next shift."

Faith took a deep, shaking breath. "I think the river counts as running water."

Greg's heartbeat began to speed with interest at that possibility. "Wait, you think he deliberately left both bodies near some kind of water?"

"Running water," she clarified. "I'm not sure what it means—"

"Witches," he said softly.

"What?"

He sat back in his chair. "You must have heard the old superstition. My grandmother used to tell us stories about it, the same way she'd warn us not to walk under ladders or say the devil's name three times. People once believed witches can't cross running water."

"So at least there's something he's afraid of."

Greg stood, excited now. For Greg. He was almost cute, worked up like this. "I'd better call the station, tell them about the hair and the water. You know, Faith, you're very good at this. If you finished your degree, I think you'd be an asset to the staff. That is…not that you aren't already. An asset."

Now he looked uncomfortable, which was also cute. Greg proved many of the generalizations about science nerds, but the city was damned lucky to have someone this smart. "You only meant to say that what I do now doesn't take such specific skills," she clarified for him. "Or pay as well."

"But you do it with excellent skill," he agreed, "and deserve to earn more." He smiled, and it lit his bearded face, like sunshine through the clouds. He suddenly looked younger than she'd thought he was.

Then he stopped smiling, as if he feared being too forward. He was trying so hard not to cross the supervisor/employee line, Faith almost felt guilty for having drawn the line in the first place.

"Thanks, Greg. For everything. I'm…I'm sorry for the scene I caused, the other day. When I got mad at Detective Chopin in your office, I mean. It was unprofessional of me."

"I admire Roy a great deal, but he could drive anyone a little crazy. Especially if you're…dating?" He turned to examine a folder with feigned nonchalance, but his pale eyes sought her out over the top of his glasses.

"We're not dating," she assured him. But since she respected him, she wanted to be completely honest. "I'm not sure what we are."

"Why don't I just say that I hope everything works out for the best. How's that for appropriately vague?" But his heartbeat and breathing, which had evened out as they discussed her education, were increasing again. Was he worried about something?

She hesitated, then asked, "Is there something I should know about him?"

"What do you mean?"

"I shouldn't have asked. Never mind."

Greg's squint sharpened, and his shoulders went back. "Has he been bothering you?"

"No! He called in the middle of the night, but that's probably nothing…."

"And he telephoned your mother when you broke a date," Greg provided. He took a deep breath as he considered his options, then said, "This doesn't leave the office, all right?"

Faith nodded, needing to hear what he had to say, half-afraid to.

"Roy Chopin is a stand-up guy and a first-class detective,"

said Greg. "There are few people I'd rather have at my back. But I've heard rumors—and I stress that these are *rumors*—that he's a little rough on the women he dates."

Faith felt a chill of unease at the implications.

Greg's eyes widened as he seemed to recognize the implications at the same time. "No! I don't mean physical abuse, not that I've heard about. But he's got a temper. My guess is, someone that big and that loud can get pretty scary, even if he doesn't mean to be. If he's a little jealous, maybe a little possessive…"

Like the kind of guy who wouldn't take no for an answer? Who would call her mother when he got Faith's answering machine, just because she broke a date? Who would call her at three o'clock in the morning?

He'd seemed almost sweet, but she wondered now what his mood would have been like if she'd been out at the time.

Damn.

"I shouldn't have said that much," said Greg quickly, efficiently. "You're a grown woman, you can certainly handle your own dating life. And I like Roy."

"I know," said Faith, standing, trying to hide her uncertainty. "Stand-up. First-class detective."

"Are you going to be okay?"

"Yes. Thank you." Faith even dared to lightly touch his sleeve. "You're a good guy yourself."

He held her gaze for a moment—and she sensed feelings off him. The interest. The attraction. The dilemma over that attraction. "I care about you," he admitted softly.

Before she could think of what to say, he shook off the moment. "I care for all of my staff," he added, picking up a sheaf of files as a distraction. "Anyway, I thought you should know. About Nessa French."

Since he seemed uncomfortable with praise and thanks, almost as uncomfortable as he was with what he clearly saw as an inappropriate distraction, Faith simply smiled her gratitude before returning to her desk.

Instead of beginning her data entry, she started work on a computer search. There were benefits to being able to access the NOPD's records this way.

Crime: Homicide. She would also look up suicides and accidental deaths, just in case. Sometimes the investigating officers got it wrong.

Method: Strangulation. She also included choking, garroting, suffocation and hanging.

Extent of Search: Three years. She resigned herself to going back further if necessary.

Victim: Female. Psychic. Blond.

And after searching for all of that, she began hunting for victims whose first names began with a *P.*

The search took a lot longer than she'd hoped, especially since, for the sake of fairness, she made herself stop to work on her actual job now and then. She ate at her desk. She exchanged smiles with Greg as he went out to lunch and looked quickly away when—smiling amiably back—he bumped into the doorjamb. But by late afternoon, just as she was giving up hope, Faith found someone.

Penelope Lafayette had been eighteen four years ago when she was found strangled in her Algiers Point apartment, across the Mississippi from the French Quarter. There were clear discrepancies, which was why Faith hadn't found her more quickly. Penelope had been strangled with what the coroner thought was a curtain string. She wasn't a practicing psychic reader, instead working concessions at the Superdome. But one of the angles the *Times-Picayune* had brought out—Faith had double-checked the newspaper database on each possibility—was that this might have been some kind of satanic killing. They reported that Penelope had been involved with tarot cards, Ouija boards and witchcraft.

Faith made note of the woman's name, intending to call Celeste as soon as she was away from work. If anyone could confirm Penelope's identity, it would be someone who spoke to the dead for a living. It looked like Madame Cassandra might have to place another call to Butch Jefferson.

Then Faith hit a detour in the form of a call from a friendly sergeant at the 8th District police station. Three young men matching descriptions that she and Evan had given had been brought in. Could she come down to the station and pick them out from a lineup?

"Yes," she agreed. "Of course." But her heart sank. For one thing, she wanted to pursue the lead on Penelope Lafayette. For another...

Well, she didn't necessarily like the police station.

Bad enough that the gangbangers had attacked Evan, had threatened her. The inconvenience of being an official crime victim was going to drive her crazy.

Or maybe it was just exacerbating how crazy she already was.

Faith had hated going through the mug shots the previous week. Every time she'd touched a page, she had sensed lingering emotions and ugly feelings. Almost every person who'd turned those pages had been in some way victimized. People who'd suffered rape or robbery, who'd seen killings take place. Emotions that powerful didn't just go away. They stuck to what they'd touched. Worse, the whole station was just as highly charged. Except for the police and the lawyers, almost everyone who spent time there, perpetrator or victim, did so on what for them was a very bad day. It was like a stain that would never come out.

Faith promised to come right over, and she did—after stopping at a public phone.

* * *

"—about a voice, Butch, it's in the eyes!" Having been sent back by the desk sergeant, Faith heard the now-familiar bellow easily above the cacophony of ringing phones, insistent voices and office machinery from copiers to typewriters. "That's why she'll never meet with you. She knows you'll see that she's full of shit."

Faith rounded a corner and saw them, amidst the usual chaos. Butch Jefferson and Roy Chopin stood by a high-piled desk, having what could kindly be termed an animated conversation. Roy had his back to her, suit jacket off. His pin-striped shirt, sleeves rolled to the elbow, almost completely hid his partner.

"I'm beginning to think maybe *neither* of you wants to be disillusioned, there," he challenged.

"You have a suspicious nature, son," protested Butch pleasantly. He wasn't shouting at all, but now that she saw where he was, Faith could easily follow his voice. "Could be the lady just wants to do her civic duty while protecting her privacy. I say we give her that chance."

"Bullshit. Reporters can't act on anonymous tips—why the hell should we?"

"Because the girl was right." Butch caught Faith's eye around the barrier that was Roy's waving arm, and he smiled. He had a great smile, cheerful and wise. If she'd ever had a grandfather, Faith could imagine him being just like Butch. Just not black.

Roy made a strangling sound of pure frustration. "It's not like half the crazies in the city weren't already calling him a serial killer. It's not like she said he's six foot two with a mohawk and lives at 2348 Marsais Street."

"Am I interrupting?" asked Faith, intrigued.

Roy spun so fast, coffee slopped out of his cup.

"Not in the least, Miss Faith," said Butch, his grin broadening while his partner glared at him. "Roy here and I, we were just debating the merits of anonymous tips."

Cassandra. Faith struggled to keep her features only vaguely interested. *They're discussing Cassandra.*

She said, "I suppose you're getting a lot of those, huh?"

Roy looked strangely stiff. "Uh, yeah," he said. Then he looked down at his coffee and his wet hand. He seemed confused for a moment before putting the cup on the corner of the desk and wiping his hands on his slacks. Plainclothes detectives, Faith knew, wore suits because they were supposed to present a professional image despite not being in uniform. Roy stretched the definition of the word *professional.* "Everybody loves a serial killer."

Faith blinked at him.

He seemed to realize just how stupid that sounded, and changed the subject. "What are you doing here?"

"Now, son, that is no way to address the lady," scolded Butch, but Faith wasn't bothered. Roy was definitely big, just like Greg had warned. And he'd been shouting. So why didn't he seem scarier?

"I got a call that they arrested some of those gang members. I get to do a lineup."

"Ah." Butch nodded. "Speaking of ladies doing their civic duty."

"You want my advice?" asked Roy, then gave it without waiting. "They're not boys. They may not have been boys even in Huggies. Think of them as perps. It'll be easier to press charges."

That's when Faith noticed the charcoal sketch on the desk. It was the sketch she'd described to Evan. The killer looked even less threatening in two-dimensional black-and-white than he had when he'd hesitated in Celeste's doorway—but Faith knew what she'd smelled, sensed and heard. It was *him.*

Celeste must have delivered it, just as she'd promised.

And now it sat on top of an open book of mug shots?

Butch must actually be using it, looking for matches. God, she loved Butch.

"You do still want to press charges, right?" asked Roy, through her distraction.

She started, then tried her damnedest not to look guilty. As far as they knew, only Celeste and Cassandra had seen the man in that drawing.

"If I can find the lineup room, anyway," she said, tipping her face up toward Roy.

"Follow me," he offered, and said over his shoulder at Butch, "If you can survive without me for a few minutes?"

"You kids take your time," chuckled Butch, as if they were heading out on a date.

Roy rolled his eyes. "Yeah, 'cause serial killers are known for waiting around until we make a little time to investigate them. Get the address on the brother-in-law—we'll head out as soon as I'm back."

It was kind of cool, watching them together. Their affection was palpable. And now that she noticed...

Strangely, as long as she'd been focused on Roy, Faith had barely registered the disturbing undercurrents of leftover energy around here. In fact, as the detective walked her to the back room, she became aware of something else. Okay, two things. But the first was simply that she liked the view of his rangy body from the back. That wasn't surprising. At least one woman there—who, by her dress, seemed to be under arrest for prostitution—was ogling him with blatant interest.

More important, Roy had such an assurance about him, such a mixture of aggression and confidence, that the misery of this place didn't seem to touch him. Faith didn't know a whole lot about auras. She was no Nessa, thank goodness. But from how she'd heard them described, she wouldn't be surprised if Roy had some kind of natural, auric shield. If so, it was sizable. As Faith followed his cocky saunter, well within his personal space, the air felt neutral. Clean, even.

Several of the police officers stared as Roy and Faith passed. Only one person, a skinny guy with a yellow buzz, handcuffed to a desk, dared comment. And he barely managed to start—"Looky here, looky what walked in,"—before Roy turned on him.

"You got something to say?" he demanded, low. He took one threatening step toward the guy and leaned into his space, suddenly seeming bigger and wider than he ever had. His smile was pure predator. "Wanna share it?"

The skinny guy shrank back in his chair. "No sir."

"I didn't think so." Roy extended his hand, an after-you gesture for Faith. She noticed he didn't drop his eye contact with that particular offender until after she'd passed.

"How'd you learn to do that?" she asked over her shoulder, aware of his bulk close behind her. Her best way of dealing with that kind of scum would've been to ignore him. Roy's way had been far more satisfying to watch.

He looked honestly confused. "Do what?"

Throw your personal energy around like a weapon. But that would sound way too psychic-y. "Get him to shut up?"

"That guy? He was just posing. Here you go."

They'd reached the room that she recognized from dozens of movies and TV shows, with a two-way mirror and everything. But it was empty. Apparently she was early.

"So aren't you going to say it?" he asked, shifting his weight, shoving his hands in his trouser pockets.

Say what? "Thanks for the directions?"

He rolled his eyes, shook his head, and bent nearer her. He did that a lot, when they talked. "No. *I told you so.* You believed the note. I didn't. You've got to have heard about this morning's vic."

"Nessa." She nodded. "I didn't know her that well."

"Thank God for small favors. Well, you were right, I was wrong. It's a serial."

Suddenly, Faith didn't like the way that sounded. "It's not like I made some big prediction or anything."

"Actually…" He leaned back against the doorjamb, with a quick glance down the hall. Apparently they had a few more minutes. "Boulanger says you're the one who noticed the missing hair and the running water. That's not half-bad."

"I can be observant." Faith glanced toward the empty chamber beyond the mirror, wishing for a distraction.

"Yeah, but at least you're observant of reality. The crackpot calls have already started to come in."

"Crackpots?" Did he mean Cassandra? The very idea annoyed her.

"People claiming to be the killer—we have to follow those up. People claiming to know the killer. And then there's my favorite, the psychics who claim to have otherworldly information about, of course, the killer." He laughed, freeing a hand from his pocket to spread expressively. "The other night some broad who claims to talk to the dead says she's seen him. Alive, mind you. And how'd she know who he was? His dead victims ID'd him."

Faith stared at his obvious amusement. "Some of my best friends are psychic readers," she reminded him coolly. "You know, you really are—"

An ass. But Cassandra had called him an ass just the previous night, hadn't she? Better to minimize their similarities.

Roy waited, eyebrows arched in exaggerated expectation, clearly still amused.

"Very, very annoying," she finished weakly.

He shrugged. "I get that a lot. But if it makes you happy, I'll say one nice thing about the lady. At least the medium had the guts to identify herself and come down to the station, which is more than most of the crackpots will do."

As opposed to Cassandra.

Was he calling Cassandra a coward?

Finally the lights came on in the chamber beyond the mirror. Blinds were pulled. A police officer came in and introduced himself to Faith, letting her know what to expect, then hurried out for another delay.

Roy took a step back—probably to go to someone's brother-in-law's house—then hesitated, his body pivoted toward the door, his head turned toward her.

"About this morning," he said.

Faith waited, curious.

"When I first saw her…Nessa French…" He wasn't smiling. "For a minute, she looked like you. That's why I called, once we were done for the night. Logically I knew who she was, but still…"

He shrugged again, scowling.

Then he turned and left her to her lineup.

Between his departure and her surprise at his confession, the negative energy of this room swept onto her full-force. But this time, Faith didn't let it drag her down. She took a deep breath and imagined her own auric shield, part swagger, part cynic. She had a job to do—ID the perps, then find out what Celeste could tell her about Penelope Lafayette.

It worked. Instead of drowning under all the previous instances in which someone in pain had stood right here, forced to stare at the people who'd hurt them or someone they knew, she was able to feel strong in herself. Neutral. Clean.

So that was the secret.

Maybe she could handle police stations after all.

Chapter 10

It was a lot easier to be Cassandra-the-anonymous-contact when she waited until Butch was off duty Tuesday. There were far fewer interruptions.

Even then, though, Faith couldn't stop imagining what Roy would say if he were listening in. He would complain that Cassandra wasn't specific enough. That Cassandra was a coward. That Cassandra was a fake.

Well...as an individual, Cassandra *was* a fake. She didn't exist and Faith, who gave her voice, wasn't really psychic. Not exactly.

But the information Cassandra passed on—that was always real. Like this time. She'd confirmed it with Celeste.

"One of the earlier victims," she drawled, telephoning from the library on her lunch hour, "was named Lafayette. Penelope Lafayette, with a *P*? She died February 18, four years ago."

She had to clench her fist to keep from offering the address.

It wasn't just that she thought the detectives should do some of their own work. It might sound too much like what she'd overheard Roy demanding, like describing the killer as six foot two with a mohawk, living at 2348 Marsais Street.

But, she thought with grim satisfaction, she did now have the address if he needed it.

"Miss Cassie, you are a wonder," said Butch. "I will surely look up that child as soon as I get to the station. But I'm afraid I have an even bigger favor to ask."

"You ask it, Detective Sergeant," she said. "I'll let you know what I can do."

"Would you do me the honor of meeting with me?"

Damn. This had to be Roy's doing. He'd been pushing for a face-to-face meeting from the start.

"Now Detective Sergeant, you know that's not the kind of relationship we have. Let's just keep ourselves long distance, shall we?"

"Aw, Miss Cassie. You know I wouldn't ask if it weren't important, don't you? That sketch your friend brought to the station for us, it was mighty helpful. But when I pulled some mug shots, I'm afraid Miss Celeste just couldn't be sure of any matches. All I'm asking you to do is meet with me, look at the pictures and tell me if any of those boys is our killer."

At the station? Faith thought. The energy there she could handle. The chances that she'd be recognized, on the other hand…

She managed to retain her Virginian drawl when she said, "I don't believe I should do that."

"You don't trust me," sighed Butch. "That's it, isn't it? What can I do to convince you otherwise?"

"Stop trying to guilt me into a meeting just to prove I trust you?"

He laughed. "You name the place, Miss Cassie. You name the time. You don't even have to get close to me—I can put the pictures down and back off to give you space. You can choose any of them what looks like the man you saw, and put it separate from the other shots before you go. Then I can come in closer and see what you chose. Maybe we can just wave at each other."

Now Faith laughed. He really did seem to be bending over backwards. Except… "I'm just a li'l ol' psychic, sir, but it seems to me that my ID wouldn't be enough to justify a search warrant, let alone an arrest."

"No more than your anonymous tips have been, but they surely do point us in the right direction. Once we know who we're looking for, you leave the justification to us. You could sure save us a mountain of time, all the same."

Faith couldn't believe she was even considering it—but she was. He was right about how much time it would save them, to have a name on which to focus their investigation. That was time in which another psychic might not die. How could Faith even consider weighing her anonymity over that? And was it even that great a risk? She did trust Butch, more than she trusted his partner anyway.

And besides…

That's why she'll never meet with you. She knows that you'll see she's full of shit.

Wouldn't it be nice if the NOPD put this one to bed because of the help of someone Roy had called a coward and a crackpot?

"St. Louis Cemetery," she decided, choosing a location in which it would be very, very easy to lose someone. "Thursday morning. Dawn."

"Number One?" Butch asked. It was a fair question. There were also St. Louis cemeteries Number Two, in the Garden District, and Number Three, near the Fairgrounds.

"Number One, in the French Quarter." And across the street

from the 8th District police station. But the cemetery was much, much larger. "We'll meet by Marie Laveau's tomb."

"You do know, Miss Cassie, that the cemeteries don't officially open until 9:00 a.m., don't you?"

She smiled. "And you do know, Detective Sergeant, that folks manage to get in all the same, don't you?"

"I reckon I'm willing to risk a trespassing charge if you are, ma'am," he chuckled. "And I surely do appreciate you taking our relationship to this next level."

"You'll come alone," she instructed. "If I see anyone else there, especially that partner of yours—"

"I promised discretion, and discretion you shall get."

So why, when Faith hung up and looked around, did she feel so uneasy? No other library patrons had come near the pay phones and bathrooms as she'd spoken to Butch. Nobody was watching her.

And she did trust him, on a gut level. He had no reason to betray her. It's not as if she—Cassandra—were wanted for any sort of crime. Butch needed her help, not just on this case but on who knew how many other future cases with which she might assist?

And Faith might be able to see, hear and smell very well, but she didn't get psychic hunches.

She decided what she was feeling was simple anxiety at leaving her comfort zone, the same cowardly feeling for which she'd broken her date with Roy. She shook her head and told herself to grow up.

It was time to get back to work.

And now she had to put together some kind of disguise for Madame Cassandra's first and only appearance.

Faith had to tuck her gauzy skirt up into its waistband before she could scramble over the iron fence that surrounded the cemetery. The trick was to carefully stand on the top rail, so as not to impale yourself on the spike-topped bars. A ground fog cloaked the whole of the Vieux Carre, the French Quarter, that morning. The railings were slick with dew. But she dropped fairly easily onto the grass inside the fence. She just hoped that Butch, as an officer of the law, would manage an easier way in. It wasn't the kind of climb you'd normally wish on your grandfather figure.

It wasn't the most cheerful of locations, either. She'd chosen it because, unlike most of the other obvious landmarks in the area, this one should stay relatively private until 9:00 a.m. But she'd been thinking of the cemetery as a tourist attraction.

She'd all but forgotten it was also a cemetery!

Not just that, but the oldest and probably the creepiest cemetery in New Orleans. Especially with ground fog cloaking the architecture of death that spread before her.

Since much of New Orleans was below sea level, graves had to be kept above ground. The St. Louis cemetery had hundreds of raised tombs, crisscrossed by dozens of alleys and paths. There were wall vaults, multiple tiers of graves two and three levels high built from whitewashed bricks, most of which had lost the majority of their white. There were step tombs, partly buried, with stone slabs rising perhaps a foot above the ground; platform tombs, easily as high as they were wide; and the even taller sarcophagus tombs, as large as buildings. Some of the crypts had huge cracks running through them. Over two hundred years of hurricanes and heat waves would do that. Some tombs were no more than ruined lots of crumbling brick. Then there were all the monuments—weeping angels and oversize urns and lambs atop children's graves—and rusting, ornate ironwork and railings. The place was such a labyrinth that tourists were warned to avoid it except in groups. It offered too much concealment for muggers and other ne'er-do-wells.

Like, Faith supposed, herself. Or maybe like Cassandra.

She loosened her gauzy skirt from her waistband so that it fell almost to her ballet shoes, drew on her elbow gloves and fastened across her nose the veiling she'd borrowed from Moonsong, whose main form of exercise was belly dancing. She was already wearing her black wig and a decent amount of Krystal's old jewelry—the mystical jewelry that Krystal's mother hadn't wanted. She'd used Absinthe's gothic eyeliner and mascara. Copiously.

She didn't plan on letting Butch close enough to get a good look at her. But just in case, she had every intention of looking like someone named Madame Cassandra, not Faith Corbett.

And if Butch recognized her anyway…well, she'd default to simply begging him to keep her secret.

The problem with meeting at dawn, she decided as she made her way from one tomb to the next cloaked in the stillness and the mist, was that to get there early, she had to arrive *before* dawn. The sky wasn't even graying yet. She had excellent eyesight, even in the dark, but still…

She kind of hoped Butch was armed. For his own safety.

Many of the tombs which Faith passed had flowers and votive candles, or offerings of food and hoodoo money. But none had more offerings than that of the notorious vodoun queen, Marie Laveau. Her vault stood twice as high as Faith, its plaster finish worn off the brick in many places, and it was marred all over with *X*'s that had been scratched into it by believers and amateurs alike. Legend had it that if you drew three *X*'s, or tapped on the tomb three times, or turned in three circles and made a wish, the long-dead queen might yet grant it.

Waiting nearby, in the shelter of another tomb across the alley from Laveau's, Faith wasn't particularly tempted to make a wish. She wasn't sure what she'd wish for—and she definitely didn't like entering bargains without knowing the price.

Luckily, even as the sky edged toward gray, she heard Butch coming. He wasn't trying to be particularly quiet. In fact, he was softly whistling a jazz tune that she'd heard him whistle before.

Creepy as this place was, Faith appreciated his effort.

"Why, Detective Sergeant Jefferson," she drawled, stepping out from her shelter when he got close enough. "Aren't you prompt?"

He started, then grinned through the mist at her. "Miss Cassie, as I live and breathe. May I say that it is a pleasure to meet you at last."

But he didn't try coming closer. She appreciated that, too.

"You said you had some pictures for me to look at?"

"I do. It's a mite bit dark, so I brought a flashlight, too. How about I leave them right here for a few minutes?" And he placed the folder he'd carried, as well as the promised light, on one of the platform tombs.

Then, as promised, he backed away.

"You are a gentleman, sir," said Faith, stepping up to the ghostly white tomb and opening the folder. The elbow gloves, she thought, had been an excellent idea. Less chance of fingerprints.

Also, as she looked at one photocopied picture, then the next, then the next, she didn't run as much risk of picking negative energy off of them as she had at the station.

Unfortunately...

"I've got some bad news for you, Detective Sergeant," she said, closing the folder. "None of these boys is your killer."

"Are you sure?"

"My night vision is excellent, and so is my recall. You're looking for somebody else."

And she backed away, though not as far as she'd started.

"Well, that is a shame," said Butch. "But I do appreciate

you helping us cross those fellows off the list. Have you gotten any more…?"

"Visions?" she supplied. "I suppose that's as good a term as any. Nothing since yesterday, but I promise you, Detective Sergeant, I will keep my radar turned on. Have you learned anything more about poor Penelope Lafayette?"

"Not very much, but I will confess to you, Miss Cassandra, I've been working that lead alone so far. As you have so aptly noted in the past, my partner is something of a…" He searched for the right word.

For some reason, her nose itched. "I believe I called him a horse's ass?"

"I would have used the word cynic, ma'am, as it does him more justice. But as soon as I can make some connection that he will believe, we will follow up on that excellent piece of information. If you—"

Faith heard it then, the softest of footsteps, and her head came up. She lifted a gloved hand. "Someone's here," she warned, straining for the sound of breathing, of a heartbeat. "You said you'd come alone."

"I promise you, Miss Cassie, if anyone's here, it's not of my—"

But something clicked as he spoke, a soft, metallic sound. Twice. Three times. And Butch didn't finish his sentence.

Someone shot him first.

Butch dropped to his knees, clutching a hand to his chest, looking surprised.

Faith cried out, more from shock than fear. She tried to step closer to him and spin toward the flash of muzzle flame at the same time.

Then she saw the muzzle of the gun pointed at her, and instinct took over.

She dove for cover, even as another shot exploded through the silence. Its echo ricocheted eerily among the crypts. She suspected they would muffle its noise from the nearby station.

Oh God oh God oh God. How had this happened? Why hadn't she sensed the man's presence, at least smelled him? She still didn't smell him, but she could hear him now, the thrumming of his excited heartbeat, his footsteps crunching closer.

"Cassandra?" he whispered eerily, and her heart almost stopped. "I know you're here."

He wasn't after her as Faith. He wasn't even after the cop he'd just shot.

He was after the contact?

Beyond the whisper and the footsteps, she heard Butch moan.

The gunman had to already know where she was. She took a chance and screamed, "Butch, call for help!"

Then she scrambled to her feet and ducked around another tomb, even as the gunman's footsteps sped toward her cry.

Butch only moaned again. She felt sick with the fear that, between pain and his gurgling breath, he couldn't call for anything. It would be up to her.

And she didn't have a gun. Or even a freaking phone!

The gunman—the serial killer?—came nearer.

Faith ducked around another vault, into the mist.

It was a game of cat and mouse—and she'd never wanted to be the mouse. But go figure, her one night of self-defense for women hadn't taught her how to disarm someone. The basic rules concerning armed attackers were pretty simple. If they want something you can live without, give it to them and live. If they want more, like to take you to a secondary crime scene, better to run. Except for trained professionals, most shooters missed most of the time, at least from a distance of over five feet.

It occurred to Faith that the man creeping after her had hit Butch with his first shot, in the fog, from at least twenty feet away. That didn't sound like an amateur.

But who?

In any case, she wasn't leaving Butch.

Seizing inspiration, she tied her excess skirts into a knot and used the wrought-iron fencework around an oversize family crypt to clamber onto its stone surface. She slid onto its white-washed roof, onto her stomach, and peeked over the edge. Her perch was maybe as high as a garden shed, maybe a garage.

She saw the gunman now, a man dressed in gray, wearing a stocking over his head and creeping in her direction. He still had a pistol in his hand. And damn it, she didn't.

She had to get rid of him, not just for her own protection but to go to Butch!

Then Faith realized how she could solve both those problems at once. Butch had a gun!

If only she didn't have to cross an entire alley, ten feet of open space, to get to it.

"Madame Cassandra?" The gunman had circled the tomb that first hid her. Now he was looking down the different paths she could have taken—still, thank goodness, looking at the ground. He was still hissing his words in a strange whisper, eerily unlike a human voice. "Come out and die."

Faith peered over the edge of the crypt, judged the distance to its neighbor as a workable four feet, and carefully rose into a crouch. One…

She tried not to be scared.

Two…

It was only what, twelve feet to the ground? Thirteen?

Three! She ran. Jumped. Landed and dropped to her bare knees with the barest scuffling noise before, she hoped, he could see her. Then she listened.

His footsteps sounded farther away. "You can't avoid me forever, Cassandra."

Oh yeah?

She did it again. And again. The third time, she misjudged the distance. One of her feet slipped as she landed, and she scraped her shin. But she managed to clamber back up to safety, then to look over the edge of that tomb.

The sky had definitely lightened to gray, but it was overcast. Wisps of fog still drifted amidst the City of the Dead. The gunman was a ways down the alley, nearer Butch—she didn't like that part—but not looking this far for her. She had to take the chance of sliding her feet off the crypt roof, then her legs, then—

Her gloved hands scrabbled at whitewashed plaster as she slid all the way off and dropped to the grass below.

"Even if you run, I'll find you," warned the gunman. From his voice, she could tell he was facing the opposite direction.

Faith took that chance and dodged across the alley. She pivoted behind another tomb, panted and began to work her way back. Closer to Butch. Closer to the gunman. Closer to Marie Laveau.

Now she knew what mice in mazes must feel like, with walls rising up on all four sides and too many tantalizing openings to all be a worthwhile choice. She still didn't like being the mouse. But she tried to move as quietly as one anyway, listening to be sure of where the gunman was.

"Why, what an intriguing sketch," he whispered hoarsely. He must be looking at the folder Butch had brought. "I wonder who drew it?"

She moved from one tomb to the next, pressing herself tight against whitewashed brick or crumbling plaster, listening, then moving again. Closer, then closer, by frustrating increments. Only when she realized that the crypt she'd pressed against was scratched with X's did she know that she'd made it.

Now came the hard part.

To get to Butch, and to Butch's gun, she had to distract the gunman. And to do that…?

"Did you run away, little psychic?" demanded the gunman, his whisper too damned close to Butch's weak moans. "Then I suppose there's nothing left for me to do except tie up loose ends, is there?"

Faith crouched, picked up the first thing she could grab—a large conch shell left by some hopeful petitioner—and threw it. Hard. Across the alley.

It clattered satisfyingly.

Even more satisfying was the sound of the killer's footsteps jogging in that direction. While he did that, Faith circled Marie Laveau's tomb, then ran to Butch and fell to her knees by his side. She swallowed back her own moan at the sight of all that blood.

His eyes drifted open, focused slowly on her face. The veil had pulled loose, in all her climbing and jumping. Her wig might or might not be straight. But she didn't give a damn whether he recognized her or not.

All she wanted to do was to hold him, to call for help, to press her hands on the bleeding hole in his chest. But first, she had to get the gun on his waistband holster.

Luckily, he was wearing it.

She unsnapped the holster and withdrew the gun, which was much, much heavier than she'd expected. She'd never held one before. She hoped she could do it now.

"Safety, darlin'," murmured Butch on a gurgling exhale. For a moment, she thought he meant for her to be careful. Then she realized he meant the button on the side of the pistol.

She slid it back, heard a click. The safety was off.

"Two…" He coughed. Worse, he coughed up blood. "…handed."

"Where's your cell phone?" she demanded. "I have to call for—"

Then she heard it—the thrum of the gunman's heartbeat, which had been moving away from her, turned back. His amazingly silent footsteps were returning.

Butch was right. She didn't have time for the phone. She used both hands, her left bracing her right, like she'd seen in movies, and she lifted the pistol to hold it, arms extended, over Butch's body.

From the mist, she heard that same tiny series of clicks that had preceded Butch's being shot—a hammer being pulled back?

She was in the open, wide open, and the gunman wasn't. She had only one hope, and that was to shoot first. So she did.

Blindly. But straight at the clicks.

The pistol leaped in her hands. At the same time, with another explosion, she saw a flash of blue flame from across the alley. Rocks sprayed upward from only a foot beside her, but she wasn't leaving Butch again. She shot at where she'd seen the flame. So this was what people meant by cover fire.

"We're across the street from a police station!" she shouted. "Think they've heard us yet?"

To make her point, she fired again.

Then she heard footsteps. Running footsteps. Running away.

Leaving behind misery, gunsmoke and the lingering scent of... She sneezed. Was that cayenne pepper?

Desperate, Faith searched Butch's coat pockets for his cell phone. She found it, tried not to fumble it with her stupid gloved hands, dialed 9-1-1.

Butch's lips moved. If she didn't have such excellent hearing, Faith doubted she'd have heard him whisper, "Taping you... *Cassie*...."

When she met his fading gaze, she saw recognition there...recognition, and the sweetest grandfatherly smile pulling at his bloodstained lips. This close, he knew damned well she was Faith. He was warning her to protect her identity.

"You'd better…get. N—" Butch choked. *"Now."*

"Don't worry about me," she muttered, pressing a wad of her skirt to his wound as she held the phone to her ear with her other hand.

On a low, lingering breath, Butch sighed the name, "Roy."

The operator asked Faith to state her emergency.

"Officer down," she said, instinctively adapting Cassandra's Virginian drawl. "Marie Laveau's tomb in the St. Louis Cemetery. He's been shot—Detective Sergeant Butch Jefferson has been shot. Send EMTs. Hurry!"

"Is the shooter still on the scene?" asked the male operator, with the kind of calm that only a trained professional could manage.

"No." God help her, Faith hoped she wasn't lying. But she might well have lied to get help here faster. "He ran away. Please hurry!"

"We're already dispatching emergency teams, ma'am. Just stay on the line. Could you tell me your name?"

But Faith hung up. They had what they needed to know.

And Butch's eyes, still open, couldn't see anything anymore. Her skirt wasn't stopping blood, because he'd stopped bleeding. She couldn't hear his breath. She couldn't hear his heart.

Oh, God. Not Butch….

Hearing sirens and shouts, Faith realized that she had a decision to make. She could either wait for the authorities and implicate herself seven ways to Sunday—in disguise, holding a gun, powder on her hands…or at least on her gloves. Or she could slip away, let the fictitious Madame Cassandra take the heat for the anonymous call, and escape to keep looking for the killer.

Butch had told her to "get." She hoped this was what he'd meant.

She ran.

Gun, cell phone and all.

Chapter 11

*R*oy.

The last word on Butch's lips had been his partner's name.

After she'd gotten well away from the cemetery, from what would surely be a manhunt the likes of which New Orleans had rarely seen, Faith made her way across the backstreets of the French Quarter to the Mississippi. She wasn't sure why. Maybe she needed the sense of eternity that the huge, slow river offered. Maybe she needed to decide what Butch had meant with his dying word.

Or maybe she just needed to sit at the base of the levee, water lapping at her feet, and stop shaking. Stop crying.

She stared at the bloody gloves she wore, gloves that had pressed against Butch's wound, gloves that had fired a gun. Chances were, she'd left fibers from them all over the place. She stripped them off her arms, like stripping off another identity. She had to get rid of them. And the gun.

And Butch's cell phone. Especially if it had some sort of global positioning satellite chip in it, she couldn't risk keeping it with her for very long. But she had to do something first, and she had to decide how to do it.

Roy.

Surely Butch hadn't meant that the gunman was Roy—had he? Could even he have recognized his partner, with that stocking over the man's head? Faith couldn't believe Roy was guilty, and not just because of how painfully her chest contracted at the very idea. She'd watched the gunman move, sly and nearly silent, like some kind of commando ninja—had Roy ever in his life managed to be silent? Roy had power to him, not grace. She thought the gunman had been smaller than Roy, too, though he hadn't gotten that close to her. And she'd heard his heartbeat....

She blinked, belatedly recognizing something.

She'd heard the gunman's heartbeat, rapid with excitement...and she hadn't heard that strange skip she'd come to fear.

This may not be the same man who'd killed Krystal and Nessa. Was she now dealing with *two* killers?

She made her decision from plain, old-fashioned decency.

By now, the EMTs were probably arriving, probably trying to revive Butch. Would anyone have thought to call his partner yet? She doubted it. Not during the lifesaving efforts.

Roy at least deserved to be told.

Looking at the phone in her hands, Faith quickly figured it out. She'd been through four cell phones, all of which she'd managed to break or lose before giving up on them. This one was like her third. Press the button under Menu. Then Contacts. Then Roy at Home. Press the green button to call.

The phone rang, and she wondered how the hell she was going to do this. Any way she could, she guessed, as it rang again. She began to worry, on the third ring...

Then, with the rattle of a handset fumbled from a table,

Roy's voice answered with sleepy, affectionate annoyance. "What the hell are you doing calling this early, you old fart? How do you know I don't have a girl with me?"

Faith's breath caught with something close to a stabbing pain. He had Caller ID. He thought...

Well, it was obvious what he thought.

"Detective Chopin," she half-drawled, half-whispered. He'd spoken with her as Faith too often, lately. But she'd learned this morning just how effectively whispers could disguise a person's voice. "I'm afraid I have some bad news."

His voice deepened to an immediate threat, sharpened by worry. "Who the hell is this?"

"It's Madame Cassandra, Detective."

"What the fuck are you doing with my partner's phone?"

There was no way to do this except to do it. "He met with me this morning, to show me some pictures. There's been a shooting, detective. He's dead."

Roy.

For a long moment, she heard silence on the other end of the line. Silence and a ragged, stunned breathing.

"The EMTs are with him at the St. Louis Cemetery, by Marie Laveau's tomb," she continued. "But it's too late. Whoever it was had come for me. I am so sorry...."

"You—" His voice choked off. When he tried again, his words resonated with a darkness she'd never imagined. She heard shuffling now. The sound of someone trying to get up, get dressed, without hanging up the phone. "You'd better be joking, bitch. If this is real, if you set this up—"

"Listen to me," she insisted. "You need to know something. Two somethings. Whoever shot him was not the serial killer—"

"And why the hell would I think it was?" He really *didn't* buy that the killer had come after Cassandra. Damn.

"Also, Butch's last words were concern for you."

Then she hung up.

The phone rang in her hand, almost immediately, but she turned it off. He had to finish getting dressed, getting downtown, finding out that she'd spoken the truth.

In something of a daze, she tucked Butch's cell phone into one of her gloves, then tied both gloves around the gun with multiple knots.

Then she threw the whole ugly trophy into the Mississippi, a river famed for never giving up her dead…or many of the living that went into it.

Goodbye, psychic contact.

Then Faith went home to get out of these awful, tragedy-stained clothes before the morning light made her too conspicuous.

"I don't know which kind of psychic killer is worse," said Moonsong at breakfast two mornings later. She put down the newspaper, which Absinthe, in a rage at the headline, had stolen from a neighbor. "Someone who kills psychics, or a psychic who kills."

"If the psychic kills a cop, that's definitely worse." Absinthe stood at the refrigerator, staring inside as if some kind of better food would magically appear. "We need their protection. It was bad enough when they suspected us of being rip-off artists. Now—"

"Now they think we're all in some big conspiracy to hide this Cassandra person," finished Evan, who'd settled for dry cereal. "If you say you never heard of her, they ask why not? You were smart, Faith."

Faith looked dully up from the Pop-Tarts she'd toasted and now couldn't eat. She hadn't eaten very much during the past two days, knowing full well that her secrets muddled the investigators' understanding of the twenty-four hours before Butch had died, and watching the twenty-four, thirty-six, forty-eight hours after his death pass with no arrests. She'd had nightmares. She'd felt downright brittle at work. Luckily, Greg, who knew she'd known and liked Butch, had done what he could to make things easier for her. "Smart? How am I smart?"

"Not letting anyone know you're psychic. You haven't had the police hounding you at work, asking stupid questions you can't answer."

No, she thought. *I've just had Butch's corpse laid out in the back room.*

"I'm not psychic," she said.

"Oh, give it up." Absinthe slid the plate with the Pop-Tarts away from Faith and to her own place. "Of course you are."

"No. I'm not. I…" Faith searched for a way to explain it— hard to do, when she still didn't understood herself. "I can smell things—that Moonsong spent time with a smoker last night, that Evan spent time with a *pot*-smoker last night and that Absinthe had sex the day before yesterday with someone who wore a lot of patchouli."

Her three roommates were staring at her now, intrigued.

Absinthe said, "Hey, I showered."

"Yes, you did. Twice. You used my soap this morning, after your run. I can smell that, too."

"I ran out of mine. So sue me."

"I can hear things," Faith continued. "Evan's heart is beating faster than Moonsong's or Absinthe's—he's taking this more seriously than you two are. His breathing is more shallow, too."

"You never explained it this way before," he said.

"And if I touch you, any one of you, I can feel things."

Absinthe took a bite of the Pop-Tarts. "Like, say…a psychic?"

Fine. Faith held out her hand.

The others exchanged significant looks. They knew how she felt about touching people. But of all of them, Absinthe was least likely to shy away from a dare.

She put her bare hand with its chipped black nails into Faith's.

Sensations poured through the connection between them—more subtle than touching a stranger would have been, easier than if Faith hadn't been braced against the touch, but still powerful.

"You've got a toothache," said Faith. "There's a tightness in your jaw from it. You've been eating a lot of peppermint lately—I can taste that. You…"

She concentrated.

Absinthe pulled her hand free, cocking her head, staring a dark challenge.

"You used to be anorexic," decided Faith more softly, interpreting what she'd sensed. "A few years back, before you learned it was healthier to tell the world to go to hell. It left scars in your heart and your kidneys, and it weakened your joints, like the way a year of drought shows up in the rings of a tree."

"I guess I was wrong." Evan sat back from his cereal. "You're not psychic at all."

"I'm not! I mean—I know I'm *something,* I would never claim to be normal, don't think I'm saying that. Being psychic would be normal compared to me. But it's more like I'm hyperaware. Moonsong could touch your forehead and tell whether you have a fever. I can touch your forehead and tell if you have a hangover. Absinthe could smell if you've been in an herb garden in the past hour. I can smell if you've been in an herb garden in the past few weeks. It's just…it's like the volume's turned up. But a psychic…"

They continued to stare at her.

"Okay, here's what I *can't* do. I'm not empathic, like Moonsong. I can't tell whether Absinthe is pissed off or relieved that I just said those things about her. Her heart sped up a little, but that was it."

Absinthe shrugged. "Like I give a shit."

Moonsong translated, "She doesn't mind. Oh. Well, she minds me telling you that. Sorry, Absinthe."

Absinthe handed Moonsong a piece of Pop-Tarts. "Shut up, Goldilocks."

"And I can't look at a spread of cards the way Krystal would and tell you where your worst problems are coming from, or how things will resolve themselves. Even if I can sense that someone's lying, because of the way their body changes, it doesn't mean I have the slightest hint about what the truth is. And I can't even begin to see the future."

"Not all psychics can," Evan reminded her. "Just clairvoyants."

"But most have pretty good instincts. I don't even have that." If she had, maybe Butch would still be alive.

As if to prove several of Faith's points, Moonsong said, "You're really upset over Butch's death, aren't you?"

Faith nodded, but said nothing else. While the others finished their breakfast and headed out—Saturdays were big days for the tourist trade—she stayed home and felt...confused.

She wished she felt she could confess her involvement to her roommates, could let them know who Madame Cassandra really was. But Celeste, who'd called her that first morning after Butch's death, had warned her to keep quiet.

"The partner of that dead detective, he came looking for Cassandra and he's out for blood. Take my advice, girl. You do not want a piece of this."

Poor Roy. "But he's wasting time looking for Cassandra

while the real killer's getting free. Maybe if he just understood—"

"He *won't* understand. I said *out for blood,* not exploring possibilities. When I told him I didn't know anymore about you than your description—the black-haired gypsy description—the man picked up one of my statues and threw it into the wall and broke both of them—the statue *and* the wall. He's got himself quite a temper, does Detective Chopin."

Faith could imagine Roy doing just that. Considering how close he'd been to Butch, she could imagine him doing more. Celeste was right. She didn't want a piece of it.

Which was too bad, since she already had a piece. Extra large.

"Besides," Celeste had added. "Butch doesn't think it's a good idea."

Did she mean...? "Celeste, you *didn't!*"

"I'm a medium, girl. That's what I do. He thinks his friend's gonna need you as *you,* and that won't happen if he knows you're Cassandra."

"But—"

"Okay, here's another reason. You said the man who killed the detective was gunning for Cassandra, right? If word gets out that you're Cassandra, then he'll know where to find her. Now you lay low, you keep your mouth shut and you let them catch the real killer first."

And so far, that's what Faith was doing.

But she felt like an unforgivable coward. And worse...

Worse, she felt guilty. It didn't help when Celeste insisted there was no Cassandra—there was, and she was Faith. The fiction of Cassandra was, at least in part, the reason Butch was dead. The fiction of Cassandra was the reason Roy had been stalking the French Quarter like a madman with a badge, risking his job and apparently not giving a damn.

Celeste had shrugged off his outburst. "I needed to replaster anyhow." But if Roy lost his temper around the wrong person, the NOPD could be out two good detectives instead of one. And it would, at least in part, be her fault.

Advice or no advice, Faith knew what she had to do.

She stopped by work, despite it being Saturday, and looked up Roy's address on the database. He might be working this case all hours—against all regulations, considering that the death of a partner should bar him from the investigation—but he still was used to working nights. It was Saturday morning, now. Unless he'd gone home with someone else, he'd be there.

She caught a cab.

She had no idea how much she would tell him. But she knew she had to tell him something.

And she couldn't make the proper judgment over the phone.

Detective Roy Chopin lived in the Irish Channel, a narrow stretch of the city between the Garden District and the river. Other than how much fun St. Patrick's Day was supposed to be in the area pubs, the neighborhood had a lousy reputation. Faith was surprised to see more than one of the faded old houses being renovated. It looked like even the Channel was starting to benefit from the magic of urban renewal.

Roy's home was a turn-of-the-century shotgun house, long and narrow, painted blue with grayish-white trim. When the taxi driver dropped her off, he asked if she was sure she had the right place. This block didn't look impoverished so much as...old. Most of the homes were bumpy with window air conditioners instead of central air. Cars sat in the driveways or on curbs or under carports, since shutting anything up in an old garage in this kind of humidity was asking for trouble. A white-haired old woman sat on the porch across the street despite the increasing heat of the day, eyeing Faith's arrival with interest. Farther down the block, an old man walked his mutt.

If Faith concentrated, she could hear the sounds of children's cartoons or a shower turning on, smell someone cooking pancakes or squeezing oranges or smoking their first cigarette of the day. This was the sort of place where people had paid off their house and then kept the house in the family which, to Faith's way of reasoning, made it safer than some of the snazzy newer developments with garages and central air.

The name Chopin looked to have been written on the mailbox longer than she'd been alive.

As the cab pulled away, she made her way under a magnolia tree and past a yard that needed mowing to the front stoop. She rang the bell.

And waited. While she waited, she looked around her.

A maroon-colored car sat on the oyster-shell driveway—oyster shells were the Louisiana equivalent of gravel. It was a big car, kind of square with little headlights, also probably older than her. It seemed to have been kept in good shape.

She rang the bell again and heard footsteps inside the house. Roy. He seemed to be moving slowly. She could hear when he reached the door, and then he hesitated for a long moment.

When the door unlocked and swung open, she could see that she'd woken him up. His jeans were zipped but not snapped. He'd pulled on what was clearly an unwashed shirt but hadn't bothered buttoning it. His cheeks and throat and stubborn jaw were bristly with shadow and his eyes were sunken—but, at the moment, remarkably alert.

And he was holding a gun.

As distracting as the sight of his bare chest was—dark, hairy, naked—it was the gun Faith found herself staring at. It looked just like Butch's gun.

After a moment of staring at her, Roy looked down at the gun, too, as if surprised to find himself holding it. Then he moved it to his other hand, flicked the safety on and tucked it into his waistband, in back.

He unlatched the screen door, brows furrowing. "What are you doing here?"

"I came to see how you're— Why were you holding a gun?"

He snorted, shrugged one shoulder. "We still don't know who killed Butch. I wasn't taking any chances. I guess I'm just not that lucky."

Oh, God. "You *want* someone to kill you?"

His smile was truly menacing. "I want someone to try. The same bastard who did Butch. I want him to give me an excuse."

At least he hadn't said he wanted Cassandra to give him an excuse. That was a good sign, right?

But everything else, all of this, felt like bad, bad signs. He smelled of beer—lots of beer—and exhaustion. She sensed a disconcerting energy about him, like he was vibrating, pulled so tight he might snap at any moment. Someone like him snapping would be a bad thing.

Now he held open the door. "You, uh, want to come in?"

Come into my parlor…. Faith had to concentrate to think clearly past the screaming memories of everything her mother and teachers and that one night of self-defense for women had taught her. What if she couldn't trust him? Chances were, if she told him she was Cassandra, trust wouldn't be high among their mutual feelings. Nobody knew she was here except the cabbie, and he'd driven away. Not only might Roy be able to take her—big as he was, armed as he was—he was a cop. If anybody could cover up a crime, it would be a homicide detective, right?

And yet…

The alternative would be not to go in. And that wasn't really worth considering.

So Faith ducked under the arm holding the screen door

open and walked past him, right through all that vibrating, angry, confused energy of his, past the smell of half-naked man and beer and sweat, and into his lair.

It was a surprisingly homey lair. The parlor had big, comfy sofas that she couldn't imagine him buying, a large television that she could, and pictures, lots of family pictures, all over the walls. Some of them looked as if they dated from the 1800s. The clothing in different family groupings placed others in different generations. Some of them included pictures of Roy—him among a cluster of laughing teenage boys with a baseball cap and a bat. Him at what looked like a family reunion, his arms draped around two older women, a child hanging off his pocket. Him maybe ten years ago, standing straight, wearing a crisp uniform and carrying some kind of certificate.

Family. History. Home. He'd lived the kind of life she'd always dreamed of. She wondered if he'd ever guessed how lucky he was.

"I'm sorry for the mess," he said now, extending a hand as if to pick up an empty beer can, then letting the hand drop to his side. Apparently he saw that picking up a couple of cans or magazines wouldn't make enough of a difference.

"That's okay." She looked up at him, studied his deep-set eyes and his lined face and his jaw-clenching pain. Now that she was here, she wasn't sure what to say.

Celeste—or maybe Butch—had been correct about the importance of keeping her secrets. *I'm Cassandra* would be the absolute worst choice.

"I was worried about you," she said instead—which, thank heavens, was also true.

"Me?" He waved the idea away with one hand. As if on an afterthought, he took the gun out of the back of his jeans and put it on the coffee table. "Don't be. It's part of the job. We all know that going in."

She could tell he was lying. She didn't need psychic abilities to guess what the truth was.

"But Butch was special," she said, pushing it.

He turned away with a jovial, "Who isn't, right?"

"Yes, but Roy, Butch was special to *you*."

When he glanced back his brows were together and he was glaring. He didn't want her to push it. He wanted her to pretend with him that everything was okay. And he was *so* pretending. She could see the war on his face. He looked like he could cry, but he also looked like the kind of guy who would put a bullet in his head before he let himself give in to that. Nothing about Roy Chopin was delicate, not even now.

But he radiated pain, all the same, and Faith couldn't stand it anymore. She had to reach out to him, even if it meant literally reaching. Bare-handed. Fingers spread.

His chin came up, mouth set, eyes desperate. She'd already warned him more than a week ago, hadn't she? He knew she didn't like to be touched. She'd worn shorts and a T-shirt. And there he stood, his shirt hanging open. No way could she hug him without skin on skin.

But she had to. It wouldn't be that overwhelming, would it? In, out, quick hug in-between. She could handle that.

So she stepped forward and wrapped her arms around him—and an explosion of unexpected, overwhelming, seismic sensation.

The sensations hit almost as hard as the power of his embrace, closing tight and hard and permanent around her.

Chapter 12

She'd braced herself against the shock of this kind of contact. She'd known he would overwhelm her.

He did.

Like a stereo snapped on at full volume, a spotlight straight in the face, a splash into icy water—no, burning water, boiling. The intensity of sensations, of images, of touch scalded her. The force of him struck too hard, too fast for Faith to do anything but cling to consciousness.

Some part of her seemed vaguely aware that, on the outside, all Roy did was hold her. Hard. Tight. He dipped his head onto hers, his face in her hair, his breath a ragged sigh of completion, of need.

Things almost seemed still on the outside.

But oh, God, what he had inside!

His forearms wrapped behind her so that his hands touched her bare arms, each fingertip a conduit into untapped electric depths. Had she thought she couldn't read emotion? His emotions arced through her. The tension in Roy's taut body wasn't just anger at his friend's death, it was rage. The strain in his neck, the throbbing in his head, which he'd tried to deaden with beer, wasn't mere guilt. *He felt stupid for not having known where Butch was that morning. He felt incompetent. His burning stomach feared that he would fail to avenge his partner. His aching heart longed for his dead mentor's advice.* All of that burned through her so loudly that the usual disjointed details stayed peripheral. *Baseball in the park. Corned beef and cabbage. Women. More than one.* None of that changed anything. It was all part of him.

All of him hurt. And as if she'd touched a live wire, all of that hurt surged from him into her, so powerfully she almost cried out from his agony.

Except…

Except somehow, as he inhaled deep gulps of her, everything in him began to relax. Slowly. Incrementally. And in some weird feedback loop, she began to relax, too. His simple embrace became a blanket. A drug. Touching him…

She'd braced herself against it for good reason.

But touching him didn't suck. Not at all.

Roy sighed, his breath hot in her hair. "You're sweet, Corbett," he muttered hoarsely, his body tensing in an effort to be a good guy. Decent. Stand-up. "Sweet and innocent. But—"

But she was so lost in him, she hardly heard. Having adapted to this much contact, adapted better than she'd ever hoped, she pressed her face to his bare chest and felt him, breathed him in return. Soft, curling chest hair and softer, tanned skin and a quickening of his heartbeat. Soap and beer and sweat and maleness. Something primal in her responded to that in a surprising rush. And then…

And then, bliss.

As if her eardrums had popped from the cacophony of him, leaving blessed silence—except that she could still hear his pulse, the catch in his breath, the funny gulpy noise when he swallowed. As if all her nerve endings had been burned away, leaving her invulnerable to pain, except that she could still feel him, feel the sudden clamminess of his skin as his body reacted to her closeness, feel the tightening of his grip, the tightening against her stomach, definitely feel the flip-flop of expectation as she recognized what his body was doing. His energy had surrounded and saturated her and now, surprisingly, she was safe there. Still overwhelmed. Dizzy even. But safe.

And without the extreme feedback from his touch, she found herself savoring every bit of it.

She lifted her face to his. "Kiss me."

His eyes narrowed, like he was mad at her. "Look, thanks for coming out, but I don't need pity sex."

His body was saying otherwise, as did his scent, but she admired him for the effort.

"That's…" Oh heavens, she could hardly breathe, he felt so good. "That's not what I asked for."

She might not know men, but she'd heard the one-thing-on-their-minds speech. What woman hadn't? Roy was a basic guy. Everything in him seemed to be screaming, full-speed ahead. His body and hers were distracting him from the troubles of the previous few days. Maybe he *didn't* need that, much less any more than that—but it was damned welcome, all the same. His breathing had picked up, along with his heart rate. She could feel extra warmth off his lips and his nipples—one of them under her ear—and, strangely, off his earlobes. And against her belly. She definitely felt heat there. But she could sense his suspicion, too. Basic didn't mean stupid.

"Have you ever dived into cold water?" she asked, and her voice sounded strangely breathless to her. Actually, all of her felt strange. Altered. Especially her breasts and deep inside her, as if her insides were shifting. "And you don't want to, and it's so cold. But after you swim even a little, it starts to feel really good, and then when you get out it's the air that feels cold—"

With a roll of his eyes and a groan, he gave up and kissed her. She didn't think he'd understood her analogy, or even cared. She didn't care either, not anymore.

Not as long as he kept on kissing her.

Understanding meant nothing compared to feeling. And oh, she didn't want to ever get out of the water.

His lips *were* warm, warmer than the rest of him, and soft, and gentle. The press of them, searching across her own sensitive mouth, singed her, charred her in the heat of him. She loved this closeness, this meeting of bodies and beings. She wanted more, more, more.

The intensity of him everywhere, in her lungs, in her mouth, spiraled through her. She shuddered in his arms, gasped her astonishment and delight.

Roy pulled back, his eyes wide. "Did you just come? From *kissing?*"

She stared up at him, unsure of anything except that even as the shuddering sensations eased, she wanted those lips back. And if his lips wouldn't cooperate—

Rising onto her tiptoes, she moved in on one of those hot, tantalizing earlobes.

"That is *so hot*," he muttered—and buried his face into her neck. His hands slid down her bare arms to her bare thighs, just under the bottom of her shorts. He cupped her butt, and she loved the roughness of his palms against her rounded cheeks as he held her against him and ravished her neck.

There was no other word for what he was doing, either. Lips. Tongue. Teeth. *Ravishing.*

When he got to her ear, sensations exploded through her and she shuddered again. He laughed a devilish laugh and deliberately kept it up.

Full-speed ahead.

Faith couldn't hold still. She wouldn't want to if she could. She wrapped her arms up over his solid shoulders, behind his tanned neck. She held tight as she writhed happily against him, pressing into him with her breasts, her stomach, her thighs. She nuzzled and tasted his sexy ear. Then she rasped her cheek over his stubble and demanded his mouth back. He gave it, openmouthed this time, filling her, owning her. She let him. She'd never thought she could feel like this, never thought she'd be able to even do this.

She'd sure never thought it would be this instinctive, this natural, this *necessary*. But this was pure man-woman action, as basic as touch came. When her hands got tired of playing with the edge of trimmed hair against the nape of his neck— and he had great hair, thick and springy and soft—she started pushing at his shirt until she was able to peel it off his broad shoulders, down his bare arms, all the way off. The hair on his arms, which had so drawn her before, felt soft under her palms for the moment before he wrapped his hard arms around her again. So did the skin on his ribs, and the hair under his arms. Then she was playing with the nape of his neck again, all the warmer, all the happier for being submerged against all that bare skin.

"*Liverons*," whispered Roy after a while, his breath tickling her ear and neck, making her shiver. With her hyperhearing, his panting already sounded like a roar, his moans a solid rumble, but she was distracted and he hadn't enunciated.

"Huh?"

He narrowed his eyes in playful warning. "Lift. Your. Arms."

She did—and like that, he'd peeled her T-shirt up out of

her waistband and over her head and arms and away. She had no idea what he'd done with it, but he sure hadn't held on to it for long. Almost immediately he was drawing his big, warm hands across her bare back—and unsnapping her bra with practiced ease. And she didn't even care. Actually, she *did* care. She approved.

Now she could writhe against him bare-breasted. His chest felt even better this way. No wonder making out was so popular.

He started ducking his head awkwardly, nuzzling her shoulders. That felt nice enough, but her shoulders weren't exactly where she wanted to be nuzzled. She hadn't realized that her frustration was partly an echo of his until he growled, took her by both shoulders, and turned her bodily around to face away from him.

Before she could even protest, he'd drawn her back against his chest, his arms hard around her again—but now his hands were on her breasts. His kisses across her ear, her cheek, and onto her neck, gave him full view of what he was doing with her breasts, too. The pressure in his jeans, now against her butt, hardened and warmed perceptibly. Oh—so *that's* what he'd wanted.

Faith loved that he wanted to see her breasts. They liked it, too. When she stretched her arms upward and back, to bury her hands into his hair again, the move lifted her breasts eagerly.

He muttered something like, "That's what I'm talking about," and did more wonderful things to her eager breasts.

She wriggled her butt into his crotch, and this time his groan resounded through her. And not just because of his mouth on her ear.

Because her groan joined it.

One of his big, rough hands left her bosom to slide down her front and vanish under the waistband of her shorts, under the edge of her panties, claiming another of her own hot spots. *Groan* was an understatement.

Explosions. Resounding, seismic explosions.

Thank goodness he was holding her up.

"*So* hot," he muttered admiringly. "C'mere."

"I thought I already was," she rasped, her head lolling back against his chest. She felt lazy and happy and she hoped he'd do that again.

He laughed and turned her again and spread his arms, expectant. "Come *here*."

Delighted to realize what he meant, she jumped him. He caught her under the thighs and pulled her up against him as she wrapped her legs around his waist, her arms around his neck. She began kissing him some more while he carried her. He generously returned her kisses.

Faith had never done this before.

She'd never been held like this, carried like this. She'd seen people act this way all the time, if not this naked. Guys carrying girls, friends with their arms around each other, easy hugs, horseplay. She'd always envied them such simple, happy physicality. She'd never thought she'd have that. Never.

Even if she hadn't been looking forward to the sex, she might have gone through with it from sheer gratitude for this. She knew that's where they were going—to the bedroom, for sex—without having to be psychic. But she was very much looking forward to it.

The kissing and the petting had sure proven better than she could possibly have imagined.

Roy turned and fell backward onto a bed, her riding him down. Then he rolled them both over so that she was on her back, looking up, and he was holding her down, his big body filling her world. "Now," he mused, his voice thick and smug. "Where were we?"

And he started kissing her again.

For the briefest moment, she'd been distracted by new sensations—*this was a guest room, not his bedroom. He knew the sheets were clean, in here. His mom sometimes visited to change them, even unused, despite his protests.*

The kissing banished those unimportant details in a hurry. He gave her so much to feel, his fingers awkward in her hair, his mouth far less awkward on her breasts, the denim of his jeans rough as she slid her legs across them. His chest under her hungry palms, then his waist under her hungry palms, then the rough denim and whatever was in his back pockets hard under her palms as she tried to get a better feel of his butt.

Obligingly, he shucked off his jeans one-handed and kicked them away, then went back to massaging her breasts with his mouth.

Oh….

She'd enjoyed the feel of denim against the sensitive skin inside her legs, but she liked the feel of his warm, hard, hairy legs even better. And now her hands had access to his butt, covered only in a stretch of briefs. Between her legs, pressing the seam and zipper of her shorts almost painfully against her, strained something else his briefs stretched to cover.

For the first time since she'd initiated this, at least since she'd adjusted to the water temperature, Faith felt a flutter of uncertainty.

Today wasn't just her first time being carried. She should probably tell him. Then again, was it any of his business?

Blindly, still kissing her, he caught one of her hands and drew it to his arousal. He groaned in obvious ecstasy as her fingers curled partly around him. As much as his underwear allowed, anyway.

She moaned her appreciation. She liked the feel of him, so hot and hard and ready for her. *Necessary.* Definitely a man-woman thing. She did ache for him where she was supposed to be aching.

But damn, he seemed big.

This might go more smoothly if she told him.

He drew up, drew back just far enough to slide his hot, dark gaze across her. She shivered, feeling it as tangibly as if he'd used his hands. Then he showed his teeth in a wicked grin of satisfaction and sank down on her again, all size and weight. He brushed those hot, soft lips against her ear and whispered, "Get naked."

It occurred to her that he was a pushy lover. He hadn't said please once. It also occurred to her that she didn't mind.

She was too busy wriggling out of her shorts and panties, both at once, to complain.

"Ooh," he said, or some similar sound of approval. He caressed her hip, then stroked his hand between her legs, explored a little with his fingers—

Her world ended. She didn't actually pass out or anything, but the next thing she became fully aware of, as the spasms subsided and the rush in her head became a mere roar, was Roy, on his side, his head pillowed on his bent elbow, brushing hair out of her face.

"Damn, you're easy to please," he marveled.

"Kiss me." See? She could be pushy, too.

"Yes, ma'am." He leaned closer and did, and soon he was on top of her again, kissing her, cradling her in his arms. He was also pushing against her with his body, the hemmed flap across the front of his briefs taking over where the seam in her shorts had been. He was clearly ready to move on.

If she needed to be more ready herself, she wasn't sure she'd survive the pleasure. Was she supposed to give him a go-ahead or something? Unsure, she pushed at the waistband of his briefs.

He had them off faster than she'd thought was possible, and now she could really hold him in her hand. Hot. Throbbing. Just a little moist. Supposedly designed to fit into her....

"Wait a minute," he grunted, arching off her to fumble in the drawer of the bedside table. *He kept his condoms in the kind of tin mints came in. Didn't want to shock his mother when she went on her cleaning tangents.*

Faith thought, *the woman can't be that stupid.* But since she didn't want to explain how she knew about him hiding the guest-room condoms, she didn't comment.

Now or never, girl. "I, uh," she said.

"Yeah?" He tore open the condom, slid it onto himself one-handed, turned back to her with a look of ravenous anticipation, and moved in to kiss her again.

"I ought to tell you something," she managed to say before his lips covered hers. "Before…"

His lips stilled completely. So did he. He drew back, looking wary now. And pissed. "You've got to be kidding."

She had no idea what to say. She could sense that whatever he thought, it infuriated him. His level of arousal just added fuel to the fire. But what *was* he thinking?

He saved her the trouble of asking. Sort of. "Which one? No, lemme guess. You're fucking positive?"

Okay, now she was really lost. "Positive about what?"

He blinked, his anger easing as surely as his lust had a moment earlier. Now they were both confused. But at least he moved into looking hopeful. "HIV positive," he clarified, as if it should have been obvious.

"No! Nothing like that!"

His relief was palpable. "Geez. Don't scare me like that." And he moved in to kiss her again. "I was clean on my last test, too."

She said, "I've never been tested," and he stopped again.

It would have been funny, if she didn't want him on her, in her, so bad she felt hollow with the need of him. He swore a little more, settled back onto his elbow looking pissed, and said, "Great, that's just great. Okay, then, hon. Give me the list."

Clearly, casual sex was more complicated than she'd thought. "The list of…?"

"You know." He waited, but since she didn't know, he just got frustrated. "Any unprotected sex? Multiple partners? Partners at risk? Drug use?"

Was he still stuck on that? "You," said Faith.

At least he got to be the one lost, this time. "Me, what?"

"You're it. A list of one. You. Now can we…?"

And she'd thought he'd been thrown by the possibility that she was at risk for AIDS?

"You're a virgin," he said, eyes wide.

"Yeah." She leaned closer and nibbled on his ear, but it wasn't nearly as fun when he wasn't playing, too.

Not that he pushed her away. But still.

"I actually used that word for you. 'One of those virginal blond types,' I said. At the time, I swear, I thought it was a figure of speech."

She gave up on his ear and sank back, now pillowing her head on her bent elbow, her nose almost touching his. "Is this going to be a problem for you? Do you—" She hated to even give him the option, but hey, guys were people, too. "Do you not want to do this anymore?"

He laughed and encircled her with those hard, strong arms she'd already come to adore. "Damn, you *are* innocent, aren't you?"

She reached down between them and encircled him and his condom with hungry fingers. "I've read books," she warned, as his eyes drifted half-closed in a moment of gratitude.

"Oh, yeah?" He was getting cocky now. He had something

of a swagger about his expression as he grazed his hand slowly, slowly down her front again. "Honey, this is nothing like reading."

What he started to do between her legs, slowly, deliberately, sure proved that. His fingers didn't exactly feel *good,* right away—not when he first moved his explorations inside. He did have big hands. But she loved lying cuddled in his arms so much, she didn't care. She loved being able to run her hands over his chest, his arms, to cup his face and kiss him. She loved his burning gaze and his whispered, husky questions. "This okay?" and "Just tell me to back off…."

No way in hell was she telling him to back off. Eventually, initial discomfort gave way to real pleasure, even awe at how easily she began to accept him. Then he tried two fingers and, after her initial gasp, that was also good. Full…but full of promise, too.

"That's right," he breathed, hot and moist into her ear. He all but vibrated with the need to do more, but he was doing his damnedest to hide it. "Just take your time…."

Then he did something clever with his thumb, and time exploded. The next thing she became fully aware of, as her ability to breathe returned, was his arrogant grin.

"You don't come like a virgin," he noted. Was she still a virgin? She couldn't tell anymore. She didn't care.

"Then maybe you're not the guy I need to—okay, I take it back," she insisted, as his brows drew down in mock threat. "You're exactly who I need."

And he was. She needed his hands on her. She needed his body on her. So… "Are we waiting for something?"

He growled out a few choice words. "You know this is just sex, right?" He said it earnestly, his face close to hers. His hand slid comfortingly over her shoulder—she loved feeling so hypersensitive without the distraction of images and information. "I mean, it's not a marriage proposal or anything. I want to see you again, that's for sure—a date wouldn't be a crazy place to start—but I just want to make certain—"

She pressed a hand to his mouth to shut him up. She really did love the feel of his lips, even under her fingertips. Especially when they were extra warm, like now. "You don't have to Mirandize me," she assured him. "I said I'm a virgin. Not a virgin from the 1950s. Nothing you say will be held against you in a court of law. Well…" She snuggled closer to him. "*This* might be held against you. But not in a court of law. I'm not an exhibitionist."

He drew back from a deep, probing kiss. "And just how would you know if you were?"

"You'd have to Mirandize me to find out."

"You're cute when you're a smart-ass," he murmured, voice husky—but he did so between more deep, probing kisses. His thick thigh, between her legs, made a great focus for her writhing.

Between the kisses, and his hands, and his hard, hot body, she suddenly felt happier than she could ever remember. Giddy, even. "Let's hear it," she teased. "'You have the right to remain silent….'"

"Yeah," he warned, moving over her again. His eyes glittered at her with a potent mix of humor and desire. "Silent. You. Like that's going to happen."

She didn't make a bet on it. Good thing, too.

As soon as he slid into her, slick and solid and *absolutely* necessary, she would definitely have lost.

Chapter 13

Roy slept afterward.

Wow, did he sleep. He worked a night shift, so Faith supposed that midmorning for him was like 4:00 a.m. for her. Add to that the fact that he'd sure earned some rest with her, and that he hadn't been sleeping well since Butch's death....

Well, it seemed important to let him sleep.

Even if part of her wanted to wake him up and demand he have sex with her again. Another equally powerful part of her wanted to slip out the front door, find a pay phone, call a cab and run. Not just back to the apartment, either. Her mother had taught her well, without Faith even knowing it. She could move unexpectedly to another state with surprising ease.

Then maybe Roy would never have to find out she was Cassandra. Or if he did, she'd be far, far away when it happened.

She lay beside him for the first hour, while he slept. At first, she couldn't have moved if she wanted to. She definitely wouldn't have wanted to.

Damn, but she loved sex! She felt lazy, and sticky, and kind of sore, and none of that mattered—at least, not in a bad way. For maybe the first time ever, she also felt like a real, physical human being. Corporeal. *Touched.* Fully, finally touched. And nothing that happened between them could ever take that away.

She owed this man for that. Big-time.

Eventually, her breathing and pulse finally eased to normal and she drifted back from her postcoital bliss. That's when she found herself watching Roy sleep in the sunlight that filtered between his closed curtains. Watching him…and worrying.

First and foremost, she didn't want him to find out she was Madame Cassandra. Not ever. But as long as he didn't know, then he was making love to someone who was just as much a fantasy creation as the fictional psychic. Either way you cut it, this wasn't good.

Also, who *had* killed Butch? Was Roy just being paranoid when he'd answered the door gun-in-hand? In one morning, he'd gone from being someone who intrigued her to someone she found almost indispensable. Oh, she wasn't such a baby as to think she was in love with him. Not real love. Not yet. But she certainly understood, now, why so many people mistook sex for love. And Roy did have possibilities. If the man who'd killed Butch came after him, Roy and all his possibilities could be cut short, just as surely—

Faith pressed a hand to her mouth at the memory of Butch dying, dying even as she tried to hold his blood in. *The killer came for Cassandra,* she reminded herself, and she tried desperately to believe it. *He had to have come for Cassandra.*

It didn't bring the comfort she'd hoped. Roy was a homicide detective, for God's sake. It wasn't a safety-first kind of job.

She didn't like the fear she felt at that. She guessed she'd have to get used to it, if she wanted more chances to watch him sleep. And she did want that. Selfishly. Needfully.

The longer she lay awake, the more problems crowded through her mind. Who would the serial killer target next? What was her mother hiding? Why the hell was Faith such a freak?

Though not, she thought as her gaze caressed the sleeping Roy, quite as big a freak as she'd feared.

Roy turned to his side with a grunt and began to snore. She decided that was her cue to get up and to do something marginally more productive than worry.

His hand latched around her ankle before she was fully off the bed. His tired eyes cracked almost imperceptibly.

"Leaving…?" he slurred.

"Should I?"

"No."

"Then I won't. I'll just…clean up."

That seemed to satisfy him. His eyes closed, and within minutes the snoring resumed. Faith was able to slide off the bed, collect her clothes from there and the living room and find his bathroom.

She liked Roy's old-fashioned, tiled bathroom—it smelled very much of him, of the unique mix of soap, antiperspirant, shaving cream, shampoo and hair gel that all went into his particular scent. It was fairly clean, although…

Faith touched the handle of the toilet brush in its plastic tube in the corner, and tried to put a word to what she felt. *Mom.* Apparently his family lived close enough to regularly drop by.

The one saving grace was that, as in the guest room, Mrs. Chopin seemed to clean up around here of her own accord, maybe even against Roy's protests. But if they weren't half-hearted protests, surely the woman would have stopped.

Oh well. So he wasn't perfect.

Stepping into the warm spray of his shower, smelling Roy all around her and on her, remembering his touch, Faith guessed she could forgive the man a little domestic laziness. Especially since Evan did most of the cleaning in *her* apartment.

Once out of the shower and dressed, her hair toweled dry, Faith took a closer look at Roy's home. It used to be his grandmother's, she decided—half this furniture had to have been inherited, and she fancied that the old house still hoarded memories of him and his brothers and sisters as children, of his dad as a child, maybe even of his grandparents moving in right after World War II.

But she had to be imagining that part. She'd imagined having some kind of family history of her own so often, in childhood fantasies, it was easy.

She loved all the pictures, countless mix-and-match collections of parents and grandparents, brothers and sisters, nieces and nephews. Police uniforms seemed to be a running theme. She wasn't quite as thrilled by the photographs of Roy with obvious girlfriends, but she supposed it spoke well of him that he didn't tear them in half once the relationship was over. And considering how young he was in some of the pictures, at least some of those relationships *had* to be over.

The place was messy, but not dirty. Roy had magazines so old, some had headlines about Martha Stewart's insider trading trial or Navy SEAL Thomas King's rescue from Puerto Isla. Fighting back the weirdest urge to straighten up, Faith decided the clutter made the place…comfortable.

As opposed to the gun on the coffee table.

Moving on to the dining room, she found more recent mail and papers covering the Formica tabletop. Apparently, Roy brought his work home. There were official-looking reports with the crescent-star logo of the City of New Orleans on them; she put those aside as private, determined not to look at them...unless she had to. A stack of library books bore titles like *Psychics Debunked, An Encyclopedia of the Psychic Arts* and *A Dictionary of Superstitions*. Strips torn from a fast-food napkin marked several entries in that last book, so she took a peek. She found an entry about hair and one about running water—both of which corroborated what she'd already thought. But she hadn't expected the third entry.

Red Cord: Protection. Power. Often used to hang or tie talismans. In Feng Shui, brings good luck. In ceremonial magic, can be used in initiation or as a belt to indicate either first-degree or third-degree status, dependent upon the group's tradition.

This killer of theirs was certainly into protection, wasn't he? Did that mean he was afraid? Was that something that could be used against him?

She moved on, increasingly involved. Past the library books lay an open folder with what looked like programs...

From local psychic fairs.

Where he'd gotten them, Faith couldn't imagine. She supposed the NOPD had their ways. But Roy had a whole stack of programs from different fairs over the past six or seven years, most of them listing participating psychics, schedules of workshops, contributors, ads and more. He seemed to have already gone through them...and underlined the name Cassandra every time it showed up.

A few years back, someone named Cassandra Armstrong had offered her services in spiritual healing.

At a psychic fair across town, two years ago, someone named Cassandra McCoy was listed in the "special thanks" column.

A year later, someone named "Cass Kent" had provided a demonstration in Kirlian photography. Roy had put a question mark by that name, then written in "Cassidy" and crossed it off his list.

He'd even circled an ad for an occult shop which included the legend, "C. Bailey, Proprietor." Beside that he'd scribbled, "Charles."

Faith suddenly felt sick. Or hunted. Or both. Maybe that was just what being hunted felt like.

She shouldn't be surprised. Hadn't she come here thinking she might confess to being Cassandra? Because of her, Roy was wasting time on a false lead while Butch's real killer was still out there. He was harassing other poor Cassandras, and a Cassidy and a Charles, in his search. She could save a lot of people a lot of trouble—but at the cost of what kind of trouble to herself?

She wished she were noble enough to do the right thing. She really did. But just now, after what had happened between her and Roy, she was too selfish and too cowardly to confess. Not yet. Not without...without thinking it through.

Her cowardice made her feel sick, too.

She heard movement from the bedroom, then Roy's footsteps in the hall, and she pushed away the folder of psychic fair programs. She met him in the hallway instead, away from all the evidence of investigation.

His investigation into her.

He'd pulled on a pair of boxers, she guessed for her benefit. Suddenly, more than anything, she wanted to be touched again. She wanted to be sure he was still safe to touch, that she hadn't dreamed how unfreakish she'd felt with him.

"Watch the morning breath—" he warned as she surged into his arms. Skin against skin. Full body contact. And she felt—

Instead of the usual shock, she felt a blissful completion. It hadn't been a one-shot deal. She hadn't dreamed it.

She didn't give a damn about morning breath. She strained

upward, demanding his lips, which he gave with enthusiasm. By the time they abandoned the kissing for air, Roy didn't seem worried about morning breath either.

He looked vaguely dazed—but not unhappy about that. "So I'm thinking, you want to grab a quick breakfast before I report to work? For you that would be lunch."

"Okay," she said, clinging to him.

"Okay?" he challenged. "That's it?"

She nodded. She supposed she should let go of him now, but she wanted to hoard this feeling. If he kept looking for Cassandra, she might not have many more chances...not that she deserved them.

"How old are you?" he asked, wary now.

"Twenty-two."

With a moan, he lowered his head onto hers, as if he didn't like her answer. "Christ, I could almost've babysat for you."

That was intriguing enough to drag her out of her own fears, at least for a moment. If she was hoarding feelings, they might as well be good ones. "So...how old are you? Are you a pervert, or just a lucky son of a bitch?"

"I just turned thirty-one, which I think puts me in the gray area. That's actually considered *young* to make detective, you know. Now suddenly I'm old."

"You may have a few more good years left in you."

"Thanks for the vote of confidence." He kissed her again, quick and decisive, before going to shower. The casualness with which he did it—just kissed her, like any normal lover, just another way to say "Wait here" or "I'm coming back"—felt new and wonderful. And way too tenuous for her liking.

But that part was her fault.

"I brought work home," he called back over his shoulder, vanishing into the bathroom. "Don't mess with anything."

"Not even your gun?" she teased.

He leaned back out the bathroom door. "No. And get used to calling that my weapon. My gun, you got pretty familiar with."

Then, with a wicked grin, he vanished again.

She stood in the hallway for several minutes, listening to the water turn on, before she thought to go back into the kitchen.

Her life had just gotten really, really complicated, hadn't it?

They didn't make their breakfast-lunch; they'd gotten so busy kissing, Roy had to just drop Faith off with apologies before speeding away to work. But she saw him briefly the next day, at Butch's funeral.

He was one of the pallbearers, in full dress uniform. Watching him move grimly through the solemn ceremony, Faith could barely breathe. The misery of the funeral, the stone faces with which the officers hid their lingering outrage, felt like standing in the middle of radioactive fallout. Butch's death wasn't just a tragedy—and even before she saw the grief in his children and grandchildren, Faith had known it was undeniably that. It was becoming something more, too. Something even darker. Something she knew she couldn't stop even if she did confess to being Cassandra.

It was becoming a vendetta.

"I swear to God I'm not ignoring you on purpose," Roy said, finding her after the ceremony. He looked very official in uniform. Martial, even. He would terrify her mother, looking like this, but not Faith. She guessed she wasn't the first woman to find a uniform sexy.

"I know," she assured him.

"Everyone's working overtime," he said. "We *want* to work the overtime."

"I know. Don't worry about me."

"You know, Butch wanted me to take you out."

She'd guessed that. He hadn't exactly been subtle. "Did *you* want you to take me out?"

A smile played at his mouth for a minute, fleeting because of where they were, and why. But momentarily, wonderfully there. "Yeah. Still do. We'll have to try it sometime, huh?"

They *hadn't* dated yet, had they? Instead, they'd just…

Faith felt her body temperature rising at the same time she felt his, but this time they both looked away.

"Will you be okay getting home?" he asked. "We're talking business…."

"I got here just fine. I can get home just fine."

So with a last, awkward nod, Roy rejoined the other men in blue, all smiles gone. She tried not to liken the energy coming from them to a lynch mob. There was a cop-killer loose out there. And when someone killed a cop, nobody rested until there was an arrest.

Whether it was the right arrest or not.

Heading home from the funeral, Faith had the strangest feeling she was being followed. She paused several times, examining all the different passersby and tourists on the sunny street around her. But no matter how hard she listened, she couldn't settle on any one sound or scent to support her unusual intuition.

She must be getting paranoid, she decided. Lynch-mob mentalities could do that to a person.

The next afternoon, at work, Roy came by to talk to Greg about the shell casings found at the cemetery. He nodded at Faith as he strode past her toward Greg's office—that was all, just nodded. He looked tall and tired and determined, and she felt short of breath just watching him move. Once he was in Greg's office, she had a hard time concentrating on her work.

She tried desperately not to listen in on their conversation about Butch. A normal woman wouldn't be able to hear them behind closed doors. Then again, if she were normal, she wouldn't be in this bind.

On the way back out, though, Roy crooked a finger at her as he passed. Still not looking at her.

Intrigued, she got up and headed out the direction he'd gone. He was waiting by the bank of elevators. He raised his eyebrows at her, feigned casual, and stepped with exaggerated nonchalance through the door into the emergency stairwell.

Pulse picking up, Faith went after him—through the heavy door and right into his arms. Sensory information washed over her, as usual. *He'd had a po'-boy for breakfast. He was overdoing the coffee again. He wasn't getting enough sleep.* But the images washed *gently*. His embrace felt like homecoming.

"So are we co-workers or not?" he demanded, neatly turning her between him and the concrete wall, his gray gaze dancing across her lips as if maybe he wanted to kiss her as much as she wanted to kiss him. "'Cause if we are, and you've got some kind of rule against it, this could be trouble. One of these days, I really do intend to take you out on a real date."

"My rule isn't that strict," she reassured him, and was rewarded by his mocking grin—for just a moment, before his kiss blinded her to everything else. She stretched her arms up over his shoulders, hanging on for dear life, tasting him, breathing him.

"Good," Roy panted, after a few minutes of that. "That's real good."

"So about this alleged date," she started. She saw his wince and felt him tense up, so she smoothly added, "I'm guessing until you get Butch's killer, you won't have a lot of free time, huh?"

"No," he agreed. "Not much. I'm sorry, Corbett...."

But even as he apologized, she could tell he was anxious to be gone—if maybe after a few more kisses. Work to do. Vengeance to wreak. It wasn't that he didn't want to be with her. It was that his need to be elsewhere won out.

"Well, until then, feel free to come by the apartment after shift some night," she offered. Evan occasionally brought lovers home. So did Absinthe. Absinthe would hang a stolen Do Not Disturb sign on her doorknob when necessary, at which point Krystal—or now, Moonsong—knew to bunk on the sofa, or in Faith or Evan's room. As Krystal had explained when Faith first moved in, it seemed safer than them going into unknown territory alone. At least at the apartment, the roommates outnumbered the visitors. "I have my own room now. The others won't mind."

In answer, Roy kissed her again. Deeply. With tongue. She shivered against him with pleasure at both the feeling of him and the memories his kisses evoked. When he drew back, all he said was, "Damn."

He said it in an admiring tone.

Then he set her carefully back against the wall as if she might fall over, kissed the top of her head and trotted off down the stairs.

Cheered, Faith headed back to her desk.

Her mood changed when she heard what Greg was discussing with Officer Leone.

"—no blowback on his hands," Greg was saying, "and all the casings are from one or more .38 Specials. There's the very real possibility he was killed with his own gun. It wouldn't be the first time. Faith. There you are."

She tried to look alert and innocent, instead of lust-starved and guilty as hell. And it wasn't the lust she felt guilty about. "I just stepped out...the bathroom..."

The bathrooms were by the elevators were by the stairwell.

"Run this through the database, will you?" Greg handed her a ballistics report and a disk. "And put a rush on it. The slug Mandelet took out of Butch is our only hope for finding a striations match. The others all hit stone."

"They think it was Butch's weapon?" she asked. She knew full well that it hadn't been. But if all the casings were .38s, and only one of the bullets was in any shape to be matched, how would anyone prove that?

Nobody knew except Cassandra and the killer.

She was an idiot.

"Unfortunately, we don't have any slugs to match it against," said Greg. "Roy was just here talking to me. Thirty-six years on the force, and Butch never had to draw his weapon. Isn't that something?"

Faith nodded, sick at her own stupidity. She worked with evidence. Panicked or not, she should have known better. When she threw Butch's weapon into the river, she'd destroyed any sure chance of proving that it wasn't the same gun that killed him.

Unless the .38 that had killed him had its own history.

"I'll run this now," she promised.

Greg continued to squint at her, his pale eyes increasingly concerned behind his wire-frame glasses. "Are you all right, Faith?"

She nodded, not trusting her voice.

"You know that you can come to me if you're having any kind of problem, don't you?"

His gentle sympathy just hurt all the more. She had to force a smile, a nod. "Thanks, Greg. But I'm fine. Really. I'll run the ballistics check now."

"Thanks." And Greg and Leone continued toward the labs, talking about the line of fire in their crime-scene reconstruction. Greg only looked back at Faith once, respecting her space...but clearly concerned.

"All over the place," Leone was saying as they vanished into the hallway.

Lying sucked, thought Faith darkly. If only she hadn't insisted on staying anonymous with Butch and meeting him in secret. If only she hadn't destroyed evidence....

And she'd gotten on her *mother's* case about lying?

Faith walked home from work in the rain, dry under her Tulane umbrella. Again, she got the strangest sensation that someone was watching her. But whenever she slowed and looked around, she saw nothing out of the ordinary. Smelled nothing. Felt nothing.

This wasn't the way her abilities generally worked.

Butch's killer had been particularly silent, too, she thought. Or maybe that was just her guilty conscience talking. Either way, she vowed to be extra careful over the next few days.

"Have you noticed anything suspicious?" she asked the others when she got home. None of them did a very good business in the rain, so they'd rented videos. It was just the sort of group get-together Faith had always wanted roommates for.

"Anything suspicious like what?" asked Evan.

"Someone...lurking?"

They shook their heads.

"Maybe you should call your detective friend and tell him about it," suggested Moonsong. "You know, people would be less likely to bother us if we have a police officer showing up now and then."

"On the downside," noted Absinthe dryly, "we'd have a police officer showing up now and then."

"I already invited him to come by after shift, so I apologize in advance if he takes me up on it and wakes anyone." In order to avoid their sit-up-and-stare interest, Faith went to the table to check for mail—and saw a Manila envelope.

From Dallas.

"He couldn't be any noisier than Bud was," said Evan. One of his old boyfriends really had gone by the name Bud, which was even more ironic when you remembered that he was gay.

Faith was hardly listening. She was picking up the envelope, tearing it open. She'd ordered this last week. After Butch died, she'd forgotten. But now...

Certificate of Birth, it read. *State of Texas. County of Dallas. City of Dallas. Parkland Hospital.*

Full Name of Child: Faith Ashley Corbett.

Her mother hadn't lied, not about that anyway. Faith's sex and date of birth were all spelled out. The form listed her weight and length at birth. There was a section where "Single Birth" was checked off, with "Twins" and "Triplets" left blank. Under "Mother" it listed Tamara's name, residence, age, birthplace, occupation and even color.

But under "Father," the form remained blank.

Name. Residence. All of it.

Absolutely blank.

More than ever, Faith suspected her father hadn't left them. Not the way her mother had always insisted he had. Apparently, Faith *had* no official father.

This wasn't something she could take care of over the phone. "I'm heading back out," she said, folding the certificate to stuff into her slacks pocket and fetching her wet umbrella.

"Don't you want to watch the movie?" asked Evan, but Moonsong's gaze was more sympathetic. Moonsong understood something was wrong. She usually did.

"Maybe I'll be back in time for the second feature."

Faith went into the rainy French Quarter.

The St. Charles streetcar stop was across Canal from Bourbon Street. That was a walk of maybe twelve blocks, nothing Faith couldn't manage even in the rain. It was a warm rain, this being August. She had hours of daytime left.

But if she'd been thinking clearly, it would have occurred to her that, in the rain, it was still dark.

It might have occurred to her to tell someone where she was going.

And it should have occurred to her, when she heard a dog crying in a close alley beside a dry cleaner, that it might be a trap. Then again, her ears weren't easily tricked. It really was a dog's sharp, ki-yi-ing cry, mixed with panicked growls, not some mimic. There was no way she could just ignore the sound of a creature in pain. So she detoured into the alley, around the large green Dumpster that blocked her view. She automatically strained her ears for the dog's heartbeat to guess just how hurt it was—

And that's when she heard the other heartbeats with it.

Slower than the dog's agonized, racing pulse, but fast for humans…except for humans in confrontation mode.

Faith spun—but not before a semicircle of young men had already begun to form behind her, shoulder to shoulder, to force her farther back into the alley.

The drumming of the rain on the Dumpster must have masked the sound of their footsteps, their heartbeats. But now there was no mistaking them. They all wore some piece of green—a do-rag, a band around the arm or leg, in one case a tattered ribbon dangling from one guy's long black braid.

They were all members of the gang from Storyville that had attacked Evan the other week. Three of them had been arrested, but now…

But now they weren't all teenagers. And there were a lot more of them. Six? No—ten.

Blocking her way.

Faith spun back to the alley and, beyond the Dumpster, saw two more. Two boys from the first attack. The ones who hadn't been arrested.

The scraggly white boy, the one with all the tattoos, held a small dog by the scruff of its neck, twisted its paw to make it ki-yi again. Beside him a familiar Asian kid with a soul patch grinned with satisfaction.

And threat.

Chapter 14

Twelve to one.

Faith didn't have to be psychic to know she was screwed.

From here on out, all she could hope for was damage control. Preferably controlling the damage to *her*.

She didn't have time to consider options. Since she'd rather handle two first, instead of ten, she bolted deeper into the alley.

Maybe they'd expected her to cower, or to vacillate. She'd definitely taken them by surprise. She could smell that much over the scent of sweat and excitement and of rain on concrete.

She shoved her umbrella in tattoo-boy's face and wrapped an arm around the dog to protect it as she bodychecked his friend. That felt like plugging into two electric sockets at once—the dog's terror and the thug's malicious glee arced through her in a single, acidic jolt. Luckily the shock passed as quickly as their moment of contact did. She drove a knee up into the thug's crotch and, as he bent with a gasp, again into his ribs. But those weren't bare skin on bare skin.

He crumpled, wrenching the umbrella from her with his weight. At least he let go of the dog, which snapped at her with a panicked cry. She let it scramble, limping, for the alley corner, even as she tried to turn to meet the second of her previous acquaintances.

Between her rescue of the dog and tattoo-boy yanking her umbrella from her as he fell, she wasn't fast enough. A wiry forearm caught her around the throat and pulled back, lifting her feet from the ground. She grabbed his arm with both hands to take her weight off her neck—

His friends had been taunting him about her since the last attack. He'd never hated anyone so much. They would make an example—

Faith kicked out and found a brace against the Dumpster's rusty side. She pushed, hard.

He only staggered backward, his brace across her airway tightening. *He'd been shot in the leg, once. His mother didn't know what he was doing today. He liked the rain—*

Struggling to concentrate, even to breathe, she drew her knees up toward her shoulders, then drove both feet back, hard, into the man's knees. They were the best she could reach. He still didn't let go.

Still, as in the previous fight, her aggression seemed to snap off a switch inside of her. She stopped reading the bastard, despite his sweaty skin against her throat and chin and under her scratching hands.

She could still feel his increased body temperature, could hear his racing heart and rough, wet breathing and smell him sharp in her nostrils.

But at least she had him out of her damned head!

She kicked backward again, still dangling. He bent, stumbled, then dropped hard to his knees. His arm across her throat loosened. As soon as her feet touched the littered concrete of the alleyway Faith pushed backward, holding the arm. She managed an awkward somersault over the boy's bent form as he fell back. She was no gymnast. She ended up on her hip in the trash. But she was momentarily free of him.

She was also trapped beside a brick wall, her way blocked by him, tattoo-boy and the other ten men who now filled the mouth of the alley and advanced.

The dog, its coat matted and one leg dangling uselessly, was barking at them as if it thought itself much larger than it was.

Faith supposed she might give the same impression.

The idea made her laugh—which had the added benefit of surprising several of her assailants. But as the men closed in on her, their threat as obvious on their faces as in their smells, she feared that she wouldn't be able to surprise them for much longer. Not this many of them.

The trick, she guessed, would be to see how many she *could* surprise—by any means necessary—before they overcame her. That, and to scratch, yank, bite and bleed as much evidence off them as possible on her way down. The only alternative would be not to fight, in hopes of simply surviving.

Another day, maybe she would. But for her, at this moment, that was no alternative at all.

They shuffled closer, past the Dumpster that would hide their actions from casual notice. They were talking big about what they meant to do, what she'd like—and what she wouldn't.

"I guess you'll know who to respect after this, bitch," warned the biggest among them, a man older than her. He had a green design painted into his shaved hair. Apparently he was the leader.

So at least they meant to leave her alive, she thought. She

reached slowly behind herself amidst the wet litter, seeking a broken bottle that she knew was there from the sound of raindrops on hollow glass. They would probably change their minds about her living, once she was done with them.

But she decided it was still better than giving up.

Faith's fingers touched a jagged edge. She readjusted her hand to close around the smooth neck of the bottle instead. She didn't like the idea of using it, particularly not since they'd be more likely to use it back on her. But it might be her only chance.

Maybe if she could take down the leader.

Maybe if she could go past him in the confusion.

Maybe...

"Is this a private tea party, or can anyone play?"

Faith was as stunned as the gangbangers when a golden-haired woman suddenly dropped into the alleyway, smack between her and the gang members. In reality, the woman must have dropped off a fire escape over their heads. But it seemed as if she just *appeared,* landing in an easy crouch, like an angel in boots and leather.

The dog backed farther into the corner, barking his confusion.

"Shit!" exclaimed one of Faith's assailants.

The woman glanced almost imperceptibly over her shoulder. "You're Faith Corbett, right?" she asked, then turned back to the gang members. "Not that I wouldn't do this one just for the sheer enjoyment of it."

In that brief glimpse, Faith thought the woman looked to be about her age. There was something strangely familiar about her. "Why do you ask?"

"I'm Dawn O'Shaughnessy. Nice to meet you. You hurt?"

"What the fuck is this?" demanded one of the shorter men, beside the leader. "This some freakin' meet-and-greet? You just dropped into a whole world of trouble, bitch."

Faith and the stranger—Dawn—ignored his posturing.

"No." Leaving the bottle amidst the litter, where it would do less damage, Faith stood and brushed off her legs. That was one pair of slacks that wouldn't see work again. "I'm not hurt. I can take at least half of them. I have before."

Several of them began to protest that. Loudly.

"Won't have to," Dawn assured her. Her pose radiated confidence. Her thick golden braid, her skintight leather suit, the boots...even her breathing and her heartbeat remained even, unconcerned. Ready. "Maybe a third of them."

Faith shook her head, confused.

Another woman, chestnut-haired, stepped out from the street beyond the Dumpster and walloped one of the gang members across the head with a piece of metal pipe.

"Three to one," the newcomer explained, with a satisfied nod.

Two of the boys turned on her. At least five of them surged onto Dawn. And the others rushed Faith.

All at once.

It didn't help that the dog kept barking, hobbling on three legs from one corner to the next. All Faith could concentrate on, at first, was the immediate—

A guy in a concert T-shirt tackled her to the asphalt. She hit her head, the impact jarring the world around her. She still managed to roll with his force, his weight, so that he was suddenly beneath her, where she could start punching him repeatedly across the face. Again. Again....

Big hands dragged her off, copping a feel. She drilled an elbow backward into the sound of breathing and felt teeth give under the blow. For a moment she was free of them—standing on her own two feet, nobody dragging her anywhere.

That's when she saw how well the other two women were faring. The smaller one, with chestnut hair, was holding off at least three bangers with her metal pipe, and to judge from the blood, that's not all she'd been doing with it. The blonde didn't seem to need weapons. She moved in a slow, ready circle, hissing beneath her breath in words that sounded Asian to Faith's untrained ear. When she struck, she struck hard and fast, kicking one boy right in the jaw, martial-arts style.

Two men already lay unconscious at her feet.

Someone grabbed Faith's ankle and yanked her down into the wet garbage. It was the man who'd tried to strangle her. She kicked out at him, sending his kneecap into a world of pain, even as tattoo-boy got her pinned by the shoulders.

"You coulda just taken it, you stupid bitch," he whispered over the frenzied barking of the hurt dog. He exuded a hatred that frightened her even worse than his words did. "Now we gotta finish it. Right here. Right—"

Then he slumped, unconscious, down onto her.

"Yeah," muttered the woman called Dawn as, having dispatched this final threat, she dragged his inert form off Faith and rolled him against the brick wall. "Blah blah blah. Don't these idiots know that they expend energy with all that bad-guy bullshit?"

Then she extended a helping hand.

Faith looked, dazedly, from her to the smaller, darker-haired woman.

That one dropped her metal pipe with a clang and swept her shoulder-length hair out of her face. "All done," she announced.

She was right.

The remaining gang members had scattered. The dog had stopped barking to hobble closer to some of the forms that lay, insensible to the rainfall, on the alley floor. It snuffled them warily, looking from them to Dawn.

They'd won.

"We should probably head out ourselves, unless we want

a lot of extra attention," said Dawn, bending to make the offer of her hand even more obvious, more impatient. "I don't know about you, but I'd prefer to stay under the radar just now."

She had unusual, green-gold eyes. Something about them disturbed Faith...but she couldn't ignore the woman indefinitely.

She took the offered hand—and the impressions that came with it.

A sterile environment—lots of white, lots of metal. Almost impervious to pain, to wounds. Powerful emotional shields... shields that had begun to crack. A circle of concerned women, strong women, seeking something. And a sense of closure, of triumph beyond the fight....

Something in Dawn seemed to say, *At last.*

And that familiarity!

As soon as she could, Faith released the woman's hand. Faith tried to hide her confusion with a fleeting smile, but she didn't need to be able to read people to know she hadn't fooled either of them.

Quickly, she bent and gathered the hurt, wet dog into her arms, so that she wouldn't have to shake the other woman's hand. Not yet. Not so soon after...

Faith wasn't sure after what. But touching Dawn had been more than enough sensory input until she at least caught her breath.

Holding the dog helped. It was quickly calming, in the cradle of her arms, which calmed her in return. Dogs were so simple. *Hungry. Safe. Hurt. Safe. Friends.*

It still cast wary looks toward Dawn, but otherwise it wiggled and licked raindrops off her arm, which calmed her even further.

Dawn stood slightly taller than Faith. The other woman, the one with the chestnut hair, was slightly shorter than her. That one smiled with a quiet grace that was almost as unsettling as Dawn's touch.

"Pleased to meet you, Faith," she said, her voice thick with an emotion Faith didn't understand. "I'm Lynn White."

She, too, had unusual eyes. And now, Faith recognized them. From the mirror.

Her world bottomed out—even as Lynn finished the introduction.

"We're your sisters."

They left the little dog with a nearby veterinarian, who insisted on keeping it overnight to give it IV nutrients after he set its leg. He said it was a cocker mix, and from its level of malnutrition, it had probably been a stray for weeks.

Faith hardly paid attention as she guaranteed to cover the bill and collect the dog the next day.

Sisters?

By unspoken agreement, none of them broached that revelation until they'd found a secluded corner in a café where they could have some privacy. The delay had given Faith a chance to process the bombshell they'd just dropped on her... and to try to come to terms with how true it felt.

Her mother's lifelong secrecy.

How very similar she and the others were in appearance—especially Dawn's hair color, and their unique, green-gold eyes.

The sense of earnestness she read off both of them.

So, cradling her coffee between two hands, Faith didn't bother arguing the idea, no matter how mind-boggling it was. Instead, she simply asked, "You're my *half* sisters?"

Dawn and Lynn exchanged telling glances. "Not exactly," said Lynn.

"You mean...my mom had more than one daughter?" The birth certificate had said *Single Birth. Older? Younger?*

"No, you're her only child. As far as we know."

Faith was out of options.

"Here's how it is." Dawn leaned across the table in her intensity. "You're the product of artificial insemination. Tamara Hallwell may be your birth mother—"

"Corbett," whispered Faith. "She's Tamara Corbett."

"—but she's not your biological mother."

"I know it's a shock." Lynn covered Faith's hand in sympathy, before Faith thought to draw back. It happened again.

Sheltered life. Scholarship. The clicking of a computer keyboard. Recent betrayal by her father figure. Love...

Faith snatched her hand free, but not before she'd gotten that last, definite impression. Lynn White was in love with someone. But she was here, instead of with him. Out of concern for Faith.

"I'm sorry," she said to her—*her sister*—at the same time as Lynn.

Lynn smiled her sympathy, instead of touching again. "I was pretty stunned when Dawn showed up and told me, too. But things were already a mess, at that point."

"Apparently Corbett is the name your birth mother took after she ran off, pregnant with you," Dawn continued. She had a more direct manner. "From what we can tell, she answered an ad to be a surrogate mother. She was implanted with three fertilized embryos, just like Lynn's and my surrogate mothers were. But somehow she convinced the folks who hired her that she wasn't pregnant. Gave up on the promise of a $50,000 payoff to do it, too."

Faith shook her head, unsure what to even ask next. "Why?"

Lynn said, "You'll probably have to ask her."

"And your mothers?"

Again, her sisters exchanged telling glances.

"You're the only one of us who got to have that," admitted Lynn. "Dawn's surrogate mother died in childbirth. She was young, a waitress who wanted the money to get her brother out of foster care."

"Justin Cohen," said Dawn. "He's an FBI agent now. He's one of the people who tracked me down."

"Mine originally did it for the fifty thou," admitted Lynn, "But...well, her story's complicated. And our biological mother, the egg donor, never even knew about us...she only started to figure things out last year."

"And then," announced Dawn, grim, "they killed her."

The rest of the story became something of a blur for Faith. It was almost too incredible to be believed. Almost, but not quite. Not after everything Faith had seen in herself. Not after what she'd sensed from these...

From her sisters.

It all traced back to the Athena Academy for the Advancement of Women, the most elite college-prep school for women in the United States. Founded almost a quarter of a century earlier, the school counted among its graduates some of the most successful women in government.

It also, against the best wishes of its founders, harbored an ugly secret.

"The name sounds familiar...wasn't it in the news, last year?" asked Faith.

"We need to start a lot earlier than that," said Dawn. "With Lab 33. It's government sponsored and top-secret. When the school was created, about twenty-three years ago, its scientists fixed on the academy's students as perfect egg donors for their experiments in genetic enhancement. The problem was how to get any of these students, who were underage and weren't fools, to make a donation."

"The lab planted two employees at the school, and chose a donor. They gave her something to cause symptoms of appendicitis. And on the way to the hospital..."

Faith listened in fascinated horror as the story unfolded. Eggs had been harvested from one of the Athena Academy's best and brightest students, thirteen-year-old Lorraine Miller, under the guise of an appendectomy. Lab 33 then fertilized the eggs with sperm stolen from a clinic. The lab team ended up with nine viable embryos to implant into three surrogate mothers.

"They wanted disposable women," said Dawn, a trace of bitterness under her matter-of-fact presentation. "Women who wouldn't be missed if they were killed after giving birth."

"So my mom…" Faith hesitated, but what else was she going to call Tamara Hallwell Corbett? The woman had given birth to her, had raised her. Tamara had kissed Faith's boo-boos and braided her hair and told her about the birds and the bees. She was more her mother than this faceless Lorraine Miller person…wasn't she? "My mom's been on the run ever since, afraid Lab 33 would find out that she really did give birth."

"Apparently," agreed Dawn. "The scientists didn't know you existed. A man named Jonas White kidnapped Lynn when she was born and raised her on his own, leaving her surrogate mother for dead. That left Lab 33 with me."

Lynn's face had darkened at the mention of Jonas White. The name sounded familiar to Faith, but she wasn't sure why. She kept her attention on Dawn.

"You were raised by scientists?" Faith couldn't begin to imagine it.

"Not completely." Dawn held her gaze. "I had my Uncle Lee." She said the name darkly.

"And," said Lynn quickly, "she got to spend a year at the Athena Academy. Everything leads back to the Athenas."

The previous year, Lorraine Miller Carrington had called an emergency meeting of her old Athena Academy friends. Keeping a sacred promise made during their school years, the women had heeded her call. But Lorraine, or Rainy, as her friends called her, never made the meeting.

"She was in a car accident," explained Dawn, who seemed to know more of the story than Lynn did. "A *rigged* car accident. A special device made her fall asleep at the wheel, and her seat belt was rigged to fail. Once the Cassandras began to investigate—"

Faith raised her hand, momentarily silencing her sister. She could hardly breathe. "The *who?*"

"The Cassandras." Dawn shrugged, seeing she would have to explain. "Every year the school takes in about thirty new students. They're divided into five teams of six each, and they have friendly competitions against each other."

"Like at Hogwarts," supplied Lynn. "Slytherin versus Gryffindor."

"But at Athena, each team picks a name from Greek mythology. Rainy Miller's group chose Cassandra. Anyway…"

She continued her narrative, but Faith heard less of it than before. She caught the pertinent pieces. Rainy, an attorney who had struggled with infertility throughout her marriage, had realized that she was the victim of egg mining. An assassin had killed her before she could tell the others.

But they hadn't counted on the determination of the Cassandras.

"One of them took down the assassin," said Dawn, clearly conflicted. "But they still don't know exactly who hired him. And they've been looking for us, for Rainy's daughters, the whole time. At first they thought I was the only one who'd survived. But then I found Lynn, and we realized you might be alive and tracked you down. It wasn't easy. Thank goodness Lynn's a computer whiz."

Lynn downplayed her role. "We can search records online that would have been impossible to access ten years ago. It helps that your mother kept her first name—and that it was an unusual one."

"So you've been following me since yesterday," said Faith softly.

"We had to be sure it was you," explained Lynn. "We tried e-mailing, on a fictitious reason of course, through your mom, but she never responded. This isn't the kind of news we'd want to give the wrong person, by accident."

"I guess not." Faith shook her head. "'Hi. We're the sisters you never knew. And you…'"

One of the points they'd skimmed past loomed into precedence now. *Experiments in genetic enhancement.*

Why else would they have needed stolen eggs? Stolen sperm? Disposable surrogate mothers?

Experiments.

Faith finished, "'And you are a mutant freak.'"

Chapter 15

"'Mutant freak' might be a bit extreme," said Dawn dryly. "I prefer 'lab rat.'"

"Give her a break, Dawn." Lynn reached out to pat Faith's hand again, then caught her own hand back. She learned fast. "You've known your whole life that you had special abilities. You were trained in them. Even my godfath—I mean, even Jonas White knew I'd been enhanced, so he made sure I grew into my potential. But this has got to be a complete shock for Faith."

"Special…" Faith shook her head, trying to digest it all. "What kind of special abilities do you have?"

"The scientists had nine embryos," explained Dawn, like a soldier making a report. "They altered them so that three would have extra healing abilities, three would have super strength and agility, and three would have super intelligence. And they kept each set of three together. Since none of the surrogate mothers had multiple births, the experiments resulted in one of each. My ability is that I heal fast. *Really* fast."

"You'll have to see her do it sometime," agreed Lynn. "It's amazing."

"And you?" asked Faith, of Lynn.

"Strength and agility."

"White put that to good use, too," said Dawn. Her tone left no confusion about her opinion of Jonas White.

That left Faith with... "But I'm not super intelligent. I mean, my grades have always been good, but I still had to study. I'm a college dropout. Something must have gone wrong with me."

So she wasn't just an experiment—she was a *failed* experiment?

"You mean you've never noticed anything that you're especially good at?" challenged Dawn. "Just because you aren't book-smart doesn't mean the alterations didn't take. Maybe you're smart with money. Or languages."

Faith shrugged. "No more than the next person."

"Computers?" suggested Lynn, and Faith shook her head. "People?"

"I'm terrible with people! Mom never wanted me getting too close, because..." She hated to mention this part. It was probably related, probably a side effect of the failed experiments, which made her abilities even more embarrassing. Still, if she couldn't tell these women...

"Because I read them," Faith admitted.

Dawn said, "Come again?"

"My programming must not have taken correctly. I'm... hyperaware. I can hear your heartbeats, right now, and your breathing, and I can smell what you had not just for lunch but breakfast, and what kind of soap you used. And when I touch someone, I get weird flashes of information about them."

"That might be exactly what they meant to accomplish," Lynn assured her. "I have some similar abilities—really good eyesight and hearing. It sounds as if your senses are just as acute, but focused differently. Focused on people."

"But how's that make me intelligent?"

"The scientists can explain it better than me," said Dawn. "But hello, which organ processes all those nerve responses?"

Faith studied the tablecloth, scowling. "My friends keep saying I'm psychic. I was beginning to think maybe…"

But there was no reason to go into the crazy notions she'd begun to entertain.

"Does it matter what you call it?" asked Lynn. "At least now you know it's real. Now you know where it comes from."

"Yeah," muttered Faith. "A test tube."

"And Lorraine Miller Carrington," Dawn reminded her.

Faith nodded. Somehow, one little detail—trivial to her two sisters—struck her as the strangest part. *How had she known?*

"One of the Cassandras," she said.

Once Faith reached her mother's home, she couldn't sit, couldn't rest. It was just too much to take.

And yet she had to take it, didn't she?

"You *stole* me?"

Her mother, hands clasped tightly in her lap as she sat on the designer sofa, did not deny it. She simply looked up at Faith with those remarkably pale-blue eyes, and she looked… broken. "I should have known you'd find out. Especially once I saw that you were…"

Her voice trailed off, and her eyes filled with tears.

"That I was a *freak?*" supplied Faith. Or, to use Dawn's term, "A lab rat?"

"Don't call yourself that. You're different, yes. You're special."

"As in special education classes."

"As in a beautiful, unique, talented woman who deserves to be cherished for exactly who she is. The way I've cherished you."

Faith shook her head, still pacing. She'd come here as soon as she left her sisters at their hotel, with promises to get together the next day. She was afraid to stop moving. She was afraid of what her new knowledge would do to her head once she slowed down enough to process it all.

"You haven't been cherishing me," she argued. "You've been manipulating me by withholding the truth. You knew I was an experiment from the start. You *knew* it!"

"No! I knew something shady was going on. I knew you were a test-tube baby. But genetically engineered? How could I guess that? Those awful people didn't tell us anything."

"So you knew there were others?" Sisters. *She had sisters!*

"When I went in for my pregnancy test, I saw another woman leaving. An African-American. She was older than me, tall and very beautiful, and the way she looked at me… It's hard to explain, but we had a moment of connection. I had to wonder…"

But Tamara didn't tell Faith what she had to wonder. She just lowered her gaze to her hands and looked miserable. She'd been looking miserable since Faith had arrived with her accusations.

But she hadn't once looked shocked.

Faith scrubbed a hand through her hair—and wondered if she'd inherited her hair from her dead mother or her nameless father. She needed to understand this. When in doubt, gather evidence. "How did you fake the pregnancy test?"

"I paid a woman for her urine," Tamara confessed. "I put it in a test tube, like a tampon, so that it would stay warm until I substituted it for my sample. That was the early 80s. Labs weren't as suspicious then as they are now. I told them I'd gotten my period, that I was sure I wasn't pregnant. They told me to stay in town anyway, just in case, but I knew our only hope was to run. So I ran."

"And left behind fifty-thousand dollars?"

"I hadn't done it for the money! Baby, you have to believe that. I'd been alone for so long. I wanted a baby so badly."

"Then why not do it the old-fashioned way?" A brief image of Roy Chopin flashed across Faith's conflicted thoughts—Roy, and what they'd done together. She could tell that for him sex was definitely about recreation, not procreation. But surely it wouldn't be that hard to trick a man, even someone as sharp as him. Provide her own condoms. Poke a few holes in them....

"I was so confused," moaned Tamara. "There were no men in my life, and I doubted finding one would make things any easier. I'll admit, when I first answered the ad, I wasn't sure what I would decide. But as soon as I began to feel my body changing, as soon as I knew you were alive, inside me..."

Faith's step slowed. She wanted to believe the yearning she heard in her mother's voice. *Her mother.* At least Faith hadn't been raised as some kind of killing machine in a laboratory, like Dawn had. At least she hadn't been used by some master criminal under the guise of her supposed protector, like Lynn.

You're the only one of us who got to have that, Lynn had said.

But how could that make up for all the secrets her so-called mother had kept from her?

The ache threatened to overwhelm her. She started pacing again.

"I suspected those doctors were up to no good," said Tamara. "I was afraid they were dangerous. But the alternative would have been to let them have you, to let them have my baby."

"Not your baby. Lorraine Miller's baby. Some man's..." Her sisters hadn't mentioned if they knew whose sperm had been stolen to create them. "Someone else's egg, someone else's sperm."

"My blood. My breath. My body to protect you. You became my baby even before your heart began to beat, and I decided right then, I wouldn't let them have you." Tamara's chin came up. "And I don't care who they send to turn you against me. I still won't let them."

"It's not your choice anymore," Faith reminded her.

"But it is still my business. You're my business. You're my *daughter.* It doesn't matter what you inherited from those strangers. I raised you. I taught you."

"To lie," Faith challenged. And look where that handy habit had gotten her...her and Madame Cassandra. "To lie, and to hide. Thanks a lot."

"It kept you safe." Tamara was squeezing her hands, her eyes brimming with desperation.

Faith turned toward the door, unable to take more of this. Not yet. Not now. "It kept me leashed."

Tamara took a deep breath. "You know where to find me, baby."

But Faith, her throat tightening with emotion, pushed back out into the humid Louisiana night.

He didn't like where she lived.

He let Himself back into the shadowy courtyard— He could do that, after all. He could come and go like a ghost. He could do things that no one knew about. He was so powerful now, He even crept up the stone steps to the front door, to look in.

But even though He was powerful, this was an apartment full of magic users themselves. So this time, after He peeked through the old-fashioned keyhole and didn't see the one He was after, He crept back down again. Just in case.

The Master had found Madame Cassandra. The Master

*wanted Him to take care of this one, before she destroyed him.
And He wanted to do it, too. He thought He was powerful
enough to take her, now.*

*But that didn't mean He must do it on her terms. Hers, or
the Master's.*

He would do it in His own time. In His own way.

*And once He'd stolen the life out of the greatest psychic in
all the French Quarter—then not even the Master would be
able to control Him.*

*After that, anything He did for the Master would be a
favor.*

Faith awoke and sat up in bed before she even understood
why. For a moment, she felt only confusion. A few magazines,
which she'd checked out from the library on her way home,
slid off her sheets and onto the floor. They reminded her of
what she'd learned, how much she still had to learn.

Lorraine Miller Carrington. *Scandal at Athena Academy.*

Had she really managed to sleep? She guessed the kind of
day she'd had took its toll on a person's strength. Even a genetically engineered superbeing.

And it's not as if she'd slept well. Waking dreams had tor-
mented her, dreams of gang ambushes and secret laboratories
and serial killers with red cords and distinctive heartbeats.

But what had woken her now?

Her bare feet hit the marble floor as soon as she recognized
the footsteps climbing the stone stairway outside. She was
down the hallway and across the dark den even before she
heard the knock, uncharacteristically soft, on the front door.

He only had to knock once before she had the door unlocked and open.

Detective Roy Chopin's eyes widened at her quick response.
Other than that, he looked wholly contained. Competent. Ready.

She could feel his exhaustion and his frustration with however his night had gone. She could also feel, as his gaze took in her boxers and camisole—and the legs and arms left bare—how quickly his exhaustion made way for a different kind of energy. He didn't bother asking if she really meant her invitation to come by after shift. He didn't explain how far after shift this was. He didn't seem worried that he might appear too eager. He was just…here.

For her. One way or another.

One thing on their minds, she thought, relief making her giddy. *Thank God.*

"So," he said, lowering his voice for the sake of her roommates as he came in, closed the door and locked all three locks behind him. "The night's crap. A domestic call that went bad. A mugging that went worse. No more frigging leads on who did Butch than we had yesterday, and every twenty-four hours they get colder. You know your gate was unlocked?"

"No it wasn't." She grabbed his tie and tugged him in the direction of her bedroom. She walked backward. She wanted to watch him. He looked amused as he followed.

"What, I'm not standing here? Start locking the damned gate."

"So what else was crap about the night?" It wasn't that she wanted him to have had a bad night. But the sheer normalcy of it, contrasted against her last twenty-four hours, made for a welcome distraction.

Almost as welcome as the heat of him, the presence of him, the scent of him trailing her across the den.

"I've got a new partner, transferred in from Baton Rouge. Name's Max. He doesn't suck, but he's not Butch, you know? What are you, Lucy Ricardo?" Now he was looking at the two twin beds while she shut her bedroom door behind them. "The innocence thing is refreshing, but damn."

Then she turned back, wrapped her arms up over his shoulders and stretched up on her toes in hopes of a kiss. "Want to shock the censors and push them together?"

"That might be helpful, yeah." Catching her against him, he covered her mouth with his. Along with his blunt scent and coffee taste and sexual energy, images flowed across her, more like a homecoming than an invasion. *Domestic call. Mugging-turned-homicide. New partner*—she loved that he was that straightforward. *Exhaustion, rapidly fading to arousal. Concern for her. Suspicions about...*

Then she'd made it past the flash of impressions and into the zone. The intensity of his breath scorched her. The wet demand of his lips engulfed her. His grip on her—weaving into her hair, sliding up her spine under her camisole—electrified almost every nerve ending in her. She pressed, hard, against his heartbeat and the sound of his breathing and the solidity of his body. She wanted him surrounding her, touching her, outside of her, inside of her, everywhere.

She wanted him to make her forget.

His tongue, filling her mouth, was a good start. She shuddered at the eager, demanding promise of him. Then she almost whimpered when he drew back, a smug gleam in his eyes.

"You're not big on wasting time, are you?" he asked, and he scooped her up and dropped her onto her bed. While she caught her balance on the bounce, he easily lifted the bed table out from between the two twins and stuck it in a corner. He shrugged off his jacket and tossed it onto the chair. Then, with one shove, he pushed Moonsong's old bed across the floor to bump into Faith's.

From down the hall, Absinthe yelled, "Shut the hell up!"

"Sorry," Faith called back. But even if furniture moving was a bit much at this hour, she wasn't really sorry at all.

"We're gonna be real popular," promised Roy, laughter in

his voice. He removed his belt holster and lay his weapon over the jacket.

"So," she prompted as he tugged his tie loose. She'd never realized watching a man undress could be this…riveting. "Crappy night."

"So Max and me are called to the old Charity hospital to talk to some gangbangers. We get there and the beat cop—first officer to respond—tells us, 'they aren't talking, but before everyone shut up, one guy let slip that some blond chick beat him up.'"

Oh. Faith's discomfort suddenly had less to do with wanting Roy to finish undressing and more to do with wanting to know how much he'd learned about today's ambush. She didn't want him to connect her to it. The ambush, and her sisters' involvement, had too much to do with the rest of her day's revelations.

The ones she was trying to forget.

She drew her knees up toward her chest, almost like a shield.

"It's déjà vu to the other day," Roy continued, tossing the tie and starting on his shirt buttons. "Sure enough, the E.R.'s holding these three shining examples of America's youth until we can talk to them. Turns out some woman called in a report about them being unconscious in an alley. But she did it anonymously."

Lynn, thought Faith. *Or maybe Dawn.* One of them must have called while she'd been busy at the vet's. Despite her discomfort with how Roy was looking at her at the moment—a lot more like a cop than like a lover—she felt glad. She liked that her sisters had the presence of mind to make sure the guys in that alley got medical attention.

"Dispatch sent a squad car to check it out," Roy continued, shrugging out of his shirt now. He wore an undershirt, but she could see his chest hair over the top. She didn't realize guys wore undershirts anymore. "Sure enough, someone beat down on these boys. But this time a weapon was used. That's aggravated assault, which is why they called us. Max and me, we take over where the patrolmen stopped questioning them. Who'd they fight with? Do we maybe have some kind of gang war heating up? Like that. But they're toughs. Now they aren't talking, not even the guy who first said he'd been smacked down by a blonde."

Then Roy paused, belt unbuckled but pants still zipped, his gaze dark and direct. "You wouldn't know anything about this, would you, Bernie?"

"I didn't assault anybody, if that's what you mean."

"Yeah." His eyes narrowed with suspicion. "That's heartfelt. Do you *know* something?"

She didn't want to lie to him. She was such a hypocrite, considering how she'd blamed her mom for secrets. Even one more, to Roy, would be several too many.

She needed him. Tonight, at least. Now. If he left…

But he had the right to leave. So she compromised and said, "Maybe?"

He groaned, heartfelt—and sat on the expanded bed beside her.

Still wearing his damned undershirt and pants.

"This is serious, Faith," he said. And it must be. It was the first time she'd heard him use her first name. "If they're messing with you, you've got to file a complaint and get the bastards off the street. If you're messing with them, I might end up having to arrest you, which would be damned embarrassing for everyone involved, meaning me."

Desperate now, Faith considered her options.

She crossed her arms, caught the hem of her camisole and stripped it up over her head.

Roy stared at her topless form for a long, silent moment. Then, with a wordless noise of defeat, he bent over her and caught her mouth with his. Lecture forgotten, his hands went to the distraction she'd offered, and she arched into his warm, callused touch.

Yes.

In only a moment, he'd lost the undershirt. He was lying on top of her and she was wrapping her legs around his waist, wrapping her arms around his incredible bare torso, doing everything she could to encourage his nonverbal attentions. She felt like she hadn't touched him, much less kissed him, in weeks instead of hours. She felt like she'd been stretched to the breaking point from waiting. And now…

Oh, now.

Her whole life had changed. The normalcy of him, of this—despite the fact that this, too, was a new development in her life—meant a hell of a lot more than whatever some top-secret laboratory might have done to her before she was born.

At least in the short-term.

And for now, tonight, short-term was all that mattered.

The next morning, when she reluctantly left her bed—and the nice, solid man in it—to take her shower, everything was great. Surprisingly great, considering how awful the previous day had been. Morning sex and lingering kisses, she guessed, could do that.

She thought she heard Roy's cell phone ring while she was in the shower, but she tried not to listen in. She might have genetically altered superhearing, but that didn't mean people didn't deserve their privacy. And it wasn't like Roy said much.

Then, when she got back to her room, clean and ready for the promised breakfast and ride to work, she was surprised to find him not only dressed but standing there, waiting.

Staring at her.

Something dark and hurtful sharpened his gaze. His mouth had definitely returned to threatening mode. And a sense of betrayal roiled off of his taut posture. Faith hesitated, confused. Why…?

Then she saw the small pile of clothes lying on her bed. Gauzy, gypsy clothes. With a black wig.

Roy shook his head only once before stepping forward and coldly snapping a pair of handcuffs on her. She supposed she could have made a run for it, could have fought him. Physically, she could have.

Emotionally, all she could do was stand there in shock.

"Faith Corbett, I'm placing you under arrest for the murder of Detective Sergeant Butch Jefferson."

He jerked the cuffs, to make sure they were secure. Hard. Angry. "Or should I maybe call you Madame Cassandra?"

Chapter 16

Five hours later, they were still questioning her. *They* included Roy's new partner, Max, who'd dragged himself in almost eight hours before his shift would actually start. Chief of Detectives Captain Frank Crawford was there. And there were a pair of dayshift plainclothesmen whom Faith had come to think of as Slick and Bubba. Slick was a thirtysomething black man, impeccably groomed right down to the gel in his hair and the pin in his tie. Bubba was, well…a bubba. With a gun.

None of them was the person she wanted.

"I'll only talk to Roy," she warned them, for maybe the dozenth time. Slick and Bubba, who were holding up the far wall, rolled their eyes at each other, patronizing. Idiots. Had she phrased that as a request?

"Ms. Corbett, as I've been telling you, Detective Chopin has been removed from this case for obvious reasons." Captain Crawford stopped pacing long enough to rub a tired hand down his skinny face, radiating stress. Considering what bits of background noise dribbled into the supposedly soundproof room, Faith wasn't surprised. The capture of even a suspected cop killer had lit a fire under this station. "He's in no position to help you—"

Faith laughed. "I'm not asking for his help, Captain. I doubt he'd give it."

She faintly heard Roy's bitter voice, behind the one-way mirror. "She's got that right."

Of course, nobody else in the room heard it. "*I'm* offering *him* something, not the other way around. *Information,* you morons," she added, for Slick and Bubba's edification.

Captain Crawford said, "Well, if you'll tell us, we'll be happy to pass your information on to the detective who brought you in. A little cooperation will go a long way."

But she'd recently learned the secret to surviving police stations. She had her sense of self firmly in place. "Yes, it will, Captain. So cooperate. I talk to Roy."

"We put a lab rush on the clothing found in your room, Ms. Corbett, and even waiting for DNA results it doesn't look good for you. Traces of blood. Gunpowder residue. Goodbye, job. Goodbye, clean record. Goodbye freedom—you're facing serious time, or worse."

Faith wondered if Greg Boulanger had run the tests, or if he, too, had been removed from the case. "No, I'm not."

Okay, so she wasn't quite as sure as she pretended to be.

The captain slapped a Manila folder onto the table in front of her. "We've got the sworn testimony of a citizen who saw a woman of your height and build, with black hair and clothes matching those found in your room, leaving the scene of the crime."

Roy hadn't mentioned that part. "Anything else?"

"As a matter of fact—" But Crawford stopped himself, eyeing her warily. "We're the ones conducting this damned interrogation, Ms. Corbett, not you. So how about you start answering our questions? What did you do with Sergeant Jefferson's gun?"

She said nothing.

"Who was involved in the killing with you?"

She said nothing. But she felt relieved they didn't believe she'd acted alone.

Corbett slammed a hand down beside the folder, leaning over her now. "Why did you want Butch Jefferson dead?"

That, she couldn't ignore. "I didn't! Butch was a wonderful man. How could *anyone* want him dead?"

"Obviously someone did. Maybe you can shed some light on who that might have been?" Before she could stop him, the captain tapped her under the chin to make her look up at him.

He and his wife were in separate beds. They'd become strangers. His one real joy was his young son. He—

She swung her head away, pushing her chair back from him—its feet squealed on the concrete floor, and the handcuff that attached her to the table pulled taut. It was either that or head-butt the guy, which would be trouble. "Don't touch me!"

Captain Crawford reared back almost as quickly at her reaction. "What the hell?"

It was Roy's new partner, Max Leonard, who intervened. "We've already established that she doesn't like to be touched, Captain. Ms. Corbett, sweetheart, he wasn't trying to hurt you."

Faith gritted her teeth, embarrassed by her reaction, angry that they'd gotten her to talk at all. She hadn't said he was trying to hurt her, damn it. She just didn't want…

Okay, so maybe she was feeling the stress after all. The booking process alone had resulted in a few too many casual, normally harmless touches. Time to practice Krystal's quiet breathing.

"As Roy told me," she said tightly, "I have the right to remain silent."

"Let me give this a try," suggested Max, drawing the captain back. Roy's new partner seemed like a nice enough guy, stocky, balding, fighting a middle-aged spread. He wore a wedding ring and a Mary medal. Instead of looming over Faith the way Captain Crawford had or intimidating her with his ability to move around the room while she had to stay in her little chair, Max sat on the corner of the table and held her gaze. Not touching her. "I'm sure Chopin also told you that you have the right to an attorney, sweetheart. Are you sure you don't want us to send for one?"

"No," Faith assured him, dragging together the threads of her poise. "Not yet."

Not until she'd talked to Roy.

She'd tried, after the initial shock of the arrest. Handcuffed in the back seat of his car on the way over, she'd tried to explain. He'd just turned up the volume of his radio, zydeco music blasting out the windows, so that he couldn't hear what she had to say. To judge from the way he was treating her now, the Faith he'd made love to not an hour before the arrest could have been someone else. Or dead.

Faith understood his arresting her. If she'd been a cop and found the backpack, she would have arrested her, too—though how he'd found the backpack was a whole other issue. What her secrets had done to their budding relationship, though—that pressed on her heart like a ten-ton weight.

They were through. She got that, and she knew she'd brought it on herself, through her secrecy. She wasn't looking for sympathy. But he had to hear the truth from her, or he might never hear it…and not knowing would be even worse for him.

The first thing any attorney with half a brain would tell her was not to talk. And she sure as hell couldn't count on ever getting an audience with Roy if this went to trial.

One problem at a time; that was how she'd take things.

"Do you want another cola?" asked Max gently. "You need a bathroom break?"

"I'm fine, thank you."

"See, Faith—can I call you Faith?" Max's good-cop routine was almost as skilled as Butch's had been. It would have been funny, if only it weren't so damned effective. Everything about the interrogation room was set up to make her feel alone and helpless. The lack of windows. The industrial-white walls and low-watt bulbs. The rudimentary table and plastic chairs, with her chair farthest from the door. Even the one-way mirror, with the threat of who knew how many unseen people watching her through it, played its role in Faith's intimidation. Against all that, a little niceness went a long, long way.

But not long enough to make her forget what she had to do.

"You don't look like a killer to me," Max continued, deliberately soothing. "Like you say, you didn't want Butch dead. I believe that. If you wanted him dead, why would you have called in help for him? I'm thinking someone else did the shooting, someone you could help us catch. You kept it secret because it was maybe an accident? Maybe you got scared? But we can't help you, sweetheart, until you tell us how it went down."

"And I will," Faith assured him. Four relieved exhalations followed her promise before she added, "As long as Roy's here to hear it directly from me. Otherwise, I'm not saying anything."

Crawford slapped a hand against the painted brick wall and swore. "That's it. Clear out, boys. Maybe once Ms. Corbett has a chance to ponder her fate for a while, she'll figure out that she's not a guest here, she's an accused murderer."

Slick and Bubba headed out first, exchanging amused glances. An apologetic Max followed and, finally, Crawford.

Then Faith was alone, one wrist still handcuffed to the table, in the hell room. Alone with her secret weapon.

One of her secret weapons, anyway.

They had no idea that she could hear what they were saying on the other side of the mirror.

"So send me in, Cap." Ironic, how comfortingly familiar Roy's voice seemed, even now that they were on opposite sides of more than that wall. At least he'd heard her say she didn't want Butch dead, whether or not he believed it. "If it makes her confess, where's the harm?"

"The appearance of partiality is the harm, Roy! I shouldn't have to tell you that."

"I only look partial if I don't burn her lying little ass with this."

"Yes, because we all know that boyfriends who've been played for a sap are paragons of impartiality. *No.*"

Faith pretended to study her ink-smudged fingers, knowing that she was being studied in turn. She'd been okay with the physical contact when she'd been fingerprinted, but that's because she'd been braced for it.

"So why isn't she asking for a lawyer?" That was Max.

"She's a blonde," said someone who sounded like Slick. "Who says blondes have to make sense?"

"I'm not questioning it, I'm just counting my blessings," said the captain. "I've known stupid public defenders, but we won't find one in this city stupid enough to leave this arrest unchallenged."

"And they'd be wrong!" Roy protested.

"Really, Detective? 'Cause I'm thinking it wasn't a search warrant you had in your pants when you showed up at her door last night."

Faith scratched her nose, just in case her lips twitched.

She would have heard Roy's yell even without genetically engineered superhearing. "Screw that!"

"Hey, Chopin." Maybe his new partner really was a good cop, and didn't just play one for interrogations. "The captain's just saying what the D.A.'s office will tell you. Calm down."

"You're talking like I tried to hide what went down. Don't think I wasn't tempted. But I've been a freakin' Serpico on this one, Cap. I've been one hundred percent forthcoming."

"Oh, really? You were *boffing* the suspect!"

"I didn't know she was a suspect at the time!"

"And how do we know you wouldn't have considered it if you weren't boffing her?"

"Whoa, now." Max again. "Let's all calm down. Chopin, how about you take us through this one more time before we make a decision."

Faith pretended to be distracted by toeing a worn spot on the floor. She wanted to hear this as much as anybody.

Roy groaned—but he talked. "It's maybe seven-thirty in the morning. I've been there since two, two-fifteen. Corbett's in the shower."

"Alone?" That would be Slick again, giving Roy a hard time.

"Yeah, *alone.* She's got three roommates and only one bathroom between 'em. Also, she's got a job to get to."

"Not anymore, she doesn't." Slick, again.

"Can the commentary," the captain warned. "Let the man give his report."

"So my mobile rings. I don't recognize the number. I answer. And it's another freakin' anonymous contact, this time a guy. He says he's got a tip."

Faith bit her lip. So whoever knew about the clothes in her backpack was a man?

"I don't recognize the voice—he's whispering. But he says, 'You and Cassandra have a good time last night?' I ask what the hell that's supposed to mean, and he says, 'Check the backpack on her closet shelf.' And he disconnects."

"Well, that's a comfort. Any rookie knows that evidence stuffed in a backpack and kept on a closet shelf counts as plain view." Captain Crawford treated sarcasm as an art form, didn't he?

"Except I don't look in the closet right away. Sure, I'm curious, but I'm no idiot, and this smells like a setup. I pull on some clothes and I head out to the kitchen, where two of Corbett's roommates—the guy and the black girl—are making breakfast. They say hi. I say hi. I figure the girl, Moonsong they call her, is the most gullible so I say, 'This is a great place. You mind if I look around while I wait for Faith?' And she says 'Sure, do you want pancakes?'"

Slick laughed. "She offered you pancakes?"

"I say 'yes, thank you,' and I head back to Corbett's closet. Part of me still thinks this is a joke, but…there it was. The girl said 'sure,' Captain. She's lived there a lot longer than Corbett, and she said 'sure.' That's consent."

"She knew you were a cop?"

"I interviewed her after Krystal Tanner's murder. In case she'd forgotten that, I had the badge pinned to my belt. We're covered."

Faith considered all that, her expression deliberately neutral. Poor, manipulated Moonsong.

"Good. Good work. But we'll need more than that to make a case against Little Mary Sunshine in there. Max is right. She did call for help. She doesn't look like a murderer, and don't think that won't count with a jury. *And* she has no record."

"We're setting up a lineup for the witness," said Bubba.

"And don't forget, her roommate's the one who drew the sketch that Butch had with him when he died," added Roy. "Whether or not it's a picture of Krystal Tanner's killer, it links

Corbett's roommate to Celeste Deveaux and to Madame Cassandra. That links Corbett herself. A, to B, to C."

So they knew that, too. The number of people Faith had involved in her masquerade were starting to stack up, weren't they?

Not for the first time in the five hours that had passed since her arrest, she considered what she was going to do once she got out—and she had to assume, had to hope she would get out, or she'd be lost. She'd alienated her lover, her roommates, even her mom…her surrogate mom, anyway. Even if the charges didn't stick, she doubted she could or should keep her job for long—the air of suspicion would interfere too strongly with her work. It was almost a year since she'd dropped out of school.

Maybe her sisters showing up yesterday hadn't been an accident—not in the universal scheme of things. Maybe it was time to get to know Lynn and Dawn. Maybe Faith should seek out the Athena Academy and the Cassandras, to learn about her biological mother…and help find whoever had hired her killer. Maybe it was past time to confirm who and what she really was.

Once she knew that the psychics of New Orleans were as safe as she could make them, that is.

The argument, outside the interrogation room, was going on too long. Soon she *would* have to use the bathroom, and she wasn't looking forward to the logistics of that. "It was a man," she said, loudly. "With a stocking on his head."

Beyond the one-way mirror, all conversation ceased. She'd figured they had an intercom on.

"I don't think he came to kill Butch. I think he came to kill me."

The door cracked open and Captain Crawford stuck his head in. "You're ready to talk now, Ms. Corbett?"

She fixed him with as cool a stare as she could manage. "To Roy Chopin, I am."

Crawford narrowed his eyes and slammed the door shut.

Nobody on the other side of the mirror said anything for a moment, so Faith guessed it was all being conveyed with expressions. Then, finally, Crawford said, "Fine. But not alone."

"I never said he had to be alone," said Faith.

Now, when the four detectives filed into the room, Slick and Bubba looked unnerved. They didn't know how she'd heard that. Max looked curious, and Roy...

Roy looked pissed.

"So I'm here," he said, coolly spreading his arms. At some point across the morning he'd loosened his tie, unbuttoned his collar, rolled his sleeves up to his elbow. Only because she could hear his pulse, his breathing, could she tell just how angry he really was. "Talk."

"It's true," she said, meeting his gaze. "I'm Madame Cassandra."

His gaze narrowed, almost imperceptibly. His jaw hardened similarly. But he simply folded his arms, shrugged and said, "Tell me something I don't know."

She guessed telling her to go to hell wouldn't count as a good interrogation technique. The point was to keep her talking, not to shut her up.

"Okay—the first thing you should know is that Madame Cassandra isn't exactly a psychic. She's a...a persona I made up when I tried being a psychic for a few days, about a year ago, back when I met Krystal and the others. I thought if I were psychic, that would explain some things...."

Roy never looked away from her. "Why would it matter?"

Faith shrugged. "By then, though, I'd gotten to know some of the French Quarter crowd. I liked them. They trusted me. So when they told me things they thought were important—

things they'd overheard, or gotten through a reading—I started calling Butch to pass on the tips. In order to stay anonymous, I said I was Madame Cassandra, but Madame Cassandra doesn't exist."

"So who was with Roy in the cemetery last Thursday?" demanded Roy.

"I was. Faith. He saw past the costume. He knew me."

The words squeezed out past his teeth. "And you *killed* him for *that?*"

Max put a hand on Roy's arm. Roy shrugged it away, shaking his head at Faith in outraged disbelief. So much for holding back his anger.

"Of course I didn't! Cassandra wasn't a secret worth killing over, and I'm no killer. I was *glad* he recognized me. It was a *relief.*

"I didn't lure him there either—yes, the location was my choice, but Butch is the one who insisted that we meet, so that I could look at some mug shots." Holding Roy's accusing gaze, Faith related everything she could remember about what had happened in the cemetery. How strangely silent the killer had been. How he'd called her Cassandra. How she'd made her way back to Butch. How he'd instructed her on the use of his weapon.

How Butch had smiled at her, and said Roy's name… and died.

By the time Faith finished, even Slick and Bubba looked haunted. Even Max, who probably hadn't known Butch very well if at all, had bowed his head.

Roy moved first, finally. He bent across the table, planted one hand to the right of her, one hand to the left of her, and leaned close enough that she could count the eyelashes surrounding his blazing gray eyes. His jaw had never looked so much like a dare. His voice was a hiss of menace.

"So *why'd. You. Run?*"

"Because Butch told me to."

He shook his head, straightened and turned away, like he couldn't stand to look at her. Maybe he couldn't. It was Max who gently asked, "Why do you suppose Butch would tell you something like that, sweetheart?"

Faith frowned down at the worn table, on less solid ground here. "I've been wondering that myself," she admitted, eliciting a snort from Roy. "Really. And it's only been here at the station, surrounded by cops, that I've come up with a theory."

The detectives waited. Even Roy turned back long enough to widen his eyes in exaggerated anticipation.

"Butch must have realized the killer was there for me, not him," she said. "For Madame Cassandra, anyway—how would anyone know that was me? I didn't tell anybody I was meeting Butch, but even if someone had found out through me, they would've known who I really was. The only way someone would have shown up at the cemetery thinking Cassandra would be there, instead of Faith, was if someone found out about the meeting through Butch."

She looked up to meet Roy's gaze, a chill of horror accompanying her full realization as she said, "Chances are, anyone he told about the meeting was a cop.

"Butch was protecting me and my identity as Cassandra from one of you."

Chapter 17

Roy exploded. "So now you're saying *I* killed Butch? Right down to the dying declaration. Great story, hon, just like all your lies."

He cut himself off, shaking his head, raising his hands as if to keep from doing something with them that he'd regret.

"Of course I'm not saying that! I called you right afterward, didn't I? I slept with you! You think I would have done that with someone I thought was a killer?"

"Yeah? Well, that makes two of us."

"Butch probably wouldn't have told you about meeting Cassandra because he knew you were such a cynic about her. He might have told someone else, though, someone more open to the idea. That's why he wanted me to leave before the police arrived. He thought he'd tipped off the serial killer, and he didn't want him—whoever he was—connecting Cassandra to me."

"Did he tell you to take the gun, too?"

"No." Faith took a deep breath, turning her attention from Roy's rage to her own predicament. She'd done what she could to give him a little closure about his partner. Maybe someday he'd even realize that she hadn't set out to keep secrets from him. But for now...enough was enough.

"I panicked," she admitted. "I'd never seen anybody killed before, especially someone I cared about, not even Krystal. And someone had been shooting at me. And once I ran, I was kind of committed to going fugitive. Letting Cassandra go fugitive, anyway. So, I did what a fugitive does. I got rid of the evidence."

"Where?"

"I threw it in the Mississippi."

Four men groaned in unison. Outside the mirror, Faith heard cursing from the captain and a few other men who must be watching.

Well, she deserved that. "It was stupid, I know, but I wasn't thinking clearly. I threw the gun, the gloves and the phone in the river, and I went home and stuffed everything I was wearing into my old backpack. I thought about throwing that away, too, but thought someone might find it in the trash, and if I burned it, someone might remember me burning something. So I figured I'd just wait until things quieted down, that it would be safest in my closet. I didn't know there was blood on it."

That's when she heard something interesting happen with all four men's heartbeats—a subtle quickening. A tightening of their bodies. With just one of them, she might not have noticed. Not even now that she knew her abilities were real, if artificially engineered. But four of them....

"There *wasn't* blood on the clothes?" she challenged. "The captain *lied?*"

None of them admitted anything; they weren't that stupid. But outside the room, where he thought she couldn't hear, the captain said, "Half a year working evidence, and she thinks we can get lab results back that fast?"

Or that the police would always tell the truth in an interrogation. Damn! "What about the witness who saw Cassandra leave?"

"Saw *you* leave," Roy countered with a finger stab at the air between them. He neither confirmed nor denied the witness, but he positively smelled of righteous fury on this one. "Saw you leave with evidence and an eyewitness account that could've caught Butch's killer, assuming *you* aren't the killer."

"Have me take a lie detector test."

"How's three days in lock-up sound for a lie detector test? Spend enough time with the hookers and the druggies, I'm thinking you'll be ready to tell us anything."

"You'd be wrong."

"Okay." The door opened and the captain came in. "Chopin, you're losing what little objectivity you had. I'm stopping this before you make a real threat and get her case thrown out."

"You don't have a case," Faith admitted. It was time.

Roy's eyes widened, and his parted lips took on new levels of mockery. "Oh, I think we do!"

Max stepped between Roy's fury and Faith's chair, where she was still handcuffed. "No offense, sweetheart, but we may need more than just your word to drop the charges of murder."

Captain Crawford added, "Not to mention we just got your confession to obstruction of justice."

"No, you didn't."

"Hello? That story you just told? Leaving the scene of a crime? Destroying evidence?"

Time for her second secret weapon. "It's not admissible."

That shut them up, at least for a heartbeat or two. Faith suspected it was more her use of the lingo than the point she'd made, but she ran with it. "The search was invalid, so Roy didn't have probable cause for the arrest."

"Bullshit!" challenged Roy. Right. He'd been a freakin' Serpico, whoever that was.

"Ms. Corbett," interrupted the captain, "your roommate gave Detective Chopin permission to look around the place. That means he didn't need a search warrant."

"For the shared rooms, sure, but not for my bedroom, and definitely not for my closet, where I have a reasonable expectation of privacy." Now the men exchanged sharp glances. *Reasonable expectation of privacy* was a solid legal term, and they knew it. They knew she knew what she was talking about.

Their very scents reflected their growing concern that she might be right.

"I may have brought Detective Chopin into my room, even into my bed, but I never gave him permission to go into my closet. So the search was invalid. Which means the arrest was invalid. Which means the confession was fruit of the poisonous tree. I'm officially asking for a lawyer now, but trust me, he or she will just confirm this. So will the D.A."

The police stared at her.

"Michael Manning?" she reminded them, as if they might have forgotten who their district attorney was. "The one who publishes those great murder mysteries? My mother works for him. I interviewed him last year for an essay I was writing, about just this topic, and he was very clear on where the courts stand."

The police still stared. Even Roy.

"That would be when I was still in college," Faith explained. "When I was majoring in pre-law at Tulane."

And damn, that felt good.

She wondered if her biological mother, Rainy Miller Carrington, had ever gotten this strong a sense of satisfaction from practicing law. She hoped so.

Maybe Faith's choice of a major hadn't been such a fluke, after all.

Not an hour later, they had to let her go. She'd called her roommates to reassure them of her fate and had picked up her personal effects before Captain Crawford intercepted her with the inevitable question.

"Ms. Corbett? Why in God's name did you let all of us, yourself included, waste the whole morning if you knew your confession would be inadmissible?"

"I'm not your legal consultant, Captain." Faith looked past him toward where Roy stood with Max. Roy wasn't any less angry to see her walk. "I wanted Detective Chopin to hear the truth from me, and this was the only way he would. My apologies if that turned out to be a misuse of the city's time—but I'm not the one who initiated the arrest."

Then she headed out to the waiting room—and a surprising champion.

Greg Boulanger pushed to his feet from a plastic chair, his normally vague expression telegraphing relief. "Faith! Are you all right?"

She considered that. She was a genetically engineered lab rat. It was possible a police officer was gunning for her, especially now that the cops knew she was Madame Cassandra. She doubted even Greg could keep her job for her, not after she'd confessed to destroying evidence, whether that confession was admissible or not…if she didn't resign, they'd just invent a reason to get rid of her. The authorities had to be able to trust their evidence technicians. She didn't blame them.

Whoever was killing psychics was still out there. Whoever had killed Butch was still out there. Hell, whoever had ordered a hit on Rainy Miller Carrington was still out there!

The first and only man she'd ever slept with, a man she cared about, now hated her guts. And even before that, when he got an anonymous tip that she was withholding evidence in a murder case, he hadn't questioned it. From what she could tell, he'd never once considered that the bag could have been planted.

It hadn't been. But since she'd been in the shower, washing his touch and scent off of her even as he searched her closet, it would have been nice if Roy had at least wondered.

Maybe anonymous contacts were fine, in Roy's book, as long as they didn't claim to be psychic.

Was she "all right"?

"I've been better," she admitted wryly, too overwhelmed by the detritus of her life to feel any of it as sharply as she knew she soon would. "What are you doing here?"

Greg pulled his glasses down on his nose to peer over them, his pale eyes insulted. "I'm your boss, Faith. When you didn't show up for work, I called your apartment. Absinthe told me you'd been arrested, so I came to make sure you were all right, to see if you needed help with bail."

Faith blinked at him, taken aback. That was so sweet. So… *Greg.* "You don't think I'm guilty?"

"No."

"Thank you," she said, her throat tight.

His modest smile flickered across his usually solemn mouth, there and gone, before he shrugged off her gratitude. She recognized the feel of him pulling back. He'd been doing it ever since she'd told him she didn't date co-workers.

"Well now that they've released you, can I at least give you a ride home?" he asked. "You've got to be exhausted."

"I quit," said Faith.

Greg stared, clearly taken aback. "What's that?"

"Nobody's going to want me working with evidence—"

"That's not their call to make." Damned if Greg's shoulders didn't square slightly, at the very possibility that anybody would try to fire her. Maybe still waters really did run deep. "You work for me, not them."

"I don't blame them. You shouldn't either. Besides, I think it's time I went back to school, finished getting my law degree."

Greg's brows had pinched together. His concern was touching. "And I can't talk you out of this?"

"No. But what you can do," she added, "now that I'm not working for you, is take me out for a late lunch. No matter what else I've got to work out right now...I'm *starved.*"

It took a long moment before understanding dawned in Greg's eyes. When it did, his smile lingered longer. He wasn't half-bad-looking, when he smiled.

He offered his arm like some old-fashioned gallant, an effect his beard enhanced. Since he was wearing a long-sleeved shirt, Faith smiled back and took it.

Only as they reached the Plexiglas door to the street did Faith feel someone's attention, hot and accusing, on the back of her neck. She glanced over her shoulder as Greg opened the door for her.

It was Roy, arms folded, staring after them.

He wore a look of pure hatred. For the first time, he truly frightened her.

Faith quickly turned and hurried out of the police station, unsettled by his Jekyll/Hyde act. What if she hadn't really known Roy after all? What if he'd only been keeping her alive for the sex? What if Butch's dying declaration had been some kind of warning?

Roy.

No. She refused to believe it. But did it matter? She would
have to be particularly careful around cops from now on, either way.

She would have to be particularly careful around everybody.

So this was what an actual date felt like. It had been so long
since her Tulane boyfriend disaster, Faith had almost forgotten.

Greg surprised her with a playful side she'd never guessed
he had—though perhaps she should have, considering the way
she liked his balloon smell. He took her to lunch on one of the
popular, two-hour Mississippi riverboat cruises. Faith hesitated
only a moment when he suggested it. While Greg couldn't discuss active cases, he could still help her plan her next move. And
surely she could take two hours to recover from her morning!

So they boarded the *Antebellum,* a white, four-deck, stern-
wheeler steamboat. They barely made it up the gangplank, to
the sound of a steam calliope straight out of the Golden Age,
before the copper bell rang out and the twenty-five-ton paddlewheel began to turn, churning the water of the Mississippi
to push them away from the landing. In minutes, Greg had
them settled at a window table in the second-deck dining
room, where they could watch the harbor over lunch. The *Antebellum* provided indoor and outdoor seating, but it was still
August. Even on the river, August in Louisiana was hot.

And Faith was hungry. She'd gone through two helpings of
fried chicken, red beans and rice and a bowl of gumbo—as well
as some French bread and several glasses of iced tea—before
she noticed Greg's bemused expression as he watched her.

She flushed. "I skipped breakfast this morning. I was busy
getting arrested."

By the man I slept with last night. And this morning.

"On the basis of some pretty flimsy evidence, the way I
hear it," said Greg. "I don't want to pry, Faith, but…"

But he'd taken time off work for her. He'd been there for her, even moreso in the end than Roy. And she'd kept enough secrets for a lifetime. So, with the sound of the steam calliope playing outside, she repeated to Greg what she'd told the detectives.

Who Madame Cassandra was, and how Butch had died.

He looked stunned—but, being Greg, it was a quiet stunned. "You think the killer was a cop?"

She sighed, shook her head. "I have no way of being sure. All I know is, he's someone who might have learned about the meeting from Butch…and Butch told me to run. If Butch actually knew the killer, you'd think he'd have named him."

Then she remembered Butch's last word. *Roy*.

No. Surely she would have sensed something. "Whoever he is, I've got to stop him. I don't think I could leave town, knowing that my friends are still in danger."

Greg looked concerned. "I'm really not sure what to tackle first. You leaving town, or you thinking you can take down a serial killer single-handedly."

She thought of Lynn White and Dawn O'Shaughnessy, with whom she had dinner plans for tonight, and the interesting things they had to discuss. "I may not have to do it single-handedly. And I'm not leaving town for good. I like it here. My mother…"

But she still wasn't sure what she thought of Tamara, after yesterday's revelations.

"I've learned about some family I hadn't known before," she said, by way of excuse. "I thought it might be nice to go visit."

For all she knew, Rainy Miller Carrington had parents. Siblings. Cousins. In any case, the woman certainly had a grave. Surely Rainy's friends—the Athenas, the *Cassandras*—would be able to advise Faith of how much her family knew, maybe even make introductions.

"Family? That's great!" Perhaps glad to steer the lunch conversation away from serial killers, Greg told her how he'd come from a fair-size family—always trouble, and always loved. Faith admitted little about her own discoveries, for obvious reasons, but she enjoyed listening. The jazz concert started, adding a great Dixieland flavor to the whole afternoon. It almost felt...normal. Especially for someone who'd been held on murder charges mere hours before.

Maybe she just had to take her normalcy in small doses.

While Greg talked, Faith tried to consider him as a date. He wasn't bad-looking, for a science geek, with his curly black hair and his beard and his pale eyes behind his glasses. More important than that, he was *nice*. He cared about his people. He cared about his job. He clearly cared about his brother and sister.

He smelled of latex gloves and balloons, which she couldn't help liking.

She considered it, and she felt guilty. With all that in his favor, why wasn't she more attracted to him? Why, instead, did her thoughts stray back to the sheer physical release that she'd gotten that morning, naked and sweaty and gasping and open in every possible way—with someone else?

With a backpack full of evidence just beyond her closet door. Thinking of the backpack, Faith frowned.

"It's not that bad," Greg assured her, thinking she was reacting to his funny family anecdote. "My brother stopped wetting the bed eventually...whether we let him forget it or not."

"No—I just had a really bad thought. The man who called Roy this morning. The anonymous contact. How could *he* have known about the backpack in my closet? How could anyone?"

Greg seemed to resign himself to this newest, dark turn in the conversation. "Your roommate Evan?"

It was possible. As Roy had told her early on—the first rule of investigative work was that everyone lied. But…Evan? *Her* Evan? She shook her head.

Greg nudged his glasses down, as he sometimes did when particularly serious. "You can't imagine—Faith, you don't think Roy made up the anonymous contact, do you?"

That was a more likely—and even worse—possibility. Especially if he'd started nosing around her room, the way she'd snooped around his place after their first time together. If he actually found the backpack, found the wig, he would need some reason to legally justify the search. He could call a friend, maybe his partner, and have them call him back. And then…

Strangely, now that she and Roy were over, Faith found herself hoping that was exactly what happened. Because the third possibility…

Her stomach clenched at the thought. *Someone had left the gate unlocked, last night.* "Or maybe someone else had been in the apartment. In my room!"

Wouldn't she have smelled lingering traces of an intruder?

She'd been more than a little distracted when she'd gotten home last night. She hadn't *tried* to smell anything. Now the idea that an intruder, maybe the killer himself, had been in her room gave her chills.

"I've got to call my roommates again," she decided, pushing her chair back to stand—then looking, crestfallen, out the window. A wide expanse of the Mississippi lay between them and land. The *Antebellum* had left the French Quarter and the distinctive Huey P. Long Bridge well behind it; to judge from the narration she heard on outdoor loudspeakers, they were passing the site of the Battle of New Orleans. They easily had another hour of cruise before she could use a pay phone.

"May I use your cell phone? I'll keep it short."

"Sure." He fished it from his pocket and passed it across the table to her. "Why?"

"I need to make sure my roommates are okay." The signal line on his phone's display wasn't particularly strong, and the jazz band, though really good, was also fairly loud. "Would you mind if…?"

"Not at all. Want me to come with you?"

He'd been great, so far. But she didn't need a bodyguard just yet. "No, stay in the air-conditioning. I'll be right back."

Easygoing as ever, Greg nodded and turned his chair to better watch the concert, signaling the waitress for more coffee.

Faith headed out onto the deck, which was marginally quieter now that the rooftop calliope had stopped tooting out its carousel melodies. She hurried up an open stairway, away from the sound of the jazz band but closer to the churning wash of the two-story paddlewheel not far beneath her. At least the signal was stronger here, standing by the outside railing. She dialed her home number, covered her outside ear with her hand to block out the worst of the noise, and waited.

The phone rang.

It rang a second time.

It rang a third time.

The line clicked as the answering machine picked up. It was Evan's voice, following Tamara Corbett's theory of safe answering machines. "Hi! You've reached our apartment, but you haven't quite reached us. If you want to leave a message for—"

Faith disconnected, still nervous. Her roommates were psychics. There was a killer on the loose who murdered psychics and who might very well know his way around their apartment.

After only a moment's hesitation, she dialed a new number.

"Detectives Division," answered a tired voice, on the second ring. Behind him the distinct bustle of the station sounded almost as loud as the paddlewheel Faith was muffling.

"I need to talk to Detective Max Leonard, please." Faith winced. Well, she couldn't very well ask for Roy. Not the Roy who'd glared hatred at her as she left the station. Not the Roy who wanted to burn her ass.

Max had recently transferred from Baton Rouge, he'd said. If Faith had a chance at objectivity with anybody...

"Hey, Boulanger, *comment ça va?*" That was Cajun for "how's it going?" Max must be reading the caller ID.

"It's not Greg, Detective Leonard. It's Faith Corbett. I have a favor to ask."

"Really?" Max pitched his voice a little louder, stiff with the awareness of an audience. "How can I help you, Ms. Corbett?"

The expletives that sounded near him were unmistakably Roy's. Faith ignored them and the distinct click once the expletives stopped, which meant Roy had picked up on another line.

"I'm worried about my roommates," she continued, hating that she had to ask for help but unwilling to risk her friends. Especially if the killer was really after the fictional Cassandra. "They aren't answering the phone. Hopefully they're just working the Square, but it's rare for all three of them to be out during the midday heat, and if somebody got into my apartment once, to see what I had in my closet.... I know you don't owe me any favors, but since whoever was in the apartment might be the psychic killer—you know, since he called me Cassandra...."

She stopped talking in order to listen closer to the strange shuffling on Max's end. When Max spoke, it was halting, as if he was going off someone else's script. "Why is it you can't check on them yourself, sweetheart? Are you afraid to go in alone?"

Okay, so his dose of niceness came with some condescension.

"I'm stuck on a riverboat."

"A riverboat?"

"Greg took me to lunch. Look, I'm worried, and since the psychic killer is yours and Roy's case, I was hoping you'd check it out. It's simple behavioral psychology. If he's been there once, he'll go back. The only way to catch—"

But she didn't finish her sentence.

She caught a whiff of danger on the air—of power, of lust, of *evil*—only as something dropped past her line of sight.

Something red.

The serial killer drew the cord taut, catching the phone, then yanking Faith's chin up and backward. The dropped phone skittered away from her, over the side—and into the churning wash of the twenty-five-ton paddlewheel.

Chapter 18

If Faith hadn't been on the phone, she would be dead.

As it was, the cord cut deeply against the underside of her chin. It cinched the heels of her hands, hands that had thankfully been against her ears, hard against her jaw. Hardened residue of dried blood bit into the skin of her wrists, her throat, and with it—

Nessa's horror that she would never see her mom again....

Krystal's surprise, her terror—and a sense of recognition. Chet?

Oh, God. The horrible, gargling noise from her own throat as she lost her breath mingled with a borrowed memory of the noises Nessa and Krystal had made, and Penelope Lafayette, and the nameless first victim. Faith was dying four times at once, sliced deep with the immediacy of what those poor women had gone through, telegraphed into her through their blood. But she knew how to stop it, this time.

At least, she knew how to stop the feedback.

She dragged downward with her hands against the red cord, keeping it from crushing her airway completely. She snapped her head backward.

Right into the killer's face.

A blast of light, the pain of impact, blinded her momentarily. A cough wheezed out of her, with nothing to replace it. But like before, like when she'd fought the gangbangers, striking out somehow blocked the influx of images. Now, blessedly, it was just her, some guy and the churning paddlewheel below them.

Only one murder, hers, not the other four. *Attempted* murder. But damn it, she couldn't breathe!

Faith swung her head back again, impacted his face, and the universe reeled.

The killer wailed wordless protest and pain, the sound wet with fresh blood. The rope dug deeper into her throat. Faith stomped down, hard, on the foot behind her, glad to feel her heel crunching across his toes. The rope dug deeper still. Faint with dizziness now, hurting and breathless, she slammed her head back a third time.

Blackness threatened her vision from the outside in. Blackness and nausea. But this time, the killer stumbled.

It was just enough for Faith to gasp a sharp, painful breath. She dropped to her knees, ducked her head, let her own body weight pull her free from under the slackened cord.

Numb hands still caught in it, she rolled on the deck to face her bent assailant. Brown hair. Quiet eyes.

The same man she'd seen at Celeste's. The one Butch had been trying to ID when he'd died.

The serial killer.

His red cord had twisted cruelly around her hands, with her turn. She still didn't let go. It wasn't merely the best damned evidence she was going to get on the guy.

It was this bastard's weapon of choice.

Still down, using her weight in their tug-of-war, she kicked at him. She wished her shoes were harder as she connected with his shins, with his knee, each impact lurching through her. She was losing the feeling in her hands, could see her fingers turning white from lack of blood. The killer wore protective leather gloves. He pulled the rope tighter, lifting her half off the deck with his strength. Despite the churning paddlewheel below, she could hear his distinct heartbeat now, the strange miss to its rhythm. His pheromones of conquest were turning rank with frustration.

"Let go," Faith ordered, surprised to hear how raspy her voice sounded. And she pulled something that her repeated head butts into his face had given her. *"Chet."*

His eyes widened. Faith could feel the bones in her hands crunching together under the twisted cord. Since kicking at him didn't help, she slid her legs under her and rose, hard, right into him. He stumbled backward. She helped, with a full-body tackle.

He fell back onto the deck. She landed on top of him and his unusual heartbeat, on purpose. She tried to dig her elbows into his chest, her knee into his privates, but her now-numb hands stayed trapped.

Still playing tug-of-war with the murder weapon.

For a moment, she could feel wetness on her face. Spray from the huge blue paddlewheel slicing past, mere yards below them. Then the killer rolled with her, slammed her against the railing—and one of Faith's legs slid under the rail, right over the edge of the deck.

Into the nothingness above the mighty Mississippi.

Damn it! If she had to be genetically engineered anyway, why couldn't *she* have gotten the superstrength?

Well, she hadn't.

But she'd gotten something. The killer—was his name really Chet?—thrust himself against her again in violence, in fear, in something even uglier. Faith's hip slid over the sharp wooden edge of the deck.

She could feel the paddlewheel's spray across her ankle now.

Using every bit of strength left in her arms, no longer able to tell she even had hands where the cord had cut off all feeling, Faith leveraged herself a few inches higher, drew the man closer and buried her bare face into his bare neck.

And bit his jaw, like the vampires Krystal had feared.

And now, *now* she got Chet.

He'd gone off his antipsychotic meds.

He'd been burning incense and scented candles. Their scent was almost as powerful on him as the scent of death.

He'd spent time in an institution, where they'd taken his shoelaces. Now he had a room at his mother's old house. Someone took care of him. His—

Jealousy. *Jealousy so sharp that it burned in her gut like a sympathy pain. Particularly jealousy of one person…the Master. A woman got naked for the Master once. She laughed at Chet when they caught him watching. "I'm psychic," she'd said.*

He needed to be psychic. Nobody would laugh at him again.

He needed her!

With a wordless wail, he shook Faith away from his neck and shoved her, hard, more precariously across the slick wooden deck.

Her other leg fell over the side of the boat. She lurched abruptly downward. Only her hands, tangled in the cord he held, and her shoulders against the bottom rail kept her from falling. From the deck below, she heard someone scream.

She held on in every possible way. "Who's the Master, Chet?" It felt like talking past sandpaper. Her throat ached. She wanted to throw up.

But at least she got words from him. "Shut up!"

"Who was the woman? The one who laughed at you. Was she your first? The first one you killed?"

"Shut up! You don't know anything!"

"I know *everything!*" Remembering Roy's book of superstitions, Faith said, "This cord drains people of their energy, right? Well I'm draining your psychic energy, Chet. *Right now.* Every drop you got from Krystal. Every drop you got from Nessa. If you don't let go, you won't have any left at all."

She was lying, but it worked.

"No!"

"They'll put you back in the asylum." God. She actually felt cruel, saying it. As twisted and evil as this man was....

But what was her alternative? "They'll laugh at you."

"Shut up!"

She tried to swing one leg back up onto the deck. "Going."

Chet shook his head.

"Going," she repeated. "Every bit of stolen power. I've got Penelope's now, too. You're just some weak, stupid boy again, Chet. Stop this before I get everything."

Their gazes held, linking them just as tightly as the cord.

"Gone," said Faith.

And with a howl of despair, Chet let go of the cord. He vaulted over the white railing and dropped.

Released, Faith dropped too. Body weight slid her downward. Wildly, she swung her arms at a rail-post and, with a lurch, she caught it with her elbows and hung.

Only then could she look. Had he dived into the river, into the deadly wash of the paddlewheel?

No. He'd swung lithely to the deck beneath her.

Swung, landed and started running.

She swung, too—just as she saw Greg racing up the stairs, horror on his usually inexpressive face. "Faith!"

One thing at a time. Faith wasn't as graceful about it as Chet had been. Her hands were still bound, still deadened. But after two swings she arched through the air and landed, only slamming one hip against the second-deck railing. She barely had time to bruise a knee as she fell before she was up and running after the killer.

Trying to twist her hands free at the same time.

Like before, when the killer had fled Celeste's, Chet's main method of escape was to push past other people, using them as obstacles to her pursuit. He slammed an old woman against one of the dining room windows and sent a toddler sprawling perilously close to the boat's edge—that cost Faith more time as she slowed, before she saw that the child's mother had snatched him to safety.

By then, Chet was almost to the bow.

Faith tore after him, finally wrenching one hand free of the cord. Jazz music from the dining room, "When the Saints Come Marching In" taunted her with its jaunty familiarity. Chet didn't have much choice of where to go. He skidded down the open stairway, rabbiting toward the bottom deck.

Faith slid down the painted railing for speed, landed on the polished wood floor, and kept after him. He was heading for the stern again, the stern and the turning, thumping wheel, which looked even larger from here than it had from above. He stopped before he got there and spun, his head pivoting from Faith to the river to Faith.

"Don't do it," she warned him, shouting over the churning wash. Feeling was starting to come back to her hands in agonizing throbs. She kind of wished it hadn't.

He shook his head. His jaw was bleeding where she'd bit him.

"Even if you survive the wheel, the river will kill you. She won't protect you, this time. She doesn't give up her dead."

And we may never know who you were. Why you killed. Who your first victim was. We may never prove your guilt.

Or my innocence.

He shook his head again.

"I'll give you back some of your power!"

Chet's eyes widened, more disbelief than hope.

"I've...cleansed it now." Wow, was she making this up. "Like running it through a filter. Now it's not just power, it's good power. It won't..." She tried to put words to the sense of desperation, of need, that she'd gotten off of him. "It will last better than the other times. It will *taste* better."

Chet took a quick step back. He was pressed against the rail now, paddles of the blue wheel rolling downward right behind him, like some wet, dizzying backdrop.

Slowly, Faith lowered the red cord with one stiff hand and reached out with the other. "Come on. Look, you don't have to steal my energy. I'm *offering* it. That's how powerful I am."

And slowly, warily, the killer reached outward.

His gloved hand closed around hers. But if she concentrated—

He felt like *pain*. He felt like *humiliation*. Most frighteningly, he felt like *a sucking void—there was a hole in him, a gaping, ragged hole where pieces of his humanity should have been, and they were gone*. The parts that kept most people from killing just weren't there.

Their absence had turned him vicious, pain or no pain. He wasn't safe for the rest of society. Ever.

Maybe Chet saw something in her face as she fully comprehended that, comprehended that he could kill for reasons so foreign to her, he could never be predicted. That he would kill again and again. Or maybe this had just been a con. He spun and threw her against the railing, her head too close to the paddlewheel now.

And Faith…she went somewhere dark herself. She threw herself against him, wrenching her hand free of his, hurling them both down onto the deck. She caught him across the throat with one arm as she landed on him. And before he could fight back, she drew the cord slowly across his face, where he could see it.

His eyes widened in horrified recognition of who could take whose power now.

"Goodbye, Chet," Faith rasped.

Then she slammed the flat of her hand into his nose, breaking it and knocking him unconscious.

Not an hour later, Faith sat in the open back of an ambulance at the Toulouse Street Wharf. Her feet dangled, and her hands and throat were bandaged. She'd already been photographed from all angles by the police crew to support a charge of assault. Luckily she had no damage that required disrobing. The bruises on her hip and knee were from swinging around a riverboat like Tarzan, not from Chet. Her hands and her neck, though…

They hurt. But nowhere near as badly as Krystal's must have, or Nessa's. The secondhand memories of what had happened to them clogged Faith's throat, as surely as the swelling from her attack.

Faith sincerely hoped assault was not what they nailed this guy for.

She'd already watched one ambulance shuttle Chet off toward the Charity Hospital, complete with a police guard. Now she was watching Roy and Max—who still had the serial killer case whether or not Roy had gotten back onto Butch's—as they interviewed fellow passengers. Watching, and eavesdropping.

They asked the standard questions. "Did you notice anything unusual?"

"Did you see the man any earlier in the cruise?"

"When did you see the blonde leave the dining room?"

Sometimes they tried to trip someone up, just to confirm their story. "So the girl pushed little Timmy out of the way? Oh, okay. Yeah. It was the guy who did that."

Faith wasn't completely comfortable with the direction some of the questions took—or their answers. The *Antebellum* had been nowhere near full, not for an afternoon tour on a workday in the blazing August heat. Chet had been surprisingly careful; nobody had seen him attack her, and people had only noticed the scuffle once Faith's legs appeared dangling off the third deck. Even Greg had had to admit that he didn't actually see "the suspect" initially attack Faith. He'd only seen them fighting.

"But come on," he'd added loyally. "Either he was trying to push her off or to pull her back up. Which do you think's more likely?"

"I wasn't there," said Roy bluntly. "So what happened next?"

What happened next, by all accounts, was that Faith chased the suspect down two decks, including one flight of stairs, and then broke his nose. The authorities' best proof that Faith had been the victim of this encounter, and not the perpetrator, was her word and the ligature marks on her throat. And considering the circumstances of the morning, Faith didn't expect the police to give a lot of credit to her word.

Roy and Max were still conferring over their notes when Roy muttered, "Told you she was a Bernie."

"I apologize for not believing you," said Max, easygoing as ever. Faith still didn't know what a Bernie was.

"Timing's awful suspicious, though."

"You still thinking conspiracy?"

Roy shrugged. Sitting with the EMTs, across the wharf from the detectives, Faith sighed. Great. She and Greg had delivered a serial killer into the detectives' hands—and they *still* suspected her.

"Why don't I do the follow-ups," suggested Max, but Roy shook his head.

"No way in hell. This one, I gotta hear."

So they strolled over to her, as casual as if this sort of thing happened every day. Maybe for them, it did.

"Sorry we have to meet this way," said Max. "We already had a patrol check on your roommates and they were fine."

"That's because the killer was on the *Antebellum*." Faith's scratchy voice sounded funny in her own ears. It still hurt.

"Yeah." Roy withdrew his ever-present notepad....

Well, thought Faith, not *always* present. It would be a long time before she stopped thinking of sex when she thought about Roy Chopin. And that was a shame.

"About that," he said. "Any idea how he ended up on the same cruise as you? Was it maybe...*magic?*"

Faith flipped him off.

"Enough of that," chided Max. "Both of you. It's a valid question, Ms. Corbett. If the accused really is the killer we've been after—and I'm not saying he isn't—do you think he followed you onto the boat? Or was there any reason he would've known you'd be there?"

"Like what? *I* didn't know I'd be there! It was Greg's idea, but he didn't know I'd go to lunch with him until, like, ten minutes before the *Antebellum* left dock. Neither one of us exactly called ahead." Did she imagine it, or did she note a slight acceleration of Roy's heartbeat when she mentioned her date with Greg? "If Chet followed me, he would've had to be waiting outside the station. I guess it's possible he would know I was there, if he's the one who called Roy this morning. But how would he know I'd be released?"

The detectives exchanged telling glances before Roy challenged, "So you're saying this wasn't a prearranged meeting?"

"That's what it sounds like to me, Detective."

"We need you to tell us again what happened," said Max. "In as much detail as possible this time. Do you think you're up to that, sweetheart?"

Roy rolled his eyes.

"I'm fine," rasped Faith. "I was on Greg's cell phone…"

They listened to her story with minimal interruption, like good detectives should, though she sensed Roy's muscles tightening several times as he had to physically fight the urge to make snide comments.

"…by then, Greg had gotten there with the security guard. They handcuffed Chet, and we called back to shore. And that's that."

The detectives exchanged that look again. "You keep calling him Chet," said Max.

"So?"

"So the guy doesn't have any ID on him," clarified Roy, each question like a shove. "No wallet. Just a pocket full of salt. So how do you know his name? Did he introduce himself, or were you previously acquainted?"

Oh, great. Faith had been wondering, since her sisters' announcement the previous day, just how deeply her genetically enhanced sensitivity went. It unnerved her that she could guess someone's actual name—something you'd think wouldn't just come across with acute sight, hearing, or smell. But it sure wasn't imagination this time. "I guessed."

Even more unnerving was the intensity of Roy's stare. *He knows,* she thought, and felt sick about it. *He knows I'm a freak.* Why wouldn't he? He knew she was Cassandra, now. And he'd seen her respond to something no normal person could have heard, back in the police station.

She met his gaze in a silent dare, waiting for the disgust, waiting for the dismissal.

Waiting for him to turn away.

Instead, Roy continued in cop mode. "Well it will be interesting to see who he ID's as."

"Yes, it will. Do you at least believe he's the killer?"

"We can't discuss open cases," hedged Max.

"You know that when the tests on that cord come back, my epithelials are a lot more likely to be on it than his are. He wore gloves. I was bare-handed."

"Why don't we wait until the tests come back to worry about that, sweetheart?" asked Max.

She nodded, and they finished their notes. Most of the other police had gone on, witnesses dismissed, evidence collected. The EMTs tried to talk her into going to the hospital, just to make sure none of her injuries were more serious, but Faith declined. She'd had enough people touching her for one day, and enough of small rooms.

Her hands hurt, but they would heal.

The rest of her...

Greg had waited, the whole time, though he'd stayed back while she was questioned—one of the first rules of interview work, apparently, was to separate the witnesses. Only when Max beckoned him over did he return to Faith's side.

She looked from one man to the next. Greg, analytical and bespectacled, his mouth tight from the violence of the afternoon. Roy, exhausted from even less sleep than she'd had, pretending not to care. His jaw was still a dare, though, and his posture pure disapproval. And Max, the newcomer, least burdened by the subcurrents of everything that had happened, best able to stay objective.

"Chet's the serial killer," she told them in her wounded, rasping voice. "You know that, don't you?"

"We only know what the evidence tells us," said Max.

"Yes, but what do your instincts tell you?"

It was Roy who answered. "You're the psychic, Cassandra."

His words seemed especially taut. This time, Faith didn't bother to argue it.

"Correct me if I'm wrong," said Lynn as her fingers danced across the keys of her laptop. The dresser's mirror reflected the top of her bent, chestnut head. "But didn't everything turn out for the best? The charges against you were dropped. The killer has been caught."

"One of them," Faith reminded her. "But it doesn't feel... finished."

"You're the psychic," said Dawn, from where she sat on one of the chairs by the window. "You should know." Her posture was casual, one booted leg hooked up over the chair's arm, but Faith knew that, even without an imminent danger, Dawn was keeping watch. The three sisters were in Lynn and Dawn's hotel room. As soon as Lynn and Dawn had seen Faith's injuries, when she'd shown up for dinner, they'd dragged her up here for an explanation.

It had been a long explanation. After that came Faith's request.

"I'm in," announced Lynn, and vacated the chair to sit on the bed behind it. "It was easy, with your password as a starting point. Apparently with all the excitement this afternoon, nobody got around to blocking you out of the system yet."

"But nobody can see that I accessed it?" Faith took the chair. She'd unwrapped the bandages from her swollen hands, but they were still stiff and sore. She would have to type very slowly to see what needed seeing.

"You're cyber-invisible," Lynn assured her.

So Faith pulled up the files on that afternoon's arrests,

scrolling past larcenies and drug busts until she found the one she was looking for. "Here it is—Toulouse Street Wharf. They ran his prints and he turned out to be…Chester Elliott Simpson. Thirty. They've got him under psychiatric observation."

There were even some initial notes by the admitting doctor. *May suffer from paranoia-based delusional disorder. Thinks women are witches. Perceives safety in superstitions like salt/running water. Violence against women—rebellion against perceived powerlessness? Investigate childhood/familial history of psychiatric disturbance.*

"Apparently he's crazy," translated Faith.

"I suppose that's a start," said Lynn. "So what will it take for you to believe it's over?"

"Understanding why he did it."

Dawn looked over her shoulder, here with them and yet somehow, sadly, apart. "*Because he's a nutjob* doesn't work for you?"

"And a life sentence without possibility for parole."

Faith could see Lynn's wry smile reflected in the dresser mirror. "Considering today's legal system, that could take a while."

"And finding Butch's killer." That was the biggest, she decided. Of course, everyone's death was a tragedy beyond measure. Krystal had brought comfort to hundreds, through her readings and her otherworldly wisdom—Chet had killed that. Nessa's possibilities were equally cut short. And Penelope Lafayette. And the mysterious first woman. But Butch…

By endangering his life every day, by reining in his younger, brasher partner, by keeping an open mind about advice from an anonymous contact who could have been anybody but had in fact been her…

The loss of Butch's goodness would haunt Faith for the longest, she thought. And not just because, if Butch were still around, she and Roy might have had a chance.

Maybe.

"So which one do you want to start on first?" asked Dawn. She was clearly not the sort of person who hung back. Faith liked that. "Comprehension, conviction, or vengeance?"

"Start on how?"

Lynn leaned forward, her elbows propped on her knees, from her perch on the bed. "You know, Faith, one of the things that happened once Dawn told me where our abilities came from was, they seemed to get a little stronger. Or maybe it was just my confidence in them that increased. Have you noticed the same thing?"

"I knew his name was Chet," Faith admitted—but then the possibilities inherent in that, in who she really was, fully occurred to her. "And I sensed some of his secrets even through gloves, when I concentrated. So heaven knows what else I can find out about him and his motives. If I just trust myself, I mean."

Lynn shrugged. And Faith made her decision.

She turned back to the computer and hunt-and-pecked another command. "Here's Chet's address, in Algiers Point. And—yes! That was quick. The detectives already executed a search warrant, so if we disturb anything looking around, we won't have tampered with evidence. Not that I suppose we can get inside...."

Lynn and Dawn snorted in unison.

"We can get inside," Lynn assured her. "Even if Chester Elliott Simpson found out, I doubt he'll be in any position to press charges for trespassing."

"Breaking and entering," Faith corrected her.

"Sis," Lynn's green eyes looked particularly mysterious. "I never have to break.

"I just enter."

Chapter 19

Dawn declined to accompany her sisters on this particular reconnaissance mission. "I've got things to do," she'd said, without telling them more.

So Lynn and Faith headed out alone. Luckily, Lynn had a rental car. They caught the Canal Street Ferry across the Mississippi to Algiers Point, a historic neighborhood opposite the French Quarter, and followed their printout map until they found—and deliberately passed—the Creole Cottage-style house listed as Chet Simpson's primary residence.

"It's barely a quarter mile from the ferry landing," noted Faith. "He could walk that far no problem, and ten minutes later he's at the Quarter. He doesn't even need a driver's license. No wonder he likes to think running water will protect him. It's not just a common superstition. He crosses the Mississippi every time he comes back to his lair."

The house was built on four-foot brick piers with a sharply

slanting, continuous gable roof, a full-front gallery, and an exterior stairway to the second floor. It was dark.

"So you really think you might be able to sense something in there?" asked Lynn, turning the corner and driving on. She'd explained that they wanted to case the place before they actually stopped the car.

"I don't know. But when I was in Roy's house…he's a friend…was a friend…" Okay, so Roy was complicated.

Lynn slanted an intrigued glance her direction, but said nothing. And she wasn't even the psychic.

"It felt as if the house had memories. At the time I half figured I was imagining it, but now that I know I was engineered this way…maybe I can read this one, too. If we can get in."

Lynn grinned. "Oh, we can get in."

Not ten minutes later, the car was parked around the corner from Chet's home and the two sisters were securely inside the front parlor, the door shut behind them.

"I learned to pick locks," Lynn whispered, flexing her hands in their expensive gloves, "at a very early age."

They stood in a front parlor, its double French doors framed on either side with ceiling-high shuttered windows. The ceiling showed exposed beams. The old fireplace had a wrap-around mantel.

The TV set and stereo speakers, standing like a miniature Stonehenge, seemed almost blasphemous amidst the history of the building.

"You don't need a light, do you?" asked Lynn.

"Nope."

"Neither do I."

The sisters exchanged smiles in this darkness that, somehow, their eyes could penetrate. That momentary connection helped remind Faith of what she was here to do.

To trust her instincts.

And whatever she was, to trust herself.

She took a deep breath and closed her eyes, laying the back of her hand on the mantel, to better connect with the home's energy without leaving fingerprints.

Bustling. Searching. Frustration. She could smell the powder used in lifting fingerprints, could smell the luminol sprayed into a few key areas in the vain search for bloodstains. Mostly, she could feel Roy's presence, smell his scent from where he'd stalked through here, pissing off the crime-scene unit with his often unnecessary suggestions, arguing with Max.

Then again, she was particularly familiar with Roy's scent and his energy, for obvious reasons. "The police only left an hour ago," she reported, surprised at how certain she felt about that little bit of information. "They found some things they could use, books and I think…yes, a flyer from the psychic fair. But they're afraid it's all circumstantial. They didn't find the hair he took off his victims."

The Creole floor plan led to rooms on either side of the parlor, to rooms behind those, and to an open porch, or loggia, in back. Every room had doorways into every other connected room. There were no hallways.

As Faith and Lynn slowly moved from one area to the next, Faith began to pick up on the house's less recent history. "Some of it's just…just a blur of normalcy. Several families were raised here since it was built. It almost feels as if the house resents having just one person living here, now. It was built for families…."

Stopping herself, Faith looked at her newfound sister. "Like some people are."

Lynn returned her smile.

Faith went back to reading the house. "The parts that stand out seem to be the periods of extreme emotion. Here—" she pointed at a rocking chair. "This is where a woman was sitting when they told her that her husband had been killed. That was maybe thirty…no, thirty-five years ago, I think. And over there—" she pointed into the kitchen "—that's where her daughter walked out on her, after a screaming argument. The mother thought the daughter was throwing herself away on some guy. The daughter thought the mother was trying to run her life."

Amazing. It wasn't so much that she could see or smell or hear the confrontations. It really was like imagining it.

Except whatever Lab 33 had done to her, the things she "imagined" were already true.

"And Chet?" prompted Lynn.

"He watched them. From here. He was really upset to see his sister go. His mother said…" Faith concentrated, feeling the emotions more than hearing the words, but some words seemed to just fit. "She predicted that things would turn out badly for her daughter. You know how people are—*you'll be sorry,* or *don't come to me when he leaves you.* Like that. Later, the boyfriend did leave the sister, and that made Chet afraid. He thought his mom predicted it, maybe made it happen."

"Chet's not all there, is he?"

"Not really, no. But I think that mainly comes out when he's excited, or upset." When his heart started its strange, irregular rhythm.

They headed up the stairs to find two large rooms with long, slanting ceilings, connected with a door in between. It was the far room that offered a door with outside stairs down to the porch.

"This was the girls' room," explained Faith, crossing it. It seemed to be used for storage now—unused exercise equipment, old vinyl record albums, boxes of belongings nobody meant to ever reclaim. "I think that was an old Creole tradition. Daughters get the indoor stairway because they aren't supposed to be coming and going a lot. But the boy's room has an outdoor entrance, to give them their privacy when they go catting around."

"That's awfully…" Lynn considered her words, then settled on, "sexist."

"You said it. It was here…" Again, she touched the doorjamb, careful to use just the side of her hand. It felt as if the house was calling her toward something, toward a touch of familiarity, so Faith leaned her cheek against the wood for a deeper sense.

And with a hum of power, like that, the scene played out in front of her.

A preteen boy, Chet, banished to his sister's room. But he wanted to know what was going on. He came to stand here, right here, and peeked through the doorway. He was surprised to see his big brother and his girlfriend Claudia in the bed, doing things they probably shouldn't be doing in his mama's house. His brother got away with everything, and it wasn't fair. Still, it sure was interesting, what she looked like naked, what they were doing….

Until Claudia began to giggle. "I'm psychic, you know," she told his brother, who until then was just grunting. "I can tell when we're being watched!"

And she sat up a little, as much as his brother's weight would let her, and she pointed right at Chet. Then his brother saw, too. He roared, and leaped out of bed, and ran at him. Chet had never seen him like…like that…and he was scared.

"Who am I, you little turd?" demanded his brother, pushing him down onto the floor, like always, planting a knee on his back. "You forget who I am?"

It was an old litany, one Chet knew by heart. "You're… you're the Master."

"Damned right!"

Faith's eyes opened. She pulled away from the doorjamb, scrubbed at her cheek with her aching bare hand as she wished she could scrub away the snippets of understanding that were still rolling into her mind, as if on some kind of delay. "She wasn't really psychic at all."

"What?" asked Lynn.

Faith recounted the vision, the borrowed memory, whatever it had been. The more she described it, the more upset she felt. "And what's really tragic—for Krystal and Nessa and Penny, I mean—is she wasn't even psychic. Chet was a mouth-breather. Claudia heard him."

"And what about this brother? This Master?"

"I can't see him," said Faith—too quickly, even to her own ears. The silence, after her confession, echoed.

"Doesn't that strike you as kind of odd?"

Faith didn't have an answer for that.

"You were able to see Chet, right?" insisted Lynn. "You could see this Claudia person. Why can't you see the brother?"

That's when Faith knew why. She just hated to face it. "Maybe for the same reason I went so long without realizing how many secrets my mom was keeping from me. It was there all the time, and I didn't see it until I was ready to see it. Because I don't want to know."

Lynn raised her eyebrows in the darkness and waited. Faith wondered how much her sister resembled Rainy Miller Carrington, at that moment.

"Or maybe I don't want to see him because of what he did to Chet."

"Which was…?"

Faith shook her head and took a step backward into the girls' bedroom. The one where Chet had been exiled so often, accused of being just a girl himself. "I can't do it, Lynn. I can't look at it straight-on. I know the brother tortured him, but how far it went past normal big-brother bullying—I'm not sure, and I don't want to see it."

But there were some things she had to see, weren't there? Understanding was more important than her cowardice. So Faith took a deep breath, squared her shoulders, strode into the middle of the boys' bedroom—and concentrated.

"Chet hated feeling so powerless," she announced, translating the swirl of impressions that registered within her as surely as sound and smell and temperature. "Then one day... it's really hot out. They don't have air conditioning yet. Claudia sneaks in before his brother gets home from...from his job? Or college classes. Since it's so hot, she strips naked to wait for him. She's been drinking, cold beer against the heat, maybe more than beer. She sees Chet peeking at her, and she's bored, so she starts teasing him about being a little pervert, about her having psychic powers to control him...oh..."

Face it.

"The bitch is teasing him about his...his reaction to her being naked. She tells him she's making it happen to him. Not like a natural response, but like witchcraft. Now he feels even more powerless. It scares him. He's telling her to make it stop, and she just taunts him some more...."

Come on, Chester. You have to do what I tell you, or it'll freeze that way.

"He's so scared. He wants to shut her up, so he runs at her, and he's pushing at her, trying to cover her mouth, but squeezing her throat works better. He's so upset, he doesn't realize she can't breathe...or maybe he doesn't care. And then—"

She had to pull back from the present-tense narration. It was too disgusting, too immediate. "He killed her. That shut her up, for good. It made him feel powerful. Manly, even. I think on some level he connected the two—her death, and the sexual rush he felt. But when his brother got home…"

What did you do? Oh my God, what *did you do?! Why do I always have to clean up after you?*

"His brother got rid of the body. Got rid of the evidence. Everything except…"

Faith looked down at her own hand, but now she was Chet, looking down at his. Skinny hand. Long fingers. And a shank of bleached blond hair that he'd twisted around his hand while trying to shut her up. He'd torn it free when his brother came in. Faith saw herself—saw him—slide it into his pocket where the Master wouldn't see.

But where did he put it then?

She took a shuddering breath, returning to the present.

"Celeste Deveaux—she's the medium I told you about. She said the spirit of the first victim was a 'bare wisp of lingering anguish.' That must have been Claudia." Maybe with this new information they could learn her last name and bring her a final, last bit of peace.

"But here's what I don't get," insisted Lynn. "Like I said. You can see Chet. You can even see the girlfriend. Why not the brother?"

Faith was ready to face that, too. "Because it's someone I know. And I don't want it to be him."

"If you're anything like Dawn and me, it's not like you have that wide a circle of acquaintances."

Faith scrubbed her hands across her pants legs, still trying to wipe them clean. "Not Evan, my roommate. He grew up in the Garden District, not Algiers Point. And he's gay."

"Check. Not Evan."

"And…and I don't think Roy." Oh God, not Roy. But she felt sure she would know his scent, know his energy, even from memories trapped in the walls and ceiling and floors of an old house. Besides... "His grandparents were from the Irish Channel. Why would his parents have moved across the river? And I saw family pictures at his house. I didn't see Chet there."

"We can come back to Roy. Who else?"

And Faith knew. It was partly process of elimination, and partly a lifting of the veil of fear. Either she owned this skill of hers or not.

"Greg," she whispered, real grief aching in her throat. "I don't know how he was able to hide the truth from me, but it was my boss Greg, before he grew his beard."

No wonder he'd gone into evidence. He'd gotten early experience, cleaning up his brother's mistakes.

Then another terrible thought occurred to her. She knew where Greg worked! "We've got to get to the station before he destroys all the evidence against Chet!"

"That would be the evidence that will clear you, right? Come on!" The sisters hurried out of the house and ran down the block toward the corner, no longer as worried about being seen. But as they jogged around the corner, toward Lynn's rental car, Faith's step slowed.

The car looked shorter than before.

That was because of the four flat tires.

"Damn!"

"Okay," said Lynn. "Don't panic. This doesn't seem like the best neighborhood. Was it a random crime, or something more personal?"

Faith tried sniffing the car—and sneezed, violently. Then again. Her nose burned and her already swollen throat ached. She had to back away from the car, eyes watering.

"What is this?" demanded Lynn, swiping a finger across one fender. But Faith knew what it was.

Cayenne pepper. *Exactly what she'd smelled when Butch was killed!*

That's when she heard the faint metallic click, echoing down the block. Then another. "Lynn, *down!*"

Both girls hit the asphalt as a shot exploded into the night. Faith found herself up close and personal with hardened tar. Window glass rained down on top of her. She pulled herself over to where Lynn lay. *Not my sister. Not my sister.* "Lynn!"

"I'm fine." Lynn shook glass out of her hair. "I move faster than you, remember?"

Faith tried to lean past the fender, but began to sneeze again. "Damn!"

"He knows what you can do," guessed Lynn.

"He what?"

"Some people use pepper to repel guard dogs, or to throw them off a scent. Apparently he just…adapted it." When Faith stared, Lynn explained, "I know security."

Faith remembered sniffing the letter that Chet had left at the Biltmore, while Greg watched. But surely that wouldn't have been enough! "Have you got a cell phone?"

"Of course I've got a cell phone. Who doesn't have a cell phone? Oh." When Faith extended her hand, Lynn gave her the phone.

This time, Faith didn't dial through the detective division. She went straight to the source.

"Chopin here."

"Don't hang up," she murmured. "If you're able to record phone calls, start recording. You're going to want to hear this."

"Gee," said Roy, drily. "You wouldn't be some kind of *anonymous contact,* would you? Got more psychic hunches for me?"

"Either you're a good detective or you aren't, Serpico." Well, whoever Serpico was, she'd gotten the impression he was one of the good guys. "Just listen for a few minutes. Oh. And, shots fired at Charbineau off Pelican, in Algiers Point."

She could hear his swearing even as she pocketed the phone, raised her hands—and stood into the open, August night.

Lynn said a less-than-ladylike word herself.

"It's okay, Greg," Faith called. "It's just me. Don't do anything you're going to regret."

"Who says I'm going to regret it?" he demanded. But although he was still pointing the weapon at her, he wasn't firing. Not yet.

Then again, he had a point. If he'd been able to hide his knowledge of the real serial killer, to murder Butch, to try to kill her—or Cassandra, as he'd thought she was at the time—and still keep all traces of guilt out of his breath, out of his heartbeat, out of his *energy*…clearly Chet wasn't the only member of the family missing some piece of humanity. Why would he regret it?

"I thought we had a connection," she said, and took a step closer to him, her arms still spread to show her harmlessness. "I know you're just trying to protect your brother. It's like you told me at lunch. Families can be a lot of trouble, but you still love them, right?"

Greg laughed. "And I thought you majored in pre-law, Faith, not psychology."

"I minored in psychology, but that doesn't mean I'm trying to play you. Didn't I go out with you, as soon as I quit? Aren't you the one I always went to, when I was upset about anything?"

Greg said nothing—until she took a step closer. Then he raised the gun, which had begun to sink. "I don't have much to lose here."

"Sure you do. I know you were trying to kill Cassandra in the cemetery, not Butch. That makes it an accident." Actually, it didn't. If he was trying to kill her, intent followed the bullet. But she wasn't telling him that.

"You don't know the NOPD! A cop killer is a cop killer."

"And an accident is an accident. But deliberately shooting me here, right in front of the home you grew up in—you can't excuse that one."

"Who'll know?"

Anyone listening to the tape Roy was hopefully making, for one. But Faith knew she couldn't count on that. "My sister. You saw us go into the house, right? Maybe you were already inside, checking for whatever the police had missed. Then we came. That's why you flattened her tires and waited for us."

"Who says I'll leave your sister talking?" demanded Greg.

Which was when Lynn stepped up beside him, grabbed his gun-hand, and said, "I do."

Greg squeezed off one shot into the asphalt before Lynn wrenched the gun free with her superstrength. Then, looking wide-eyed from her to Faith, Greg turned and ran.

Faith took off after him. "Don't lose the gun," she shouted over her shoulder. "Do *not* lose that gun! Uh…weapon."

"I didn't plan to," said Lynn, catching up more easily than seemed fair. "What's the big deal?"

"Ballistics should be able to match it to Butch's murder, that's what," Faith panted. "Hey, aren't you supposed to be able to outrun me?"

"Why not tire the guy out first?"

Good point. And Faith, either because of her genetic engineering or just because she had almost twenty years on Greg, was no bad runner either. She and Lynn stretched full out, their footsteps quickly syncing with each other's.

"We're…passing the old…gas station," Faith gasped, as they sprinted past the old historical site. That was for the ben-

efit of the police, of course, not for Lynn. "I think he's…
headed for the…ferry."

Sure enough, Greg had turned onto Seguin.

Worse, they could hear the clanging bells that announced
the ferry's imminent departure from the landing.

"Should we stop him?" called Lynn, barely winded.

"He's heading…in a good direction…." So they kept running. The clanging got louder, and she heard a scraping
noise—the ferry pulling up the skirt boards. Greg wasn't taking the pedestrian stairway. He was racing down the car ramp,
ducking past the gate arm.

"Hey!" yelled a guard. "Ferry's departing! Stop—"

The sisters, pounding past him, seemed to surprise him into
silence.

"Uh-oh," said Lynn.

Greg leaped onto the ferry. And it really was departing,
sliding out of its mooring and into the broad, dark river. Lynn
picked up her pace, quickly outstripped Faith and launched
herself outward, across the water—

Landing solidly on two feet.

"Faith!" she exclaimed, spinning and holding out her
gloved hand.

The ferry was a good four feet from the ramp now, and
drawing farther away by the second—five feet…six…

Hoping her genetic abilities went past sensory perceptions,
Faith put on an extra burst of speed, hurdled the open space—

And landed with one skidding foot, then both knees.

The phone flew out of her pocket at the impact, skidded
across the ferry deck, and arced out into the river with a
solid *plunk*.

She regained her feet in time to help her sister chase Greg
Boulanger around several cars and, finally, to tackle him to
the floor. They wrestled his arms behind him until the secu-

rity guard, already angered by their flagrant disregard for safety, made it to their side.

"You've got handcuffs, right?" panted Faith, both annoyed and admiring that Lynn was barely breathing hard. "You'd better use them, then call the NOPD…and let him know…to meet us."

She held her breath for a moment, as the guard patted Greg down, but luckily the man didn't disturb anything. Which was good, considering what Faith had just smelled.

Now she knew why Greg had gone to Chet's house.

He had the locks of the victims' hair, Chet's souvenirs of his killings, in his left hip pocket.

Chapter 20

"Police stations," said Lynn, "aren't my favorite places."

"Trust me," said Faith. "It's better on this side of the mirror."

They stood, as unobtrusive as they could make themselves, with a handful of officers watching Max and Roy interrogate Greg Boulanger through the one-way mirror. Greg was seated in the same chair Faith had used earlier that day, handcuffed to the same table.

She felt fairly confident that, unlike her, Greg couldn't hear them commenting. Especially since she and Lynn weren't actually supposed to be watching this, and so were speaking in the barest of whispers. Luckily, they both had some version of superhearing.

"We know you've been covering for your brother, Greg," growled Roy, on the other side of the glass. Sleeves rolled up and hair fingered off his forehead, he looked good doing it, too. "You let him into the morgue. You falsified evidence. And we've got the .38."

"Which Faith Corbett gave to you."

"No, which her sister gave to the patrolman who first met the ferry. Neither one of us touched it." Roy was in Greg's face now, full fury. "Yours are the only prints on it, Greg. And oh yeah—the freakin' thing is *licensed to you!*"

"Someone stole it."

"Then you committed a crime by not reporting it stolen!"

"Then I'll pay the fine."

One of the officers said to another, "He's staying pretty cool." She was right. What really surprised Faith was, Greg's pulse and breathing remained steady throughout the interrogation. He was guilty—she'd stared down the barrel of the gun that had murdered Butch. She *knew* he was guilty.

But if she'd come upon this interrogation knowing nothing, even she would have been fooled.

"I don't know what it is," she murmured to Lynn. "Either it's because he honestly feels no guilt, or because someone taught him. Or both."

"Taught him what?"

"How to control his body reactions. This guy could pass a lie detector test without breaking a sweat."

"Actually," whispered Lynn, "that's *how* you pass a lie detector test." But she wrinkled her nose, teasing, as she said it.

Faith loved that she had sisters to tease her, now.

"Look, Chopin, the bitch may have you fooled," said Greg. "But you need to know something about her, man. She's a freak of nature. She hears things, feels things—even smells things that normal humans can't even register."

"Yeah," said Roy, as if he'd already known that. Considering this afternoon, maybe he had. "And it makes her a real pistol in the sack."

That got a reaction out of Greg, just as he'd meant it to. An almost imperceptible catch in his breath, a faint acceleration of his pulse. Greg controlled it with deeper breathing. In only a moment, he'd regained his balance.

But Faith had seen him falter, all the same. And she recognized the technique. "Oh my God."

Then she recognized that the other police officers out here had noticed her—and were staring. Thanks, Roy.

"I'm sure that's just an interrogation trick," Lynn told them, shy but determined to defend Faith.

"Actually, no, I have been to bed with him." Whether or not she was a *pistol*. Most of the male cops looked impressed. A few of the female cops looked jealous. "But what I meant was—my roommate, Krystal. She taught me the same techniques. They're common, sure—controlling your body's stress through your breathing, that sort of thing, but still. She also knew about my, er, *heightened senses*."

Lynn nodded, following her.

"And Krystal had a lover sometime before her murder, even though we didn't know she'd been dating anyone."

"Would she have been gullible enough to sleep with Greg?"

"He fooled me, didn't he?"

Captain Downs, who'd relieved Captain Crawford hours before, ducked into the room. "Folks, this isn't supposed to be entertainment. Especially not for civilians. As for civilians *involved* with the case—"

Most of the police officers dispersed, but as she left, one— a pretty redhead—said, "The pistol's got an interesting theory, Cap. You might want to hear it."

Downs, a fifty-something black man with a salt-and-pepper flattop—shooed Faith and Lynn out before he raised his eyebrows and waited for the theory. So Faith explained how Greg might have dated Krystal. "Maybe they kept it quiet so it wouldn't make things weird for us at work. I don't know. It's pure speculation. But think about it—Chet went years since killing his last psychic. Why did he suddenly notice Krystal Tanner?"

The detectives had already discovered the family connection between Chester Simpson and his half brother, Greg.

Captain Downs considered Faith for a moment. Then he said, "You're not quite as big a pain as Crawford said you were, little lady." And he went inside and tapped on the glass.

It was Max who came to the door—and Faith wished she didn't feel disappointed. When the captain whispered their theory, Max nodded and went back to his interrogation. "Let's talk about Krystal Tanner, Greg."

Greg's pulse sped.

"Now out!" ordered Downs. "If you want to wait for the detectives, you can go to the booking room."

So they headed out to the desks. A drug addict twitched in one chair. Another chair was occupied by a man in a tuxedo—a man so drunk he kept swaying sideways, into an apparent hooker who kept pushing him back the other direction.

"Oh, this is better," said Lynn with gentle sarcasm.

"Weirdly, I'm getting to like it," admitted Faith. "Do you want something from the machines?"

But before she could force Lynn to choose between wrapped cupcakes and a candy bar, a disturbance from the hallway caught her attention. Faith's step hesitated when she recognized one of the gangbangers who'd attacked her in the alley. Then another. Then a third. All three of them, as before, wore some piece of green. All three of them had their hands cinched behind their backs. And all three of them sported an assortment of abrasions, black eyes, bleeding noses and swollen lips.

Behind them came an irate desk sergeant, calling for the captain....

And Dawn O'Shaughnessy.

She nudged her captives forward, then folded her arms to wait, her eyes seeking out and finding Faith and Lynn.

Dawn actually didn't show relief but, as Faith and Lynn hurried to her side, Faith sensed it off her all the same. Something in her heartbeat. Something in her scent.

Faith liked having sisters who worried about her—and sisters to worry about. "What did you *do?*" she demanded.

Dawn widened her eyes and, with a jerk of her head, indicated the gangbangers. Like it was obvious. "I dragged in some witnesses."

"Witnesses to what?" asked Lynn.

Faith asked, "How'd you handcuff all three of them at the same time?"

"They're called riot cuffs…kind of like those plastic thingies you get with your trash bags," said Dawn. "Very portable. And these guys are witnesses to whoever it was wanted Faith here dead."

Faith and Lynn stared.

Dawn rolled her eyes. "Damn, you're innocent! If it was just revenge for the earlier fight, maybe they would've sent five, maybe six or seven guys. But *twelve* of them? The more I thought about it, the more I figured they were there to take Faith down. Professionally. So tonight I went looking, asked a few questions and persuaded these nice fellows here to tell us who hired them."

She said to the captain, who'd come out in time for the last half of her story, "Call it a citizen's arrest."

"Or I could call it assault and battery," suggested Captain Downs. But all three of Dawn's prisoners reacted to that.

"That little girl didn't beat up me!" "You don't know nothing about nothing!" "I got these bruises earlier today!"

"So tell them—" started Dawn, but Faith interrupted.

"Captain, I'd like to file a complaint against these men for attacking me in an alley, yesterday afternoon. My sisters witnessed the whole thing. Would you please read them their rights, before we ask them anything else?"

The Storyville gang exchanged sullen glances, disliking the way their night had gone. Dawn cracked her knuckles. Lynn put her hands on her hips. Faith folded her arms.

Together, they made the boys *very* nervous.

Once they were officially advised that anything they said could and would be used against them in a court of law, the youngest gave in first. "Okay! Just keep these psycho bitches off me, man. It was this white dude, works for the city. Real Einstein type, with glasses, curly black hair. Maybe so tall—" He indicated. "With a beard. Like some animal growing on his face."

He'd just described Greg Boulanger—and in a way that made Faith wonder why she'd ever considered dating him.

"And how did you know him?" asked Faith.

"The man did a little pushing on the side, no big deal," said the boy with the nose stud. "A little *C* now and then. He said it was stuff he boosted off crime scenes. Anyhow, he comes to us and says blondie here was getting into too much of his personal business. Said we should shut her down."

Captain Downs beckoned the redheaded cop over. "As soon as Chopin and Leonard are through with their suspect, we need him in a lineup. Now."

"Merry Christmas, Captain," said Faith, and turned to her sisters. "I think I'm ready to go home after all."

Lynn wrapped an arm around her, carefully not touching bare skin. When Dawn would have hung back, Lynn caught her arm, too, and the three of them headed out of the station together.

"Now," said Faith, "it feels like it's over."

"Except for finding out who hired the hit on Rainy Miller Carrington," Dawn reminded them. Dawn was something of a workaholic, wasn't she?

"And finding out if Thomas King is really our father," added Lynn.

Faith stopped in her tracks. *"Thomas King?"*

"I admit, I can see the resemblance," said Tamara Corbett, trying to peer past the enthusiastic cocker spaniel on her lap to consider the magazines and pictures Faith had brought. Wilbur, as they'd named the stray dog, kept trying to lick Tamara's face. Despite her protests, Faith's mom seemed to like that.

Especially now, with its leg in a cast, the dog needed a person. And Tamara had been too lonely for too long. Faith would have taken Wilbur back home to the apartment, if her mother had hated the idea. But this was clearly not hate.

In fact, any dog that could distract a healthy, middle-aged woman from the idea that she may have borne Thomas King's child was a dog who had a permanent home.

"The Cassandras still aren't a hundred percent sure. Neither are Lynn and Dawn," Faith said now. She'd brought her sisters home for lunch, the previous day, while the dog was still staying with her roommates. Tamara had taken to them with as much love and sympathy as she was now giving Wilbur, but with a lot more respect. The way her sisters had responded to Tamara's immediate acceptance made Faith all the more aware of how lucky she'd been, to grow up with a mother.

A mother who kept secrets, yes. But Faith had no moral high ground to stand on there.

"Once we know for sure," she continued, drawing one of the magazines closer to her, "we'll meet him together."

This particular cover story was "Long Live the King," written the previous year when the Navy SEAL who'd been presumed dead was discovered in a secret prison. He had thick blond hair, like Faith's and Dawn's. Unusual green-gold eyes, like all three of the sisters.

According to the Cassandras, he'd had sperm frozen for his wife, in case one of his dangerous missions left him unable to father children. That was the sperm bank from which Lab 33 had gotten their material.

"The Cassandras are those women from the Athena Academy," said Tamara, and Faith didn't have to use her abilities to sense her mother's feelings of inferiority. The former prep-school graduates who'd been Rainy Miller's friends were all eminently successful—an FBI forensic scientist, a TV reporter and an Air Force test pilot, among other impressive careers. Once they'd learned of Faith's existence, they hadn't just answered Lynn's e-mailed announcement. Several of them had already telephoned with their welcome and encouragement.

"They sound like very special women," said Tamara.

Faith left the magazines, came around the table and gave her mother a hug. Her mother—and a very happy Wilbur. Their emotions flowed through her gently, familiarly. Now that she'd accepted her abilities, her control over them was increasing by the day. "So are you, Mom."

"Me? Oh, baby, I'm nothing special. I didn't even go to college. I never fit in."

"But that's why you were so good at keeping me safe all these years! I'm sorry I reacted the way I did, Mom. You may have saved my life with what you did. Without you I could have ended up being trained as a thief, like Lynn, or even an assassin, like Dawn. Or considering my abilities, probably a con artist. You know. Exactly the kind of person who makes life so hard for all my friends in the French Quarter. I would have hated that."

Tamara let out a broken sigh, petting Faith's hair. "Oh, I don't know about that. You may have found you liked it. You always were something of a rebel."

Faith wrinkled her nose. "I don't know. Lately, I've kind of got a thing for the law."

He was waiting not far from the streetcar stop.

Faith sensed him almost a block away, but that was because of Roy Chopin's pushy energy. Especially when he was impatient. Apparently, this afternoon, he was feeling very impatient.

He leaned against the fender of his parked Malibu, arms folded, the picture of nonchalance. But everything in him sped up when he saw her coming. His breathing. His pulse.

She couldn't tell if that was a good thing or not.

When he saw that she'd seen him, he raised his eyebrows in silent question, but he didn't make a move toward her. Instead, she detoured over to him. "Are you stalking me?"

"If I were stalking you, I woulda been right outside your mom's place. Or should I say, the D.A.'s place."

Since that wasn't an answer, Faith just folded her arms and waited.

"Your roommate Moonsong said you were here," he offered. "You're gonna have to watch that one. She's way too trusting."

Maybe she was. Faith's roommates had been surprisingly understanding about her secret identity as a police contact. They thought it was exciting. "So you're here because…?"

"I'm not sorry I arrested you." His jaw was a definite dare, just now. It went with his scowl.

Faith leaned into his space—and damned if it didn't still feel good there. Familiar. Challenging. "Then I'm not sorry I tore your arrest to shreds."

He shook his head, his mouth pulling into a mockery of a smile. "Right. You're cute when you're a smart-ass."

In the distance, Faith could hear the ding-ding of the trolley approaching. In another minute, she was sure Roy would hear it, too. "I'm more than just cute. And I'm more than just a pistol in the sack."

His eyes widened. "Did I say you weren't?"

"I'm just clarifying, here. You searched my closet."

"On an anonymous tip. Last time I heard, you were in favor of those." He considered his argument, then added, "And I found something."

"Like that justifies anything."

"Maybe not to lawyers, hon. But as far as the truth coming out, yeah."

The way he said "lawyers" made her grin. "So you really came all the way out here just to tell me you weren't sorry?"

"Yeah. That, and to ask you out."

Her own heart began to race, and her stomach began to flip-flop. But it felt good. It felt…normal. "Really?"

"We got a lot to talk about. Greg and Chet both got indicted, largely because of you being such a stupid Bernie. I figured you might want to celebrate."

"And have sex," she guessed. Not that the idea made her ill, but there were some trust issues to get past, here, too. On both sides. No matter what his body was telegraphing.

"I wouldn't rule it out, but I'm determined to cram a dinner down you sooner or later." Now his head came up. He heard the trolley, too. And here it came, the dark-green car with dark-red trim, up the center of St. Charles Avenue.

"What's a Bernie?" she asked—and he laughed, a sharp bark.

"I've been calling you Bernie all this time, and you don't know?"

She shook her head.

"Like Bernhard Goetz, the guy who shot those muggers on the New York subway. A Bernie's a ringer, Corbett. Someone who looks completely helpless, then turns around and kicks someone's ass."

The more she considered that, the more she liked it. The more she liked him for thinking of her that way. "And I'm a Bernie?"

"You went after a guy with a gun. Who'd already tried to kill you once."

"Only because the alternative would have been to let him get away."

"Agony," predicted Roy, his gaze caressing her face. "This is what you offer me."

But he was lying. And she knew it. She was genetically engineered to be able to read people, after all…and what she read, she liked. Roy was a good guy, and a good cop. Roy liked her. And Roy was someone she could touch with pleasure, instead of dread, which counted for a hell of a lot, too. Someone whose touch opened up whole new worlds for her.

People had dated for worse reasons. And yet…

She deserved better. And oh heavens, so did he.

"Maybe I do," she warned him. "Maybe I *am* agony, just waiting to happen to both of us. You may have noticed that I'm not…"

Her throat closed before she could say it.

"Not…corrupt?" he guessed, his eyes bright, mouth mocking with amusement. "Not cynical, like me and my cop friends? Not helpless and needy?"

So she had to say it. "Not normal."

The streetcar was close enough that Faith didn't need super-sight to read its curved numbers or the placard that read *St. Charles*.

"So you're special," said Roy. "Woman-of-mystery, never-boring, one-of-a-kind special. This is a bad thing?"

"You don't know the half of how weird I am." Her melodramatic conception. Her super-sisters. Her ability to sense that, amazing though it seemed, he wasn't lying now, as surely as she knew his eyes were gray. *But he didn't know.* "You don't know."

"So how should I find out if you don't give me the chance?"

Which, she realized with a rush of pleasant surprise, was exactly how normal people did it. Roy Chopin brought blessed normalcy to her life. And as for what she brought to his...

Well, maybe they could find out, at that.

"Okay," she said. "I'll go out with you."

She savored his relief. "Tonight? I know it's short notice, but tonight's my night off."

The trolley was slowing now with a squeal of brakes. "I've got plans this afternoon with my sisters, but... Give me a call later today, and you'll find out."

"I would, but you keep throwing phones into the river."

"Call me at home. Like a real date." But it had been three days. And he was addictive. So instead of strolling back to the trolley stop, Faith rose onto tiptoes and offered a kiss, which Roy took with gusto.

Yes....

His lips were warm and real. His breath struggled in his throat, which seemed to be tightening with uncertain emotion. His hands pulled her possessively closer to the tall, hard, physicality of him, and when his tongue slid into her mouth, she shuddered her release.

Yeah, this was worth another try.

"Screw the streetcar," he muttered breathily into her ear, making her shiver again. "I'll give you a ride home."

But at least one of them had to get better at delayed gratification. Shaking her head, Faith backed out of his arms. "Nope. A real date. Somewhere I can dress up."

"Oh, now you're high-maintenance all of a sudden?"

She jogged toward the streetcar. "You have no idea."

Roy followed with his long stride, but when she looked over her shoulder, he seemed entertained. There was something to be said for increased expectations. "So where do you want to dine, Your Highness?"

"Greg took me on a riverboat."

"Greg's a sociopath."

"One of many reasons I like you better." The trolley rang its last warnings, and she heard it start moving, so she turned and ran full-out. She caught the streetcar and paced it as it picked up speed. She tapped on the door-glass, and the doors slid open. She jumped on board and flashed the conductor her monthly NORTA pass.

"You oughtn't to be doing that, miss!" he scolded. "That's dangerous. You oughtn't get so close to the streetcar when she's moving like that."

But some days, Faith felt more sure of herself than others. She slid across an empty seat and hung out the open window to watch Roy's retreating figure. "Call me!" she yelled.

And he held up one hand in a single, silent wave. She knew he would.

Maybe she was special, at that. Maybe it ran in the family.

"This is nowhere near as cheesy as I would have thought," admitted Dawn, looking around the tasteful back room of Celeste Deveaux's French Quarter parlor.

"Shh!" said Lynn. 'Can't you feel it?"

So the air in here didn't vibrate just for Faith. That was a relief. Perhaps the best thing about having sisters was this sense of communion, of not being wholly alone in her abilities.

Like the ugly duckling realizing it really was a swan, after all. In Faith's case, and Dawn's, and Lynn's, they were genetically enhanced swans, but that still counted, right?

"Don't mind me," murmured Celeste, her dark eyes half closed and unfocused. The sisters shut up. Celeste's lips curved in a smile. She was used to people masking their uncertainties with humor. And Dawn in particular was uncertain about this.

But Faith's sisters were only going to be in New Orleans another day. Shouldn't they at least give this a try?

The medium's expression turned solemn. "Talk to me, spirits," she whispered, her hands spread. "I'm looking for a mother, these ladies' mother, who never knew—"

She sat bolt upright, eyes closed.

The sisters tensed. Faith could hear it in their pulses, feel it off their body temperature, both of which created a strange harmony against the slower heartbeat and more shallow breathing of Celeste in her trance state. More important, Faith could feel...

Something. Someone. Between the sisters and Celeste.

"There's a woman here," murmured the medium. "A beautiful redheaded woman. I'm hearing an R, seeing rainfall... she says it's her name. Do you know someone called...?"

"Rainy," breathed Lynn.

"She says you're her daughters. She says of course she knows you, now. How can...?"

"It's a long story." Faith searched the seemingly rich, intense air before them, seeking that sense of presence. How she would have loved to meet Lorraine Miller Carrington in life. She was certain her sisters felt the same. But maybe... "We're so sorry we never knew her. We're so sorry for what happened to her. We—"

"She's happy," insisted Celeste.

Lynn, beside Faith, caught a sharp breath of surprise. Lynn believed this was happening, too.

"She was murdered," protested Dawn, clearly less willing to suspend her disbelief.

Celeste was swaying now, her voice a weaving of husky truths. "Everyone dies, baby. She says it's not like she went anywhere. She's so happy for everyone she loves, having the strength to go on with their lives. She's…the woman's laughing, saying names so fast I can hardly keep them straight. Darcy and Alex and Kayla. Tory and Sam and Josie. They kept their promise. She's calling them your aunts, says she's living through them as much as through you three, and that you'd better all get together."

"We will," said Lynn. "Of course we will."

"She's calling your aunts…" Celeste's eyes opened with surprise. "Cassandras."

Faith nodded. "I didn't know that, when I chose the name."

"Rainy thinks you did." Celeste's eyes closed again. "Where it counts. She says you three are Cassandras, too. She is so proud of you, so very proud…."

"But we haven't done anything." That was Dawn, but this time her challenge sounded more poignant. She might not want to believe this, but she was beginning to believe, all the same.

"You're the one she wants to hug the most," announced Celeste, turning to Dawn. "The others…Rainy says they've been getting some hugging. That makes her happy, too. But you haven't yet. You deserve some. She says you've all done more than any mother could expect. If you do nothing else, ever, she couldn't be more proud of the three of you. But you will do more. It's in your blood."

Lynn sat up. "Does she know who our father is?"

Faith held her breath. *Was* it Thomas King?

"She says even he doesn't know it, yet. But stick together, and you'll find him. Does that make sense? That seems to be what your mother's most concerned about. She wants to be sure you three won't forget each other, that you'll meet with your aunts, that you won't lose touch with the people who love you. Losing touch…that's the only thing that makes this woman sad."

Faith looked at her sisters, one to either side of her.

She held out her hands.

Lynn's hand closed around hers first. Again, Faith got a rush of sensations—*computer. Craftiness. Someone waiting back home. Possibilities.*

Faith was better able to channel the impressions, now. Instead of it feeling like an assault, it became a bond. This was her sister. They *should* know each other.

Dawn hesitated a moment longer. Then, almost grudgingly, she caught Faith's hand in a strong grip. *Fighting. Training. Things to do. Loneliness.*

Longing….

She caught Lynn's hand as well, so that the three of them were truly connected.

"It's a promise," said Faith.

"A promise," repeated Lynn.

Dawn only hesitated a moment. "A promise."

Faith watched a tear of happiness slide from Celeste's closed eyes—and knew the tear did not belong to Celeste.

* * * * *

*Turn the page for a sneak preview of
the next ATHENA FORCE adventure,
Dawn O'Shaughnessy's story,
PAYBACK
by Harper Allen.
Coming to your favorite retailer in March 2005!*

Chapter 1

Status: Twenty-one days and counting
Time: 0900 hours

Any second now the man sitting across the desk from her could give the order to have her killed.

Dawn smoothed her palms on the gleaming leather of the skintight catsuit she was wearing, but as Aldrich Peters leveled an emotionless look at her she realized her mistake. She schooled her face to blankness, knowing there was nothing she could do to control the triphammer beat of her heart. After a long moment he bent his head again and resumed his perusal of Lab 33's report on her.

Her few days AWOL from Lab 33 last December had stretched into seven months—longer than she'd anticipated, but then, her assignment for the Athenas had resulted in locating not one lost sister, Lynn, but a second sibling, Faith

Corbett, who had also been a victim of genetic manipulation and who'd had no knowledge of her true origins. Together the three of them had been introduced to the man who was their biological father, Navy SEAL Thomas King…a meeting she hadn't wanted to attend. *What was I supposed to say to him, dammit?* she thought as she waited for Peters to finish reading. *"Hey, now I know you're my dad I'm kinda glad I didn't pull the trigger when I had you in my rifle sights a couple of months ago when I was working for the bad guys."*

At the time she'd almost been glad she had the excuse of returning to Lab 33 to explain her hasty departure. But as the complex's steel doors had begun sliding closed behind her yesterday evening, cutting off her last glimpse of the arid New Mexican canyons and foothills, a sense of complete isolation had overtaken her. And upon taking her first breath of the recycled air supplying the massive underground bunker, a Cold War emergency command center secretly built in the 1950s that had never been utilized, but for years now the site of Aldrich Peters's shadowy organization, her time away had seemed suddenly unreal.

For a moment she'd felt a terrible certainty that it *had* been unreal. There was no such group as the Athenas, she hadn't found Lynn White and Faith Corbett, her biological sisters, she'd never learned the truth about her existence. She was a Lab 33 assassin. She answered to Aldrich Peters. She was in a nightmare where nothing had changed.

In near panic she'd whirled around with the half-formed notion of darting back through the closing doors. At her unexpected movement the nearest guards—a commander, as she'd noted from the dull red flashes on the collar of his field-gray uniform—had jerked his weapon up into firing position, at the same time scrambling clumsily away from her. Behind his face shield she'd seen his eyes, open so wide that rims of white circled his pupils.

"*They're scared of me, Uncle Lee!*" A long-buried memory flashed into Dawn's mind. "*I wanted to play tag with them, but they shouted at me to go away. One of them called me a freak. Am I, Uncle Lee? Am I a freak like they say?*" In Dawn's memory, the six-year-old version of herself felt arms scooping her close, smelled the somehow reassuring mixture of harsh tobacco and gun oil, heard a voice whose undertone of anger she knew wasn't directed at her. "*They're the freaks, Dawnie. You're special, and don't you ever let the sons of bitches convince you otherwise. They're scared because they know you're stronger than everyone here, and I don't mean just lifting-things strong. Your strength comes from inside you. You understand what I'm saying?*" Her sobs had subsided by then but she'd stayed in the circle of his arms, happy just to be held by him. "*I guess. But you're stronger than the sunsa bits, too, right?*" The arms around her had tightened. For a moment she'd thought the unthinkable had happened and Uncle Lee was mad at her, but when he'd answered his tone had been filled with such pain that she would have gladly traded it for anger. "*Maybe once, Dawnie. Now I'm no better than they are. But I promise I'll always stay strong enough to keep them from owning you—even if staying strong costs me everything I care for in this world.*"

Aldrich Peters laid aside a sheet of paper, the crackle as he did so sounding like a gunshot in the oppressive silence. Dawn didn't flinch. Her nervousness had disappeared in the past few seconds, she realized. She supposed she should be glad it had, but all she felt was anger.

When the hell are you going to stop falling into the same stupid trap, O'Shaughnessy? She berated herself. *Every memory you have of Lee Craig is tainted. Be glad you've got something more worthwhile than your memories of him to give you strength.*

She had payback. No matter what police lieutenant Kayla Ryan had seemed to think, revenge wouldn't set things right for her. No matter that in the conversation she'd had with her sisters on the subject, Lynn and Faith had both agreed with Kayla. She had no intention of delivering Peters to justice. For one final time, she intended to be judge, jury and executioner herself.

She concealed a faint wince as the dull throbbing that signaled one of the headaches she'd recently been experiencing set up a low tattoo behind her temples. As if he sensed her momentary vulnerability, Peters slid the papers aside.

"You passed Section 8's tests with flying colors." His austere features seemed carved in stone. "The lie detector, the bio and neuro-feedbacks, the psychological work-ups by Drs. Wang and Sobie. Apparently you were telling the truth when you contacted me yesterday and said you wanted to take up your duties again."

A rush of triumph raced through her. Of course she'd passed their tests. She'd grown up here, dammit, and there wasn't a test invented that hadn't been run on her. By the age of eleven she'd known how to bend them to her advantage without even try—

"I would have been shocked if you'd failed," Peters added brusquely. "After all, if anyone could manipulate the results it would be you."

Dawn fought to keep her gaze steady. She'd underestimated him, she thought tensely. Whatever his tests and his experts told him, Dr. Aldrich Peters preferred to rely on his own instincts…and those instincts were telling him she was lying. With seconds to revoke her own death warrant she needed to go on the offensive—*now*.

"Maybe I'm being paranoid, but I get the feeling you don't fully accept my explanation for my disappearance from Lab

33 last fall," she said, allowing anger to creep into her voice. "At the risk of sounding more paranoid, I also get the feeling you're making up your mind as to whether I should even walk out of here alive. Am I right?"

The thin smile that appeared on Aldrich Peters's lips did little to soften the remoteness of his expression. "I don't call that paranoid, Dawn, I call that astute. You're right, I've got serious doubts about your story of going into an emotional tailspin after your Uncle Lee was killed. Lab 33's ultimate killing machine, the protégée Lee Craig was grooming to take his place, falling to pieces like any ordinary woman? I don't buy it."

"You don't buy it because you're forgetting one important fact." She stood abruptly, placing her palms flat on his desktop. "I *am* an ordinary woman in many respects—ordinary enough to feel pain when the only family member I've ever known is torn from me and ordinary enough to know that I haven't lived an ordinary life. I told you, losing my uncle was a shattering experience and I needed to come to terms with it."

She exhaled. "I need time to come to terms with who and what I am, too. As you just said, I'm not your usual twenty-two-year-old, am I? I'm a superbeing who's almost indestructible, trained to use my special talents to clandestinely further the best interests of my country as Uncle Lee did. After he died I felt it was time to ask myself if I really wanted to take his place."

"What conclusion did you come to?"

She answered him promptly. "That Lab 33's the only game in town for someone like me. And as Uncle Lee always told me, at least I'm working on the side of the good guys."

"Which leads me to my second question. Do you still believe we're the good guys, Dawn, or have you taken your allegiance elsewhere during these past six months?" Peters's tone held an implied threat. Slowly she let her palms slide from the desk and straightened to her full height.

"I grew up here. I've dedicated my life to Lab 33. I've demonstrated my loyalty time and again, and you still feel you have the right to ask me that?"

This was it, she told herself as Aldrich Peters held her gaze. Either she'd allayed his suspicions or she hadn't—and if it was the latter, both of them would be dead minutes from now. Her plan of gathering as much information as she could over the next few weeks for the Athenas before she made her move against him would have to be forgotten. But she wouldn't be able to stop him from hitting the emergency button on his desk that would bring the guards pouring in, and she had no doubt that they knew her Achilles' heel.

A woven-steel garotte had been part of the standard weapons issue for Lab 33 internal security for as long as she could remember…and for as long as she could remember, she'd instinctively known that particular weapon had been issued with only one opponent in mind. She could survive a bullet or a knife but as she'd told Peters, she was an ordinary human being in some respects…one of which was that she couldn't survive without oxygen.

So be it, Dawn thought with deadly calm. *If I die, I die knowing I've taken him with—*

Without warning the migrainelike throbbing shot through her head again. As fast as it had come it faded, and as her vision cleared she realized something had disconcerted Peters. His next words revealed what that something had been.

"The last thing I expected to see in your eyes when I questioned your loyalty was pain, but apparently the psych profile Drs. Wang and Sobie prepared on you was accurate," he said slowly. "This changes everything." He leaned back in his chair. "It seems I misjudged you, Dawn. Welcome home."

"It's good to be back." Her clipped reply betrayed nothing of the relief sweeping through her. *You did it, O'Shaughnessy!* she thought in fierce exultation. *You lied through your teeth to Aldrich Peters and the bastard bought it. Now nothing can stop you from—*

"Unfortunately, your little vacation couldn't have been more regrettably timed." Peters's composure was firmly back in place. "You're dying."

Books by Evelyn Vaughn

Silhouette Bombshell

A.K.A. Goddess #7
Contact #30

Family Secrets

The Player

Silhouette Intimate Moments

Buried Secrets #1205

Silhouette Shadows

*Waiting for the Wolf Moon #8
*Burning Times #39
*Beneath the Surface #55
*Forest of the Night #66

*The Circle

If you enjoyed what you just read,
then we've got an offer you can't resist!

Take 2 bestselling
love stories FREE!

Plus get a FREE surprise gift!

Clip this page and mail it to Silhouette Reader Service®

IN U.S.A.	**IN CANADA**
3010 Walden Ave.	P.O. Box 609
P.O. Box 1867	Fort Erie, Ontario
Buffalo, N.Y. 14240-1867	L2A 5X3

YES! Please send me 2 free Silhouette Bombshell™ novels and my free surprise gift. After receiving them, if I don't wish to receive any more, I can return the shipping statement marked cancel. If I don't cancel, I will receive 4 brand-new novels every month, before they're available in stores! In the U.S.A., bill me at the bargain price of $4.69 plus 25¢ shipping & handling per book and applicable sales tax, if any*. In Canada, bill me at the bargain price of $5.24 plus 25¢ shipping & handling per book and applicable taxes**. That's the complete price and a savings of 10% off the cover prices—what a great deal! I understand that accepting the 2 free books and gift places me under no obligation ever to buy any books. I can always return a shipment and cancel at any time. Even if I never buy another book from Silhouettte, the 2 free books and gift are mine to keep forever.

200 HDN D34H
300 HDN D34J

Name	(PLEASE PRINT)	
Address	Apt.#	
City	State/Prov.	Zip/Postal Code

Not valid to current Silhouette Bombshell™ subscribers.

Want to try another series?
Call 1-800-873-8635 or visit www.morefreebooks.com.

* Terms and prices subject to change without notice. Sales tax applicable in N.Y.
** Canadian residents will be charged applicable provincial taxes and GST.
All orders subject to approval. Offer limited to one per household.
® and ™ are registered trademarks owned and used by the trademark owner and
or its licensee.

BOMB04   ©2004 Harlequin Enterprises Limited

COMING NEXT MONTH

#33 SILENT WEAPON by Debra Webb
Her entire life changed when an infection rendered her deaf.
But Merri Walters used her disability to her advantage—by
becoming an expert lip reader and working for the police.
Now, her special skill was needed for an extremely dangerous
undercover assignment—one that put her at odds with the
detective in charge…and in the sights of an enemy.

#34 PAYBACK by Harper Allen
Athena Force
Dawn O'Shaughnessy was playing a dangerous game—
pretending to work for the immoral scientist who'd made her
a nearly indestructible assassin, while secretly aligning herself
with the Athena Force women who had vowed to take him
down. But when she discovered that only the man who'd
raised her to be a monster could save her from imminent
death, she had to choose between the new sisters she'd
come to know and trust, and payback….

#35 THE ORCHID HUNTER by Sandra K. Moore
She was more hunter than botanist, and Dr. Jessie Robards
knew she could find the legendary orchid that could cure
her uncle's illness—Brazil's pet vipers, jaguars, natives and
bioterrorists be damned. But the Amazonian jungle, filled
with passion and betrayal, was darker and more dangerous
than she'd ever imagined. This time it would change her,
heart and soul…*if* she made it out alive.

#36 CALCULATED RISK by Stephanie Doyle
Genius Sabrina Masters had been the CIA's favorite protégée—
until betrayal ended her career. Now she'd been called back
into duty—to play traitor and lure a deadly terrorist out of
hiding. Only she had the brains to decode the terrorist's
encrypted data, which was vital to national security. But when
the agent who'd betrayed her became her handler, the mission
became more complicated than even Sabrina could calculate….

SBCNM0205